Simon could see his father's eyes alive with old memories. "We needed shelter," Aldric said. "We had been attacked. We were cursing the fact we needed a Magician, someone who could interpret Dragonrunes, someone to speak the language, but there was no one with us. And there was . . .

"My brother, Ormand, was with me, we went to this place," he said. "We were hunting a Dragon . . . and we ended up there for the night. I remember the innkeeper, and Ormand and I went on to attack the Dragon the next day."

"Where is it?"

"Kyoto," he said, his eyes gleaming. "Ancient capital of Japan."

THE SAINT OF DRAGONS
VOLUME II

Samurai

JASON HIGHTMAN

An Imprint of HarperCollinsPublishers

Eos is an imprint of HarperCollins Publishers.

Samurai

Library of Congress Cataloging-in-Publication Data
Hightman, Jason.
    Samurai / by Jason Hightman.— 1st ed.
      p. cm.
    Summary: Simon St. George and his father, the last members of the Order
of Dragonhunters, must join forces with a group of Japanese samurai to
destroy the dragons in the Far East.
    ISBN 978-0-06-054016-6
    [1. Dragons—Fiction. 2. Samurai—Fiction. 3. Fathers and sons—Fiction.
4. East Asia—Fiction.] I. Title.
PZ7.H543995Sam 2006   2006000301
[Fic]—dc22   CIP
                                                                 AC

Typography by LL/RH
❖
First paperback edition, 2007

For my family

This book would not exist without the help of my hard-working and supportive editor, Ruth Katcher. I would also like to praise the people at HarperCollins, especially Elise Howard, for their aid, advice, and advocacy. Thanks also go to Bryan Burk and Ori Marmur for their help early on. I greatly appreciate the labors of all those who made this book a reality.

CONTENTS

Chapter 1

THE HEAT OF BATTLE

THERE IS ONE THING YOU can count on with evil. Evil will do things you never counted on. Simon St. George hated that fact as much as he detested the African sun. The heat in Kenya was unbearable, and the shadows the sun cast on the trail were hatefully dark, making it difficult to see if a Serpent was ready to leap out of the tall grasses.

And they *were* hunting Serpent. The possibility of a fiery death was always with him, and Simon found it sickening rather than exciting. His father was quite the opposite. Riding tall in his saddle ahead, Aldric St. George steered his horse with a stern energy, a quiet thrill that a fight could come at any moment.

Aldric insisted on the two of them going on horseback, for ease of movement on the rough terrain, but, looking back jealously at the car in his wake, Simon cursed his old-fashioned ways and yearned for air conditioning.

Behind him, the battered Jeep spit rocks from its wheels, slowly rolling through the ragged country—a neglected dirt road amid long yellow grasses. Beside the worried Kenyan driver sat Alaythia Moore, the beautiful New York artist who lately looked a bit awestruck by the wilds of Africa.

Simon squinted back at her, the dirt on the windows making her nothing but a pretty shadow. He rode up alongside his father. "You think she'd rather be out here with us?"

Aldric focused his eyes on the trail. "Simon, keep your mind on the task at hand."

"We're miles from the African Dragons," said Simon. "We still have to get past the next two villages. I just thought she might be lonely in there."

"It's so hot in the sun. Why the devil would she want to be out here?"

"For the company," said Simon, unhappily. Unless he was lecturing him, his British father was never much good at conversation. Simon wondered how Aldric and Alaythia spent their time alone. He figured they must always be planning strategy, going over the old scrolls and Books of St. George, learning the Serpentine language better, or designing new weaponry.

Alaythia's skills as a Magician had grown tremendously over the past few months.

Simon turned as the Jeep pulled around them and Alaythia looked out. "You have to be sick of the sun by now," she said to Aldric. "Why don't you tether the horses to the back and get some shade in the Jeep?"

Aldric smiled at her. "You mean step into the modern world?"

"Yes," she said with exasperation. "You should've left the horses back at the ship."

Alaythia, Simon thought, had just a touch of what he now recognized as New York attitude, with the slight hint of expectation that rich people carry around, which she had yet to completely lose (her grandmother had left her a fair amount of money from a Manhattan real estate fortune, which had soon dwindled away on bad investments and charity giveaways). She leaned out more, her odd beaded necklace clanging on the Jeep's door. "Come on," she prompted again. "Quit being the angry Warrior and take a break in here."

"We'll see what you say when that jalopy gets a flat tire, or the transmission goes out," said Aldric. "We do things the St. George way. We're not going to drop traditions that have been handed down for centuries."

Simon watched the two of them, surprised to see his father looking relaxed for a moment. That must have been the fifth time he'd smiled in the past two days—a record. *Alaythia could bring that out in anyone,* he thought.

"We're coming up on the next village," she said.

"This isn't the way I remember it," said the African driver and translator, as he slowed down and let the horses pass, staring at the settlement. "There should be more people out. It was a busy little place . . ."

Aldric looked alarmed as they neared the town, a sorry set of flat, boxy, falling-apart buildings in faded colors. A very old Ford sat in the high grass, ruined by time and hard rains, proof of Aldric's claim that this was no place for motorcars.

And then, beyond the junked car, a human skeleton lay in the grass.

"Halt," Aldric said to his horse, Valsephany.

Simon stopped behind him, having a bit more difficulty with Norayiss, his own stallion.

The skeleton was clean and white, left out in the sun for a long time. Flies scarcely bothered with it. Simon noted with some disgust that an arm had been lost, most likely by scavengers, jackals, perhaps. He'd seen death before, but hadn't quite gotten used to it.

The skull gleamed, a horror made ordinary by the afternoon sun.

"What does it mean?" he asked his father.

"I'm not sure," Aldric answered.

Aldric pulled a crossbow closer to him in the saddle, as did Simon. Alaythia had a rifle, its wooden stock covered in runic symbols. She held it closer, leaning out of the Jeep as the driver reluctantly drove it forward.

More death greeted them. Skeletons lined the twisting road, looking as if the people had fallen there in some attempt to escape the tiny town, and no one had bothered to bury them. It was a strange sight, and Simon felt queasy.

The path to the village became yet more riddled with skeletons and bones, and the horses' hooves crunched over them, as it was impossible to get around them. Large boulders sat on each side of the road, and Simon noted with alarm that one of the huge rocks was smeared with blood.

Blood?

Two young boys ran toward the St. Georges as they arrived. They were shouting something, terror in their eyes.

"Disease," said the translator from the Jeep. "They're yelling about disease. It is some terrible death let loose here."

"What kind of disease?" Simon asked, suddenly wanting to turn and ride away.

"They don't know," said the translator. "Many diseases in Africa. This one works fast, they say. Many days at work. Many people dead. Many dying."

"How many days?" Aldric asked.

"They want medicine," the translator said. "They expect medicine from us."

Simon looked at the African boys, feeling terrible, sensing the fear that swirled around them.

"We don't have any medicine," barked Aldric, sounding angry, and Simon recognized it as the way he always reacted when he couldn't help. His father moved his horse onward as the two boys ran alongside, pleading. "I need to know how many days since the sickness came," he repeated to their driver.

The translator tried to get an answer. "They don't know. They are children. They lost track of time . . ."

"Have there been any fires here?" asked Aldric.

The African translated their responses. "No. No fires. Just a fire in the heart. Sickness of fire."

Simon trailed behind Aldric, with the Jeep coming up behind them. The translator was becoming more agitated. "This sickness is not normal," he said. "This death works too quickly. They should've gotten word to the last town we were in. No one did."

Aldric kept moving.

"This is not right," the translator yelled after him. "We should not go farther, this is not right."

"It *is* right . . ." said Aldric, "for what we're looking for."

Alaythia offered the boys a rune-covered canteen of special water. "Drink, splash it on you," she advised them. "It will protect you."

Seeing they did not understand her, the translator took the canteen and sprinkled some of the water on himself, passing it to the children with a few hopeful words.

Simon looked back. The boys seemed skeptical of her, but they splashed the water on their skins and drank deeply all the same.

"There's not enough water," Aldric complained.

"It's something," Alaythia said, sounding annoyed. "The mixture is weakening in the sun, but it'll help them if they aren't already sick. Let them have it."

"There's not enough," repeated Aldric in a grim tone, for they had reached the center of town. He was staring ahead. Amid old, broken-down cars and trucks, there was a group of low, flat buildings. Through the open doors, Simon could see many people lying in beds. He stopped his horse and surveyed his surroundings.

The people were choking and gasping for air. Some men lay in doorways, lifting their arms weakly. And then Simon realized that every single person there had lost all their hair. The man in the doorway, the women gathering water at the well, the sick he could see in the beds—all were completely bald. It was jolting. The boys who led them in had shaven heads, or so he had thought, but now he could tell that several of the other villagers, many of them children, had lost their hair as well.

"How long has this sickness been here?" Aldric demanded. "Ask this man."

The translator got out of the car, keeping his distance as he questioned a man in a doorway. "Six days," the translator reported. "One boy arrived in town and grew ill, and from the second day, it spread to everyone. Weakness overtakes you. You have no desire to live, no strength. There is . . . only one mercy. There are five deaths every hour," the translator choked on the words. "In another day, the entire town will be gone."

Simon swallowed hard. He looked at Aldric, whose eyes burned with anger. Alaythia got out of the Jeep and moved toward the man, bringing him the last canteen.

"Alaythia, please," Aldric said quietly. "You can still catch this disease. Let Simon help him, his blood is stronger than yours."

Simon took the canteen from Alaythia, who moved back, looking helpless and angry. The boy gave the man a drink from the canteen.

"It won't do much good now," said Alaythia, and she looked at the translator. "But tell him it's strong medicine. He may believe it. It may help." And indeed, the man's eyes brightened as he took the drink.

"Now ask him if there has been anything else unusual," Aldric ordered.

The man told them there had been thousands of vultures gathered on the veldt outside the town before the disease struck.

"Thousands?" asked Aldric.

"And jackals as well," the translator explained. "Many scores of them."

"Where did they gather?" asked Simon. He knew, as his father did, that where there were ripples in nature, there were Dragons.

"I know the place," said one of the boys who'd led them here. "You bring some of that medicine to my mother, I will show you where the scavengers settled, miles up the road."

Aldric looked to Simon, who held the canteen.

"No, not him," said the boy, pointing to Simon. "The woman must bring it. My mother will not be seen by men in her state."

As the translation came, Aldric nodded in understanding. Alaythia needed no prodding; she took the canteen from Simon and followed the boy past some buildings to the first of several large canvas tents on the edge of town. The tents were leftovers from an old U.N. operation, and had been set up as a quarantine early on, the boy explained through the translator, who had hurried to keep up with Alaythia.

Vultures and jackals stood waiting a few yards away.

They had been hidden by the buildings. Their eyes followed her with interest.

Alaythia took one look back at Aldric and Simon, and entered the tent behind the boy. She heard the translator follow her with a rustle of the tent flap.

Inside, decorated blankets lay on the floor. Masks were hanging on the walls, while the sweet smell of incense filled the tent. Two old women lay in cots on either side of the tent, and their eyes begged for mercy.

A teenage boy knelt between the cots, and he greeted the first boy with a weary nod. The translator stood back at the entryway, seeming to apologize for disturbing the elderly women.

"I have medicine," said Alaythia, but she did not move closer to the women.

The translator helped them exchange words:

"What do you ask in return?" asked the second boy, suspicious.

"We're looking for something," Alaythia answered. "We need a guide. But you can have the medicine even if you don't help us."

"You are looking for the Unseen," said the boy, fearful.

"The vultures and jackals outside," Alaythia asked. "We want to know where they came from. There was a place they gathered on the first day . . . and there would have been fire near there . . . Do you know it?"

"What is there if you find it?"

"We are looking for two beasts. They are brothers, and they work together. Very unusual. They are Serpents but they look like men. They brought the disease to you. . . . They like to see suffering; they feed on it."

One of the old women shifted in her bed and propped herself up on one elbow to look at Alaythia. But Alaythia's own eyes were drawn to the flies that had gathered on the floor, rivers of them, hundreds, easing up from between the rugs. She began to tremble.

Outside, Simon had a bad feeling and began moving his horse toward the tent. Aldric followed. As his eyes fell upon the masses of jackals and vultures gathering, Aldric said, "The brothers. They're *here*."

Simon and Aldric spurred their horses toward the tent.

If they did not move quickly, there would be a new skeleton in the African sun.

Chapter 2

⚶

FIELDS OF FIRE

INSIDE THE TENT, ALAYTHIA stared at the two old women muttering at her in an unfamiliar language, and she saw the healing fluid in her canteen bubbling over, boiling. She dropped it as the metal burned her hand. The translator tried to catch it, but burned his own fingers. He yelped and fled from the tent, cradling his hand.

"Uncareful Magician," said one old woman, hissing in English. "We have long awaited you—"

"*Moritam kettisem sedosica,*" cried Alaythia, spell-chanting. "Do not cast your fire, Dragon—I have taken the power of your skin, you will not be armored against the flame."

"Lies!" cried the other woman, her eyes wild.

"You will burn with me," warned Alaythia.

The two old women lunged at her, lashing their claws as they transformed into African Tall Dragons, twelve feet of fury, each of them. Alaythia fell back and lifted a huge wooden mask for a shield, as the first Dragon, Matiki, sank his claws into it.

The two boys had already darted away and now they ran directly into Simon and Aldric, still on horseback.

Alaythia scrambled out of the tent as the first Dragon, the fearsome black-and-brown beast called Matiki, pounced upon her, sinking its teeth into her armored back, flinging his long, black braided mane.

Aldric fired his crossbow into its head. It did no harm.

But Matiki dropped Alaythia, who rolled free, as the Dragon's twin, Savagi, lurched from the tent, scrambling toward her on all fours. Simon and Aldric both shot at the beasts, landing arrows in the Dragons' arms and necks. The Dragons roared in pain, and turned to assault the riders.

Perfect, Simon thought. *We drew them from Alaythia.*

But his joy was quickly lost as Savagi leapt into the air and landed upon his horse, clinging to its neck. A huge snout stared him in the eye, and if the Serpent hadn't wasted time roaring in anger, Simon might've been crunched in its fangs. But his crossbow had one bolt left—and he shot it into the monster's throat.

Savagi screeched and tumbled back, somersaulting to land a few feet away.

Simon's horse jostled backward in the dust.

Matiki had turned on Aldric, and risen, man-like, to his full height. He slashed his long, muscular arms, trying to get at the Knight who kept his horse moving and stabbed back at the beast with his sword.

From his mount, Simon looked into Savagi's terrible yellow eyes, and knew what was coming. The Serpent reared its head back, its black throat swelling up. It was about to throw fire.

"NOOO!" cried Matiki, and yelled at his brother in the Dragontongue.

"Listen to your brother," cried Alaythia, "I've cursed your armor; you cannot burn your way out—"

Alaythia understood their words: "We have kept our magic from raging," cried Matiki to his brother. "We have come too far. We need no fire to kill these swine—"

But Savagi's rage was too much. Fire shot from his jaws.

Simon ducked and turned his horse, but the blast of black-yellow flames burned his shielded back, scorched his hair, and singed his horse's mane. The animal screamed and gave in to fear, riding them away from the threat.

The flames roared over Simon and met the ground,

flaring up in the yellow grass like a match to kerosene.

Alaythia scrambled for the well and climbed atop it, and Aldric rode his horse to a clearing as the fire spread across the parched ground. Some of the flames leapt onto Matiki, and the Dragon screeched in pain.

Simon at last got his horse to stop its run. The fire was sweeping over the veldt plains, whipped up by an unnatural wind the Dragons had brought on but could not control. Simon rode over to one of the old trucks, a rundown relief vehicle loaded with water. He opened its valves, and water gushed from it, cutting off the fire from the village.

But the veldt beyond was burning wildly. The flames were soaring across the yellow grass with such speed it made Simon gasp.

With Alaythia in relative safety, Aldric pulled a trigger on his saddle. Darts spat from tiny mounted guns on the saddle, and flew right into the African Dragons, again and again. Like a machine gun, the device riddled the creatures with silver barbs. Savagi howled and leapt for Aldric, swiping his claws against Valsephany, but the horse was protected by armor, the steel plating merely scratched and mauled in a spray of sparks.

Still Savagi did not give up. Dodging Aldric's sword, it managed to claw at him, aiming at his throat. Simon saw his father get struck below the neck. As he rode closer, Simon could see blood streaming from the cut, and he was filled with fear. He fired his crossbow, avoiding his father's body and targeting the African Dragon's head with precision. The arrow hit and the creature rocked from it, but did not let go.

Alaythia screamed and fired her rifle at Matiki, keeping him at bay, holding him off from helping his brother.

Simon could hear Aldric snarling in pain, and he wondered if he was going to witness his father's death. But galloping closer, he could see Aldric moving his sword fast as ever. He was going to be all right.

Matiki squealed in delight as Savagi swung for Aldric, but the warrior slammed his hand against the wretched creature's chest, and called out its death-spell, the sacred words that would destroy a Dragon. Quickly, Savagi broke clear before the spell could be finished. More fearsome than the Knight's sword was a deathspell.

Aldric cursed. A half-spell was of little use. Savagi fell to the ground and snapped at Simon's horse's leg in passing. The Serpent tore a chunk of muscle away, and darted for cover.

Aldric punished him with a glancing strike to the shoulder from his silver sword.

The two Dragons dove into the fire, screaming in pain, trying to escape.

"Go after them!" Aldric yelled.

How? thought Simon.

"They're going through it—so are we . . ." said Aldric, and he commanded his horse into the flames. Simon, on blind faith, followed his father's lead, and drove his own horse through the wall of fire, knowing the other side would be clear.

And it was. The Dragons had cleared a way for themselves—a passage in the fire. They ran and then galloped on all fours. Aldric and Simon rode through the field after the creatures, walls of fire flashing by on either side of their horses.

Simon thought of Moses' parting of the Red Sea, but instead of walls of water on his left and right, there were burning walls of yellow-black flames.

The Dragons had parted the raging fire on the African veldt using a desperate magic, for the flames could easily burn them as well as their enemies.

The horses were terrified, and Simon would have been, too, but he kept his mind on the targets. He tried to take aim, but he was riding too fast, his crossbow shaking in the rush. He tried in vain to slow Norayiss, but the horse was wounded, terrified, and Simon could see no way out.

Ahead, the African Dragons split up, making two passages through the flames.

Simon went left; Aldric went right. Simon saw his father ride after Matiki, and he realized he couldn't go back now. He would confront Savagi alone.

But the creature kept charging ahead down the trench.

Simon knew he had to try to take advantage. Attack from behind. He had never ridden so fast. Down twists and turns he went, as the African Dragon fled before him through a maze of fire.

Blasting away with his crossbow, Simon looked around in panic for a way to escape this confrontation; he wasn't ready for a Dragonkill on his own. But his arrows cut into the Dragon's hide, and Savagi now turned toward him and grinned pitilessly—*the boy was his*.

The cornered Dragon leapt upon Simon, landing his great jaws directly upon Simon's crossbow, which the boy swung before him for protection. Again Simon fired the bow and the last bolt emptied from the chamber, snapping the Dragon's head back. A direct blow shattered teeth in the creature's jaws.

Savagi fell upon the ground and stray flames caught on his skin and the exoskeleton at his back. The Dragon howled.

It turned, furious, and pulled at Simon, dragging him off his horse with shocking speed. His crossbow tumbled.

The injured beast's breath was labored, but he had Simon in his grasp, and was ready to crush his neck.

Suddenly, behind him the wall of flame tore open,

and Matiki went flying to the veldt ground, wailing. Savagi's huge armored ebony head swiveled to see his brother dying.

"Deathspell . . ." Matiki said, and red flames took him, bursting from somewhere inside the beast, killing it at last.

Aldric rode out behind him and jumped from his horse, slamming into Savagi. Simon was knocked loose, and Savagi was so surprised by the move, he choked, as Aldric drove his sword into his belly.

The creature struggled to hold Aldric back with his long arms, as Simon dove back into the fray, and shoved his hand upon the weak flesh at the Dragon's heart.

"Ordris africalla sadentiss ishkal," said Simon, and the deathspell took instant effect. Simon felt his hand burn as the Serpentine heart burst into perfect red fire, and the creature fell back away from Aldric in surprise at the quickness of its own death.

As the black-yellow flames around them dropped away, Simon could see lions, real African lions, running from the terrible inferno, and a group of stampeding giraffes alongside panicked hyenas, all trying to get away from the real king of the jungle . . .

Fire.

When Alaythia found them, Simon and Aldric had climbed up into a tree, having nowhere else to run.

The veldt around them was utterly blackened. The tree itself was beautifully unscarred, a random survivor of nature's supernatural wrath.

The brothers' red ashes drifted past her, where their Serpentine bones had faded to nothing. Somehow the horses must've galloped fast enough to avoid danger, for Alaythia had their bridles in hand, bringing them back. Simon had always been jealous of how she could coax them to her from anywhere by simply whistling.

"The sickness is gone," she reported. "It left the village the instant you killed them."

Simon gave a sigh of relief. His stomach had been churning ever since the fighting stopped; taking action was always better than having time to worry.

"You could've waited for me, you know," she added, brushing her long hair back from her face theatrically.

Simon smiled. Aldric squinted down at her from the tree. "You could've jumped in a wee bit faster," he replied. "Then I could be the one down there, traipsing around, casual as a Bond Street shopper."

She laughed at him. "It's a deal, then: I'll take the lead next time."

Simon groaned, for he knew there would be a next time.

And soon.

Chapter 3

OF SERPENTS AND SAMURAI

THERE WERE DECORATIONS IN the steel-walled house, but very few things that did not directly reflect Najikko's profession. What caught the eye would be the Samurai suits of armor that lined the halls. *Always keep a little something of your enemy close by. It helps you to conquer your hate.*

And how he hated the human Warriors.

Najikko's cold stare traveled past the suits of armor to a room where six new visitors awaited him. They had come seeking help, like many others. They were beautiful women, and yet all he could see were imperfections. They were ugly as sin to him.

Najikko looked out the window at one of many cities that he owned, and wondered how long it would be before a challenger came to his doorway.

Chapter 4

THE DRAGONHUNTER'S HOME LIFE

IF ANYONE ASKED, SIMON would say he lived in New England, but he was rarely there. He lived in a chilly, rundown ex-British castle—a fortress built in America during the Revolution and later modified to resemble a true baronial manor in the 1880s by a lord who wanted a touch of home in the States. And it must have succeeded in looking authentically English, for it was the only place Aldric could be convinced to make into a permanent residence. It was not yet a home in Simon's mind, just a placeholder for one, though he welcomed the cool stone walls after enduring the heat of Africa. In his first few months as Dragonhunter, he had been all over the map. Now he moped around the giant house, feeling punchy and tired, unable to sleep.

Simon felt fifty years old, and wondered how his father managed all this travel. There was Aldric, clanging around the big kitchen with all the energy of a cat, making some kind of sausage breakfast, and all Simon could do was stumble to an old chair and hope his father remembered to make him something (sometimes he didn't).

As Simon slipped past the stove, Aldric spun around, taking some biscuits out of the oven, then bumped into him, dumping the biscuits on the floor.

"Simon!" His father barked.

"Relax. I didn't mean to get in your way," said Simon, sinking into the chair. "I'm sorry."

"You're always saying sorry," mumbled Aldric.

"You're always *making* me." Simon sighed. They had grown into better coordination on the battlefield, but at home, they were all left feet and elbows and chaos. He watched as his pet fox Fenwick dived for the spilled biscuits.

Simon listened to the usual sounds of Aldric chasing the fox with a flyswatter, and looked out the wide windows at his old schoolhouse, the Lighthouse School for Boys. It was a rare, clear day, and he could see the lighthouse tower and the Revolutionary War buildings in all their rundown beauty. For a moment he wondered what the boys there were thinking of him. Crazy Simon St. George, the hermit kid, who lived in the castle and studied at home behind closed doors. Little they knew.

"You're up. I knew I heard some ridiculous tirade," said Alaythia, entering the room with a plate of sausages and a basket of piping-hot biscuits of her own. There was also the ignoble smell, Simon noted, of sulfur and ancient herbs. Alaythia often had unusual and interesting fragrances around her; Simon had found that her cooking would do that.

She strode past a surprised Aldric.

"What's all this, then?" Aldric stared.

"I decided to avoid the usual arguments—and the usual shortages, since you always forget me and Simon—and just make breakfast myself, in the alchemy lab," chirped Alaythia, and she sat down to serve the meal. "Simon?"

"I'm going to skip breakfast," said Simon, trying not to look disgusted.

"Not a great idea," she said, but didn't push the issue. She was good that way.

"Rancid stuff, smells of burned rats," grumbled Aldric. "Just 'cause yours is better doesn't mean it's good."

"Simon thinks my food is spectacular; he's just not hungry. And Simon has excellent taste, don't you, Simon?" She winked at the boy.

Aldric frowned. "His opinions frighten me."

"Well, there may have been rats in the vicinity, and they may have gotten torched—but none of them found their way into the sausages," she said and continued eating.

"I don't need any help making breakfast," Aldric said, but Simon noticed he sat down and helped himself. "I've managed well enough without your help all these years, haven't I? What I *will* say for you, is that you're getting a touch better each time out." He half-grinned at her.

"Glad you think so," she said. "There may be rats in the sausage after all."

And as they discussed this possibility in playful and somewhat aggravated tones, Simon tuned them out, and moved toward the window. He didn't like the way his father and Alaythia flirted; he wasn't sure if it was because they didn't seem serious enough about each other, or because Simon himself had begun noticing Alaythia's prettiness a bit too much, an uncomfortable thought he sent away quickly.

Fenwick stood up at the counter and pushed in his direction a stray biscuit that Aldric had tried to save from the floor. Simon actually took it.

His white horse was trotting in the field outside, and, watching it, Simon fell out of his sleepy state. Deciding he needed a ride, he grabbed another biscuit from the table and headed for the door.

"And where do you think you're going?" asked Aldric.

"Into town."

"Not for long; we've training to do. Lances today."

Simon kept going, keeping the debate to a minimum. "Training again? When am I gonna prove myself enough to you?"

"It's not about proving yourself, it's about keeping up your skills. This isn't a bloody game, is it? You can't fail at this."

Simon left the big, stone kitchen and headed down a cold hallway, but their voices echoed behind him. "You know, a little of that goes a long way," Alaythia told Aldric, good-naturedly. "You can never just let things *be*, not even for a second."

"What're you going on about? My father would knock me down if I tried to walk off like that."

"Well, you can look forward to the same wonderful relationship with Simon. You don't have to browbeat him so much, he's not afraid of hard work. He hates himself enough already."

"Oh, and why is that?" grumbled Aldric.

"Because he isn't *you*. Obviously," said Alaythia. Listening in the dark hallway, Simon could feel his face turn red. "Let him fail," she added. "It's how you learn, right?"

Simon went on to the entryway, filled with

newspapers from around the world, which might hold signs of supernatural events—the hallmarks of stray Dragonmagic.

There were circles around articles like, AFRICAN FOREST FIRES AT ALL-TIME HIGH, and STRANGE LIFEFORM SIGHTED IN JUNGLE, and so on. Simon was actually obsessed with these strange activities. They gave him nightmares, filled up his thoughts, gave every action in the world a darker purpose. Like his father, he now saw a Dragon presence in everything, and he worried constantly over every news story, from strip-mining and pollution to crime and—*right there*, he thought, his eyes on a small headline. *What is that?* FACTORY LAYING OFF THOUSANDS OF WORKERS IN UNUSUAL MOVE. *That's one of them, spreading hate, expanding its little domain of misery, that's what that is.* This was all he ever thought of now, it was just worry, worry, worry; he could hardly see the forest for the trees. Was there any end to this stuff? Was he losing his mind?

His ears perked up for a second. To his embarrassment, he could still catch the talking in the kitchen.

"He's got a girl," he heard Alaythia say.

"How do you know that?" wondered Aldric. "If he met a girl, he'd clean himself up more."

"That's why I say he's got a girl, not he 'met a girl.' If she didn't already like him, he'd have fixed that sloppy hair of his."

Simon heard the remark and left the house, patting his hair down in sudden regret. But going back would mean a lot of chatter about who she was and all that, and there was nothing he wanted less than advice from his father. His hair was a blond, wiry, standing-at-attention deal anyway, not much he could do about it.

And anyway, the horse ride to town would muss it up.

And anyway, the girl did like him enough to see past all that.

As he rode Norayiss down the long driveway, Fenwick scampered alongside. Simon wondered how the fox knew he was leaving. Aldric came to the door and shouted after him, "Be back by eleven! After training, we're going to look for Order members."

You do it yourself. What a waste of time, thought Simon, galloping down the tree-lined trail. For months, the St. Georges had been trying to find new converts to the Dragonhunting cause, and it wasn't going well. No one else could see the Serpents in their true form, so more often than not, Aldric and Simon came off looking like complete nutcases.

It used to be that the Order of Dragonhunters found soldiers from the families who had sworn to protect the St. Georges since way back in the Middle Ages. These were people who passed the job down to their sons and daughters, and so on, and so on. But the modern world had forgotten Simon's ancestor, the ancient Knight Saint George, the Dragonslayer, and those who knew the truth had been destroyed by the Serpents. It felt hopeless. There was only Simon, Aldric, and Alaythia against the hundreds of Dragons listed in the White Book of Saint George, which they had discovered only last year.

As Simon slowed his horse to a trot, watching the dusty, pebbled road pass under him, he remembered the last meeting he'd had with a distant cousin of an Order member. The poor construction worker from Massachusetts had never heard of Dragonhunting. The ordinary man had sat across from Simon and Aldric, near a half-finished skyscraper, and munched on his sandwich, looking bewildered.

The guy thought Simon and Aldric were insane, and it had been no better with any of the other six candidates they'd gone to see, all descendants and distant relatives of Dragonfighters. The Order of Dragonhunters was clearly a dead issue, but Simon's father never gave up on anything.

Simon's horse was moving now into the town of Ebony Hollow. Past the first few quiet streets, he found the novelty shop where his girlfriend—he hoped he could call her that pretty soon—was outside saying good-bye to her father.

"Simon," said Emily. "You're back from . . . where was it again, Spain?"

"Africa, actually," Simon replied, trotting his horse alongside her as he walked to school. "We went from Spain to Africa."

"On a job with your dad, right?" she said, looking at him sidelong, a bit confused. "Are you ever going to tell me what kind of job he actually does?"

I may do that, thought Simon, looking at her pretty eyes in the morning light. *I really may do that.*

"Come on, I'll give you a ride," he said, offering his hand, and she smiled, cautiously, but kept moving.

He trotted down the street beside her, crossing the trolley tracks. Anytime he had someone his age to talk to, things would come pouring out of him. It just happened. It was this desperate habit he was developing. Actually, to be honest, it was just around *her*. She was the only one he really talked to, or tried to, anyway.

"You said it was toxic waste disposal, I think," said Emily. "Why do you have to go around the world to do that?"

"Well, there aren't a lot of people who know how to handle the kind of . . . dangerous material we deal with."

"It doesn't make you glow, does it?" she said and laughed.

"Uh, it can," he said. He pretended to have trouble

keeping Norayiss on course, pulling the reins to flex his arms. He was pretty sure Emily noticed how big he was getting. He was growing stronger every day with training—*constant* training, so he knew he'd gained quite a bit of muscle—though he still wasn't as tall as he'd like to be.

"Nobody understands why you don't go to school," Emily remarked.

"It's just home schooling." That didn't sound too strange, did it? "It's not a big deal. I just travel so much, helping my dad, that I can't really . . . Have you ever thought about my name?"

"Your name? Simon?"

"No, St. George. He was a real person. The legend says he fought a Dragon, a long time ago, in the deserts of North Africa. A real Dragon, okay? I mean, it's not a legend, people say it was a real creature, whatever it was."

She creased her brow, half-amused. "And that relates to you . . . how? I don't get what you're talking about."

He paused. *What if there were real Dragons, but they didn't look like Dragons. And they did really terrible, really evil things, making all these supernatural events you hear about that no one can ever explain, and hurting people, and killing people, and someone had to stop them from doing this. Oh, no, no, no, don't say that . . .*

"Do you believe in true evil?" he asked. "The kind of evil that you can just feel coming off of someone?"

"Are you talking about the people who make these toxic waste dumps?" she replied.

"It's not toxic-waste dumps, that's not what I deal with," he said.

"What *do* you deal with?"

A species. He answered in his head, *A species that drives people to do evil, because it feeds off misery, soaks it right into the skin. It tortures people. If the Serpent doesn't actually do these things itself, it forces people to do it for him . . .*

"Maybe we can talk about this later," he mumbled. Luckily, there was no more time for talking. They'd reached her school.

She looked up and manufactured a smile. "I've gotta go. Your horse is amazing, she's really calm. So, um, I'll see you around the shop, I guess. Maybe I could finally meet your dad," she said.

"He's not real social," said Simon, embarrassed.

"Well, you can bring him by if you want."

She walked off across the grass and joined the girls, and he noticed her shoulders were raised and tight.

When she finally shot him a glance, it was strange, and Simon knew he had now put up a barrier between them. She was scared of him; he occupied a

land of fairy tales and craziness. Or was he just thinking too much?

He wished he'd kept his mouth shut.

At that moment, a terrible shadow passed across
the sun, he thought, but then it was gone before it
could be deciphered. He wondered if the menace was
all in his mind; his world always ordered by threat and
fear.

Fine. Live in your fantasy land, he thought, looking
at the mean-eyed girls with Emily. *This is real, and I'm
one of the only people in the world that can protect any of
you. You need me.* He wished they knew it.

But he had no stomach for sulking, that was his
father's habit—Aldric's little genetic gift that he probably passed down and Simon didn't want it. *Strong,
silent type. Right. What a joke. Silence is weak. It means
you're afraid.* He couldn't have gotten his father's
strength and agility, *oh, no, that would have been too
good,* so he'd inherited a total inability to talk to anybody.

Or did he? Maybe he could get along with everybody just fine if he got more of a chance to hang
around them; if his father wasn't always dragging him
around the world or shoving hard work in his face.

Stop it. Come on. Get out of your head, Simon
thought. Here he was talking to himself instead of to
other people, and he realized he'd been staring at the

girls as they walked away. *I'm not staring at you, I'm just thinking.*

He tried to figure a way to look natural. *Stop sleepwalking,* he told himself. *This is your life.*

Sometimes it seemed like the ordinary world was the one that was like a dream.

Chapter 5

A HOME LIFE DESTROYED

SIMON LEFT THE SCHOOL and Emily, riding back home, upset. He passed some of the teenagers pulling into the school parking lot, their car radios blaring, and it finally hit him that he must look incredibly stupid to Emily on his horse. *How great and impressive I thought I was. Look at me. What an idiot.* All the kids looked so confident, so *ordinary*, with nothing to worry about except homework or a Friday night date.

I don't know how to act. I don't know how to be, he was thinking. *What do people expect? I'm a human disaster. I don't even have anyone to tell this to, except Alaythia.*

As his horse weaved through the light traffic and back to the weed-sprouting train tracks, Simon passed a group of boys in suits, headed for the Lighthouse

School farther away, their hands full of junk-food breakfast from a corner store. Doughnuts and Twinkies always trumped the food they served at school.

They watched Simon pass. He was the mysterious boy, the one who had left the boys' school on Halloween night, and then came back to live hidden in the old castle outside of town.

"Simon St. George," he heard them whispering. He had always wanted to be a legend at school. He never knew it would make him feel so alone.

"Doesn't all that riding make you bar-legged?" said one boy, as if challenging Simon.

"*Bow*-legged," said another boy. "Not bar-legged. Idiot."

"Whatever," said the other. "He's so weird. He never leaves his house, his horse is his only friend." He made kissing noises. "It's his girlfriend."

Pathetic jokes. Simon rode past them. They still lived in a land of dumb humor and stupid pecking orders.

He knew things they would never know at the Lighthouse School—the darkness under life, the pain and fear of battle—and he was satisfed to know all this, but it felt like the days of struggle ahead were endless, the enemy unconquerable, and he would never be done with the fighting until he was dead.

He could see boys lining up for roll call on the field

beside the lighthouse, neat rows in neat uniforms, and for a minute he wanted to wrap himself in their perfect boring school day, to avoid the disorganized, rambling lessons he'd get later from Alaythia, and the harsh training he'd get from his father.

He saw his old friend Denman, the lighthouse keeper, heading into the tower. The gruff old Scotsman and his wife had practically raised him from infancy, but now Simon felt they were strangers, caretakers who did a job and rarely smiled. Without knowing it, Simon had been a burden, a danger to them because of the Dragons who were always hunting him, and he was a precious thing, too, the last of the Dragonhunters, bringing a responsibility that made the old couple weary. He knew his father disapproved of the way they raised him. To this day, Aldric seemed to begrudge them the fact they had gotten to see Simon's growing-up years. Simon still spent time with the Denmans now and then, but not today. There was no time.

Simon turned Norayiss, moving away, and something tore him from these memories.

As he came up the hill and rejoined the road, he noticed there were no birds chirping. The world had been enveloped in a strange quiet. When he looked down at the horse's hooves, they made no sound on the pavement. It was as if Simon had momentarily gone deaf.

He stopped his horse, worried.

And then . . . the shadows began to shift. The ones on the left side of the road vanished, and suddenly the shadows of the trees on the right side of the road began to stretch toward him. The darkness reached forward, like a set of black claws. It was as if someone had moved the sun to the wrong side of the sky.

Simon swallowed hard.

Then he noticed that the trees far off in the woods, near his home, were beginning to rustle, as if tremendously agitated. The whole forest there was shaking. A great, immense thing was moving in those trees, or causing the trees to shudder somehow. And it was headed for his house.

He spurred Norayiss on.

The horse sped down the street, and tore off into the forest. As he neared the castle, struck with panic, Simon realized he had only a small silver dagger for protection. He never dreamed he'd need body armor this close to home. He was open; easy prey.

He took hold of the knife. Silver was the finest weapon against Dragons, but it was the deathspell that killed them—and if it was a Serpent on the attack, he had no idea which spell to use, as they were specific to each Dragon.

So which one was on the attack?

There were hundreds of the beasts listed in the

White Book of Saint George.

The horse clomped through the Ebony Hollow forest, and Simon noticed with horror that the ground was rippling with beetles that seemed to be pouring out of the ground. Green-yellow insects wriggled from the earth and swarmed around the horse's hooves.

This kind of warping of nature could only mean a Dragon in their midst.

But where?

As he thundered down the road to the castle, he found no sight of the killer; just Aldric and Alaythia, outside in the field, brushing Valsephany. Simon felt calmer, thinking perhaps the Serpent had merely been spying on them, and the idle talk he caught between his father and Alaythia relaxed him for an instant.

"It's just really weird, what happened in Africa," Alaythia was saying. "The brothers knew where we were, they were ready for us, they set a trap. And they knew how to trick me into coming in first. They knew we were coming into that village, just at that time, and they knew exactly where we were."

"Quiet down," he heard Aldric say. "Simon's coming. He doesn't need to know all of this."

"Listen, something's happening," Simon warned. "There's something here—"

Suddenly, a set of claws snatched him around the shoulders from behind, and hoisted him off the horse, into the air. He screamed childishly, instantly hating himself for it, but he couldn't see what had him.

He heard the beating of terrible wings, the smell and heat of rancid breath was everywhere.

"SIMON!" Alaythia screamed, and Simon suddenly saw her down below, firing, from a wrist-device, small bolts of silver shooting toward him, narrowly missing his ear. He heard a dart plunge into the beast, but the animal had no reaction, and Simon was carried farther up, the horse pasture growing small far beneath him, and then he saw it twist away, in a terrifying spin.

Simon's head swirled from dizziness, and he tried to see what it was that had taken him. But there was no way to see, it was behind him.

He heard his father's rocket-arrows shooting up from below—Aldric must've gotten to his travel pack, left by the horse trough. The rockets hissed, whisking around the Dragon, and Simon saw in the spinning world above Ebony Hollow the white flare of their passing.

"You want to get back to your father." The Serpent laughed. "I'll make sure you do . . ."

The voice was pure terror.

A female, breathing these threats with fearsome delight.

Simon clambered to get hold of the Creature's

claws so he couldn't be dropped.

"The question," said the Serpentine beast, "is whether you go down in one piece . . ." And she dropped him, just enough so his stomach sickened, then snatched him back. "Or in many different, bleeding pieces."

Suddenly, one of the rockets connected! A silver barb slammed into the Dragon's neck.

The creature was streaming fireblood—sparks showered down on Simon from the injury, burning his skin in little pinpricks of agony. Green-yellow flames flickered lightly from the Dragon's wound.

It was enough to get the Creature to descend, but still the Dragon held tight to Simon.

Now, the Creature let loose a massive torrent of flame, and Simon felt a disgusted thrill at being *with* the Dragon as the fire charged loose. It engulfed the upper part of the old castle and the wood tiles of the roof, knocking down stones in the walls from sheer force. On the second pass, the Dragon set fire to the far side of the house, the Victorian wing made of oak and cedar.

It would all go up.

Struggling, Simon could see the castle returning to view, speeding toward him, and he realized the Serpent planned to hurl him against the tower.

"We shall leave him something to remember you

by," she said in a husky growl, and Simon soared with her, past the field, past Alaythia and Aldric rushing to take aim, and then he saw the tower coming for him, closer, closer, closer—

SLAM! A second rocket-arrow burned into the Creature, and took it off course. Simon was dropped, clattering painfully to the raked roof, then rolling in and out of the fire, and plunging to the flat top of the stables.

He was all right.

He had the wind knocked out of him, but he would've been caught breathless anyway at the sight of the Dragon above him, a green-yellow beast with long tendrils of many colors trailing behind its soaring body.

Another rocket hurtled past him, and he saw it miss the Serpent. The Creature blurred into nothingness, cloaking itself in magic. He felt it swoop past again and snap at him, invisible jaws tearing at his shirt.

It soared past.

He looked up, catching his breath, and squinted, scarcely able to penetrate the beast's magic enough to see it. But he could make it out, as it was bleeding fire into the air. He saw the Creature descend in the Ebony Hollow forest.

It needed to recover its strength.

He looked down to see Aldric yelling at him from the pasture, "SUIT UP!"

Simon swung himself to safety off the stable roof and rushed for his travel pack hidden in the hay.

In five minutes flat, they had retrieved their horses and were pursuing the Dragon, galloping at a raging speed in full-body armor.

"The Ashlover Serpent," cried Aldric, identifying it fast, for he'd memorized the White Book of Saint George, as Simon never could. Simon and Aldric rode hard through the forest, leaving Alaythia to use her magic to battle the blaze at home.

The forest crackled with an unnatural wind. They stopped at a hole, a fiery spot, devoid of vegetation and underbrush. A thin, leathery blanket stood before them, and as they watched it began to dry up and wither, curling up into nothing.

"It shed its wings," said Aldric.

Humanlike tracks in the soft ground left the area, and led toward town.

"She's injured," Aldric observed. "It will take all her strength to heal those wounds. We'll find her in town."

Simon's heart was beating hard. No Serpent had ever been fought here. No Dragon had known where the home of the Saint George descendants lay. This Creature had to be recovered. And killed.

They galloped into town, where a street of suspects greeted them. It would take a moment for Simon's eyes to adjust and see through the disguising magic. The Serpent could look like anyone.

A limping man caught his attention, but Aldric focused on a girl in a wheelchair, pushing herself away as fast as she could.

Simon watched her glide through a small crowd of people leaving breakfast at the Old Soldier Café, and the girl did indeed seem in a hurry.

He saw her blood hit the sidewalk, the red droplets turning to green, and then burning away.

Then his vision rippled, as if looking through a mirage, and he saw not a girl, but a wounded, scaly Creature limping for cover.

The Ashlover Serpent.

It turned the corner, and Aldric and Simon hurried to catch up.

As they rode down Main Street, the Ashlover slipped into the novelty shop and gave a howl and a screech, its mouth exploding with fire. Glass shattered out. The fire screamed.

"No!" Again Simon couldn't breathe—this time out of fear for Emily's family.

Green-yellow Serpentine flames lapped out of the windows. It was a bad fire. The wooden structure was old, and it would burn easily.

"Wait! It could be a diversion to get us off track," said Aldric.

"No," argued Simon, "the Thing's in there . . ." And he rode toward the fire as fast as he could, dismounting at the door in a rush.

Through the flames, he could see the wounded creature lying in a circle of green-and-yellow flames. The fire was just an attempt to slow the hunters down. Short of air and nearly unconscious, the Dragon was weakening.

Aldric pushed past Simon, walking right through the flames. As the Serpent kicked at him with its great clawed feet, Aldric wrestled it down amid the flames, and he slammed his hand upon its heart. It took many tries, the Serpent slithering out of the Knight's grasp over and over again, but at last the Creature stopped shaking, and Simon knew Aldric was reciting the words of the deathspell.

Aldric stumbled back.

The colorful tendrils of the Dragon, like wispy tentacles, pulled in and closed around its body, and caught fire . . . and the beast burned away into red ash that blew over Aldric and into Simon's eyes.

The Ashlover Dragon was dead.

"Is anyone in there?" Simon yelled into the store.

"If they were, they're dead," said Aldric, but up the street, Simon could see Emily's father rushing from the post office. He'd missed the danger.

"It's an arsonist," Simon yelled to him, climbing onto his horse. "There's smoke—I think our house might have been hit, too!" Simon turned and rode with Aldric out of town, ignoring the bewildered passersby.

Emily is safe at school, Simon thought with relief.

But his own house was burning.

By the time he and Aldric returned, Alaythia had drawn a massive black storm cloud to the house, and the resulting rainfall had, for the most part, ended the fire. But the castle was blackened, and much of its interior had been gutted.

What Simon considered home was now an ugly memento of a Dragon's evil.

Chapter 6

HOW A DRAGON TRACKS ITS PREY

"**H**OW DID IT KNOW?"

Sitting at the largest of the Old Soldier Café's tables, Alaythia twirled a tea bag in her mug, and repeated the question. "How did the Dragon find us? There's nobody to give that information away. We haven't told anyone, and we'd know if we were followed—we're always incredibly careful."

Aldric said nothing, tapping the table nervously.

"All my comic books," said Simon, "my games, everything's torched. . . . It was so hot it even melted all my metal soldier figures. I've had those since I was a little kid."

"None of those things matter," said Aldric quietly.

"They matter to me," Simon said firmly.

"That's not what I meant," said Aldric, sympathetically. "That isn't our home anymore. It can't be. If one Dragon can find us, then many can."

Simon took his remarks like a lashing. It hadn't occurred to him how bad the situation was.

"Maybe not," said Alaythia, seeing how Simon felt. "If we can figure out *how* it found us, maybe we can take steps to make ourselves safe again—to undo the problem."

There was an uncomfortable pause. "There *is* a way," Aldric said, avoiding her eyes. "It's not done very often. There are dangers to it. All kinds of dangers."

"What are you getting at?" Alaythia asked.

"The skull," answered Aldric. "If it survived the blast, even just shards of it could provide answers to these questions. If you, as a Magician, were to take hold of the bones of this Dragon, its dying spirit could enter you, and it's possible you might glimpse the Serpent's last thoughts before the spirit faded completely. But I don't think there was anything left of the beast."

They needed to find out. Simon welcomed the chance to get to Emily's shop, and he was curious to see her father's reaction to him. While at the café, Alaythia said she had grown calm enough to cast a spell on the street, so that all those who had seen Simon and Aldric in battle gear would forget what they'd seen.

"You can do that?" Simon had asked.

"Don't be too optimistic, okay? It's magic, but it's not *magic*. The memories will be gone, but the suspicion will remain," Alaythia said. "You may get people looking at you funny or asking questions for a long time."

"It's not as if they think we're an average, ordinary family as it is," Simon muttered.

A few minutes later, they were standing in the cinders before the novelty shop. Simon had seen the horror of fire before. But never in his hometown. He hadn't realized until now the Dragons could reach so deeply into his life.

Emily's father was standing nearby, talking with a worried neighbor, and then her mother's car pulled up, and Emily got out and wandered over to him, looking dazed. "My father told me what happened," she said. "What's going on?"

Simon looked at her and tried to find the right words.

He said he saw someone throw a match and run.

He and Aldric gave everyone the same story: They didn't get a good look at the guy, whoever he was; he was small, maybe even a kid, someone who had done this randomly. But there were no real suspects as far as the police were concerned.

Alaythia, however, had found evidence of the real arsonist.

As Simon was being questioned, he saw Alaythia tap Aldric on the shoulder, and they moved away from the police officers. Simon saw her showing Aldric a small shard of bone she had taken from the ashes of the shop.

It was all that remained of the beast.

"This will not be pleasant," Aldric told her, and he placed the skull shard back in her hands, and closed her fingers over it. Simon noticed how much older his father's hands looked against the smooth ivory of Alaythia's. The skull bones of the Dragon were the most useful of any fragment, but his father's seriousness made Simon feel less than fortunate. In the ruins of the castle house tower, candlelight flickered around them, and the moon pierced the uncovered window.

Aldric had decided to return to the castle, because it was dangerous to try this experiment anywhere else, and, after all, there was nothing left to ruin there.

Alaythia's face took on a deathly color almost immediately, and she closed her eyes.

"You will be able to see into the Creature's mind," Aldric told her, "its most angry, sad, or deeply held memories. You will not like what you see. You may witness things you have never imagined before. Thousands of murders may pass before your eyes, and you may see them all in terrible detail."

There was no mistaking the skull bone as anything else. It bore red, vein-like patterns, but Simon had never understood until now what those patterns might contain.

Simon reached out and touched Alaythia's arm, but Aldric moved his hand away gently. "The Dragon's spirit might enter you, Simon," said Aldric. "I do not think you would like that."

The darkness in his voice convinced Simon immediately, and he backed up against the stone wall to feel safer.

"Be careful, Alaythia," Aldric whispered. "Its spirit may want to toy with you before it vanishes from life completely. . . ."

Alaythia had gone into a trance, and now she began to whisper the ancient language of magic. For an instant, her young face looked weathered with age, then returned to normal, but her voice changed as she chanted. Soon the room filled with two voices coming out of her, one of them horrible and Serpentine. Alaythia began to tremble and Simon saw Aldric tighten his jaw.

Then she quieted, and fell back into sleep, her hands still holding the shard.

While Alaythia slumbered, Simon roamed the burned castle, his nose filled with the musty smell of a killed fire. Because of the recent rainfall, the ground was mush and mud beneath his feet, and as he ran his hand over the blackened walls, Simon counted one blessing: that Aldric kept most of his important belongings on his ship.

The few photographs of Simon's mother were kept in Aldric's stateroom onboard, hidden in a cabinet. She'd been killed by the White Dragon before Simon knew her, so those mementos were things he couldn't replace. He didn't have memories of his mother; as a young child, he'd been sent to boarding school for safekeeping from the Dragons. Those photographs were all that connected him to her.

A rustling came from the darkness ahead, and Simon clutched his flashlight tight.

Something was up there.

Simon didn't move. He was alone, his father out of earshot in the next wing. It would be impossible to get to him fast if Simon was under attack. He'd have to face this alone.

If it was an assassin, it wasn't being quiet. It was moving in the muck in the blackness ahead, then suddenly, it pounced into a puddle in the hallway, spattering water at Simon, and an animal's eyes gleamed in the moonlight.

"Fenwick."

The fox smacked his lips and then gave something

like a grin. Simon allowed himself to breathe.

"What are you doing here?"

The fox trotted through the darkened hallway and leapt to a low table that had survived the blaze, and Simon, familiar with this routine, looked straight at the animal's eyes, which slowly darkened.

The fox wriggled its snout at him, and Simon felt a tickling in his head as if whiskers had brushed over his brain, and then Fenwick held its mouth open, as if its breath held magic. And it did, Simon had learned.

He had, over time, earned the animal's trust enough to be rewarded with an old bit of mother's magic, a spell she'd left on him: Fenwick brought him things he had heard.

First, Simon saw only darkness, and heard a group of voices, all of them boys, kids he knew from the Lighthouse School. Fenwick had eavesdropped on them, and captured their conversation in the wind, pulling it into his mouth.

Now Simon saw them in his mind, talking about him:

"Weird guy . . ."

"Always by himself when I see him . . ."

"What's so weird about him? He's just home schooled."

"You ever know anybody home schooled? It means their parents are kinda out of it."

"I'm not saying that, but I see him out there practicing with, like, a steel lance, riding his horse. It's totally bizarre, and if you get close, his dad chases you away from their house."

"His *dad* is weird."

"That lady isn't weird. Is that his mom?"

"No, she's too young. . . . I think she might be a stepmom, or something. She's really nice. I've talked to her a few times in town. If it weren't for her, I'd think that place he lives in was a nuthouse."

"He always liked playing with fire when he went to school here," said one boy.

Another said, "He was always building bonfires out on the beach. . . . It's totally obvious he was the one who set fire to the joke shop, 'cause that girl who works there said she didn't want to see him anymore."

Simon groaned. Now he was the prime suspect in town for the fire that had ruined his home. Life was interesting. Very interesting.

He patted the fox, wondering if Fenwick felt sorry for him.

He would have felt sorry for himself—but a scream interrupted his thoughts.

Alaythia.

What Alaythia saw with her dream-eyes was not a world anyone would seek out. For the longest hour she'd ever known, she had experienced life, or pieces of it anyway, as a female Pyrothrax from Brazil, the Ashlover Serpent.

Alaythia saw herself burning the houses of the poor throughout South America; she saw herself consuming lost children, runaways on the streets of Rio de Janeiro, during crazed celebrations in the night. She heard the strange music in the Serpent's head and contemplated the moon in the jungle with such love she was surely insane.

When the Ashlover burned bones and flesh, Alaythia *felt* the fire leave her mouth, and it felt sweet in her throat, like ambrosia, like candy, like rainwater after a desert journey. The flames gave her visions and a sense of giddy joy, every time a different taste than the last.

The memories were a clash of events, a jumble. Alaythia would see one thing happen, then another, without knowing when they had happened, but among all these events she could hear a calling, a cry, a memory of a sound in the Serpent's head.

The Ashlover Serpent had been drawn to New England, called there, pulled by a humming in its ears, by a force, a need, and it had followed the sound all the way through South America, north through Mexico, and up the ragged North American coast to Ebony Hollow. The Serpent had been plagued with terrible dreams. It had needed to stop these nightmarish visions. And so it had gone. It had gone to the source: the castle home of the St. Georges . . . and to Alaythia.

Alaythia's love for Aldric had sent a sound and a light and a tremor into the world that she could not control; it was true of all Magicians who fell in love with Dragonhunters. All Magicians were women, and from the Old Ages, it was always a terrible risk for them to fall in love with the Knights they protected. The Dragons could feel this power emanating from the Magician and could track it. It was as simple as following a beacon of light.

The Ashlover Dragon had come for Alaythia.

More would come now.

Alaythia knew she would have to leave this house.

Chapter 7

HUNTING A MASTER OF DRAGONS

"THERE IS NO OTHER WAY," Alaythia's note read. "The Serpents can find us wherever we go, they can catch the scent of our emotions the way blood in the water draws a shark. I cannot hide my feelings for you, Aldric, or for that matter, for Simon. I don't know how to bury them. I cannot stop *feeling*."

Simon sat at the table in the dim early light, as Aldric paced the ruined kitchen.

"Dreamer," Aldric muttered. An insult, from his tone.

Barely awake, Simon ran a hand through his hair and stared at the letter again. He'd seen it first, but he still couldn't quite believe it, and he found himself reading aloud in a whisper, "If there is a magic I can learn that will disguise my feelings, to hide them so no Serpent can find us, I do not know what it is. The hope I have is that I can find the Chinese Black Dragon, and bargain with him for help. He is no ordinary Dragon, and if he helped us once, perhaps he will again. Forgive me for leaving. With all of my love . . . Alaythia."

"We've tried that, Alaythia," grumbled Aldric, speaking to the letter as if she could hear him. "We weren't able to find him, what's different now?"

"Maybe she saw something in her dream," said Simon, quietly remembering her expression in the trance. "Something from the dead Serpent that gave her a clue about where the Black Dragon went."

"Then why didn't she tell us? We could've helped her."

"Well, I guess she doesn't think so. I mean, anywhere she goes with us, the Dragons sense exactly where she is," Simon protested.

"You're being pretty bloody reasonable, aren't you?"

"You think I like this?"

"Why didn't you see this coming?"

"If *you* didn't see it, how am I supposed to know what's going on in her head?"

"You're closer to her," grumbled Aldric, and Simon felt himself turning red.

"Everything was going fine, we had it all set right, didn't we?" Aldric muttered on. "It was all working. We could've got our minds round this together . . ."

"What're you talking about?" said Simon, getting angry now. "Everything's back the way it used to be. You get to yell and scream at me, and there's no one to tell you you're wrong. There's nobody here on my side."

"*I'm* on your side."

"Yeah, right."

"You want to have a row right now? Fine. But you can't blame everything on me. You'd like to, wouldn't you?"

I'd like you to shut up, Simon was thinking.

"You've got nobody here on your side? You're a loner, Simon; you *like* being alone. You don't have friends, and you want it that way. Stop blaming me for every little thing in your life, for your *own* good."

Aldric's eyes hardened and Simon cowered inside as his father went on. "I know what you're thinking. Why don't you say it outright, then? I drove her away, is that it?"

Simon stared back. "Not on purpose, but I think, yeah, you wanted her out of here. Everything was just getting way too *normal* for you to stand it."

"That's a bunch of rot. Tell me where the note says anything like that," Aldric retorted. "She was happy. I gave her a good place to hone her talents. I was always here for her."

"You're so here for her, she's not here."

"Well, I'm going to get her back."

Silence. It took Simon a second. "We're going to go after her?"

Aldric fished around for his pipe on the charred table. "I don't see any other way," he said. "She's the only Magician on Earth. We need her to forge our weapons, give us help. Lord knows we need all of it we can get."

Aldric was tapping his pipe on his teeth the way he did when he was deep in thought, a habit that always annoyed Simon. "But figuring where to start won't be easy," Aldric said, fumbling for a plan. "She could be anywhere. The Black Dragon hasn't been seen since London. And Alaythia has a head start on us."

"A big head start," said Simon, looking at the clock on the wall. It had a small cutout for the date in its face, and if the clock was right, Alaythia had left a bit of spellchant behind. "We've been asleep for three days."

"What?" Aldric followed Simon's gaze to the clock. Alaythia had put a spell on them that kept them out of commission long enough for her to get any-where in the world.

"I thought I felt stiff when I woke up," said Simon, "I thought it was 'cause I had to sleep on the floor."

Aldric made a sound at the pit of his throat like some kind of angry animal. "That deceptive little genius."

The Ship with No Name set sail as quickly as possible, loaded with every possible weapon, device, scroll, and book they could salvage from the castle. Simon had ridden to Emily's house for a fast good-bye, but she had acted strangely, seeming not to trust him, and he feared the rumor that he was the fire-starter might have gotten to her.

But when he looked back, he could see her in the doorway, still watching him go, and he could not read her expression.

So he had that to worry about, on top of every-thing else.

Once they were at sea, however, Simon's mind was kept busy with the ship. Alaythia had left its magic intact, and there were traces of it still alive in the rig-ging and the sails, but everything about the vessel seemed sluggish and moody, like someone awoken in the middle of the night. Simon had to hammer on some of the devices and rods that worked the sails just to keep them going. Aldric scowled at that—the ship had been made by Simon's mother, the renowned Magician Maradine, and anything she touched had a sacred feel to Aldric.

His father had allowed Alaythia to make the ship her own, though, and Simon noticed the many additions she had brought in over the past few months. Not all of them were magical: homemade pottery and dried plants hung about the ship in leather pouches and slings, ornate hand-painted tea kettles, and little knitted "sweaters" for things like oil canisters and medicine bottles. She would always see herself as an artist, even if no one else did. But it did warm up the look of the place.

As Aldric set the course, stubbornly the ship took on the waves, and stabbed its bowsprit eastward, for all the good it would do them.

How would they find her?

Aldric seemed to have a plan, though he didn't seem confident it would work, and Simon had to press him for the details. Many times Simon had seen Aldric hovering around an old brass globe in a nook near the galley, and when Fenwick nosed around it, Aldric had gotten angry. The importance of it was not lost on Simon.

"It may do us no good," Aldric warned. "She's

more clever than us. But if she was in a hurry, she might've forgotten a few details. See." He allowed Simon to look closer at the globe.

The way it worked was this: Many times, they could not get close to a Dragon, only to its men, its workers, its minions, so Alaythia and Aldric had developed a technique to handle the problem. They had created a set of extremely small arrows attached to little tracking devices, homing beacons, for lack of a better term. Shoot these tiny darts into the henchmen or their clothes or cars without them knowing it, and their movements could be tracked on the globe.

It looked like technology, but it wasn't. It was the methodical work of a Magician using a kind of sorcery at least four centuries old.

"Alaythia took weapons with her," Aldric explained, "one of which was an arrow containing the tracer device. We can use that to follow her, if she hasn't purposely thrown us off the mark."

Simon nodded. A little light was glowing on the brass globe showing the beacon Alaythia was carrying. The fox gave a little whimper, and placed its snout on the signal, pointing somewhere in the middle of the Atlantic Ocean.

The clue puzzled Simon.

Was she headed to China? That was the last place the Black Dragon had lived. Back then, he had been an enemy, but what was he now? He had helped Simon when it really mattered, in the battle of the Serpent Queen, when every life on Earth was in the balance, but who was he really?

And how would he react to Alaythia on her own?

Chapter 8

THE ICE DRAGON

EVERYONE WANTED THE BLACK Dragon dead.

Rumors were swirling around the Serpentine world that perhaps the Black Dragon, or Ming Song as he called himself, had gone back to China, for there had been news reports of drought and animals dying en masse in the inland country.

But then, Serpents of every kind had been there searching for him, causing their own distortions in nature. It was a kind of mania. The Dragons had an unquenchable thirst for revenge. Their prey was elusive, though. Some Serpents had even come to believe the Black Dragon had passed through their borders, like a ghost, leaving no trace whatsoever. He was fast becoming a legend.

No one knew anything for certain.

However, in the Swiss Alps there had been some hikers who reported sightings of a small, furred creature darting its way among the rocks, something shadowy that vanished into holes and caves. The reports became a joke around Swiss mountain towns.

Such incidents were not laughed off by Herr Visser, the Beast of Switzerland, the Ice Dragon, a lowly worm in the grand scheme of things, a rare Creature who did not seek out riches or high office, but instead enjoyed smaller pleasures: torture, mind games, spreading sorrow and grief, and the occasional quiet homicide.

Not that he was without vanity. He kept his slick Serpentine skin clean and well-groomed, right down to the hairy spikes on his head and goatee, and in his human form, he always tried to be presentable—even to those he despised.

As a Dragon, the Ice Serpent bore permanent camouflage for winter. The left side of his body was perfectly black, the right side purely white. The colors split him down the middle; black ice clung to his darkened side, and frost collected on his ivory side.

He saw the world in black and white. Everything he did was pure as snow, but anyone who went against him was viewed as black as pitch, and disposed of appropriately.

Of course, he wanted to dispose of the Black Dragon more than anything.

Wouldn't that be nice, to freeze him in ice and watch him rot for the next few years?

The Ice Serpent considered the Chinese Dragon a turncoat who had tried to make himself look grand in old age by siding with *human* allies during a great battle.

Killing the traitor would make the Ice Creature famous among his kind.

Otherwise Professor Visser would remain an unimportant snake posing as an unremarkable teacher of history, even his murders unnoticed. And he had little time left to change his destiny.

The Ice Dragon was dying. Old age would get him—and soon. He had pressing things to do before that happened.

Switzerland would not be safe for him much longer, with all the turmoil in the Serpent world, with so many Dragons wanting new lands to conquer. But he was unhappy for other reasons still. His fire did not keep him warm, and no matter where he went, he felt a chill upon his skin, a frightening touch from old Mr. Death, who was on his way, reminding him each day with a white kiss of frost.

He hated snow and ice. It so happened he was born into a place that, in the past, was not often fought over by other Serpents—a refuge for a weak Dragon. Living here was no blessing, however; the cold world around him had affected his magic.

The frost settled on him after he woke each morning, and could often be seen even when he took his human form, as a blue-skinned and isolated old man. There was no magic that could keep him from looking old. He tried. The wrinkles always returned to his weak human disguise. The teeth yellowed. The eyes he saw in the mirror grew dim and veined and blurred. His powers were withering. No question about it.

But there was new hope he could make something of himself before it was too late.

The Ice Creature had followed the reports of the Chinese Black Dragon's appearance in the Swiss Alps, but when he arrived in a new ski village, he sensed the enemy had already moved on. It was only when the Ice Dragon investigated a remote crevice blocked by fallen trees that he found anything of import.

And what a thing it was. The Ice Dragon had found the remains of a cave encampment, fresh with the scent of the Black Dragon. *Ahhh,* he thought. *Here is a Serpentine soul nearly as old as myself, and one filled with barbaric memories.*

Left behind in the Black Dragon's haste was a traveling tea set, and a much-used pipe. As the Ice Creature poked his claw into the bowl, he could feel remnants of life, for a Dragon's breath contains traces of his spirit.

These were fresh ashes. And ashes speak to Dragons.

Ashes and dreams, dreams and ashes, time for the rotten to take their lashes, he thought, remembering one of his own old poems. In his mind, he was no mere history professor; he was an undiscovered poet of rare talent.

Below him, little beetles covered in frost wriggled out of the ashes of the Dragon's campfire trying to survive. The frost shook loose, revealing their black coloring.

How long ago had the Black Dragon been here? The Ice Serpent mulled it over—and had an answer sooner than he thought. Suddenly, he heard a rustling deeper in the cave. . . .

His old heart quivering, the Swiss Dragon darted back behind a rock, watching as a black shape entered the icy white den. The Chinese Dragon, hairy and hobbled and small, was returning to his nesting spot—not abandoned at all—and immediately knew something was wrong. His hair stood on edge, his nostrils flaring.

"Who hunts me?" asked the Chinese Creature.

The Ice Serpent had nowhere to run. "I hunt a *traitor*," he cried, and he leapt out and tackled the Black Dragon, the old Serpents growling like two badgers, rolling about in the ice and snow, fighting feverishly.

The Ice Dragon dug his claws into the furred flesh of the Chinese Beast and pried open its jaws. He then used the most disgusting of magics—he sucked out part of the Black Dragon's spirit.

As the Black Dragon gasped for air, its spirit-traces were invisibly pulled out.

Acting fast, the Black Dragon burst away in a flurry of sparks that bedazzled the white cave and transported himself to safety several yards outside the cave. He hobbled off down the mountain, getting away, though the trick had cost him energy.

The Ice Serpent was worse off. Older and weaker, he was in no condition to give chase.

But the icy beast had won something in the battle. In the split second that he had touched the jaws of the Black Dragon, he had tasted his spirit. It so happened the *thought* he touched upon was the memory of an encounter with, of all things . . .

Oh, to write this down, he thought, *I must record this immediately.*

Everything he knew went into his books, his *History of Serpentkind*. It was his obsession, an attempt to write all of the stories of the Dragon race, and now to have found spirit-traces of the Black Dragon, the most despised of them all, was a great treasure. The new knowledge the Ice Dragon had gained would make an absolutely perfect capstone to his work.

Chasing the Black Dragon now was only a piece of the puzzle. The Ice Serpent had gotten something *better* than a turncoat. A new plan was forming in his head.

Hours later, he went back to a little café in the mountains for the warmth of its fire, though it did him little good. He quaked from the constant cold, and his lips were turning blue, though he still managed to look human. At times his lizard skin could become visible, so he covered himself well these days. His old black trenchcoat, smelly and stained, fanned out around the chair. In its pockets were books of poetry and out-of-date travel writing from the 1950s Beat era. At the moment, however, he was doing far more important writing of his own.

He was jotting furiously in his book: "The Black Dragon must now be remembered not just for the freeing of the Saint George child, but also for this astounding discovery, which will ultimately be the undoing of the entire Dragonhunter tribe. This requires immediate and meticulous investigation. There are *two* groups of hunters, unknown to each other, but known to the Black Dragon, and now to me, both in number and location." The Black Dragon had encountered these other hunters, and the Ice Dragon had seen his memory of escaping without detection.

Herr Visser shivered and wheezed and laughed, and the woman who served him coffee looked at him with unhidden disgust. Visser stroked his goatee proudly, and he clutched the book tightly against his chest.

"Some kind of secret you have there?" the waitress asked.

"Oh, I should say it is, yes," snorted Visser, in gravel-throated German.

"You're a writer?"

"Yes, yes. To be sure," he said, looking away from her and hunching his shoulders. The place was nearly empty. Just two other travelers. Photographers, from the look of their gear.

"I like good writing," said the waitress.

"You won't find any of that here." The Swiss professor smiled, showing coffee-stained teeth. "It's a nasty little bit of writing."

"Is it a scary story?"

"Oh, yes."

"Let me take a look at it," said the waitress curiously. "Let me be a sounding board. I might have some advice for you."

"Oh, no doubt, yes," mocked the professor. "When in doubt, go to a coffee counter of an out-of-the-way restaurant for literary criticism."

"You don't have to be rude about it," the woman replied. "I read a lot of books of every kind, and it gets a little dull around here, in case you haven't noticed. Just let me take a look, give you some feedback."

"The writing's over!" Visser snarled and slammed the book down, away from her reach. "I want to watch some television, and I want some privacy, thank you very kindly." With that, he pulled from his pocket a little black-and-white television.

"And warm up the coffee," he ordered, eyes fixed on the screen, shivering again. "It's not hot enough, it doesn't warm me at all!"

The woman wandered off, confusion and a bit of humor dancing in her eyes, as if she might be laughing at him.

The Ice Dragon's chest was pounding. The discovery of the Black Dragon's little secret, the peering eyes of the waitress, all of it was upsetting his old heart. He didn't ask much of life, but he wanted things quiet, and that was hard to get these days. He considered himself a person of simple pleasures: good music, good wine, the burning of a good woman now and then. He liked to think, to prepare a little bit of a meal for his mind. And he liked a little privacy when it came to writing.

Was that so much to ask?

He scratched at his black turtleneck sweater, feeling tightness at his throat. Through his thin, dark, half-circle eyeglasses, he glanced at the waitress, who had gone into the back of the café. Good. He relaxed a bit.

He usually liked to be left alone. And yet, there was something in her interest in him that was exciting. His nervousness came out of anger.

He felt a sudden, careless desire to tell the waitress everything about himself. He was dying, he knew that, and he just wanted someone to know who he was, someone to understand. No more hiding.

And what would he say to her? What would she care to know?

He played the flute. He was a horrid player, but his magic made people hear the music as if he were a great master.

He played cards and gambled. He always won. He gave the money to women. Then sometimes he'd eat them. In summer, he sold poisoned flowers on the streets of Zurich just to talk to people.

Loneliness had driven him to find human companions, but eventually they disgusted him. One woman he rather liked had turned to ice before his eyes when he touched her, and her arm fell off with a clunk, her blood frozen inside like a Popsicle. Things he touched would often freeze. Nothing could be done. He found ways to fill his time without friendships.

He was a fan of the TV show *Columbo*. He generally watched it in a smoky café, on the tiny black-and-white television set he carried with him everywhere.

It was the only thing that ever played on the television. He was watching it now.

He spent his nights on the tops of buildings, under the stars, next to the stone gargoyles. He would read them poetry. They had no opinions, and he liked that.

His poems were bleak, and made sense only to him. He thought of them when he was burning people or freezing them to death; when his mind would think in dreamy, rattled words:

"Dark. The Souls of the People.
White. The Art of the People.
· Kiss the rage, and kill it if it doesn't look like us.
Fold the riddle over, and the riddle stays the same.
Howl and fight and it does you no good.
Eat of this darkness and I'll give you dessert."

There were others worse than that. Hundreds of them, written over two centuries, in many languages.

He wrote the poems on pages that were half black and half white—the same shades as his dirty apartment in Zurich, and his dirty office at the university.

People hated the poems. He'd tried to get them published for centuries. No magic he could conjure could get people to like them. And people hated him, no matter what disguise he took on. People hated him. And Dragons hated him.

And this was who he was.

Maybe the lady wanted to know these things about him, maybe he would tell her. Maybe he would tell the waitress that he was going to die in a blaze of immeasurable glory, and her world would grow very dark after that, for the only books that would be read would be his.

There were pieces to put in place first, however. Finding the Black Dragon was possible now, for he had torn a bit from the old lizard's mind, and knew his immediate destination. He would go after him soon. That was the simple part. Far more challenging would be to bring the hunters all together, and have them die in a single blow. *There's your fame. There's your poetry. Dead together, all at once, and you to plan it, witness it, put it into your book.*

He would write his own place in history as the killer of the Hunters.

It ought to have been a triumphant thought, but the Ice Dragon's eyes came to rest on a heap of beetles outside the window, dead from the frost. He liked to keep the beetles and gnats and bugs alive in the cold, and sometimes he'd even keep them warm in his mouth.

It struck him that if he couldn't keep his own collection of insects alive, he hardly had the strength to kill the Dragonhunters himself. *Pathetic little thing I am,* he thought. He'd require help to destroy them, but who could he turn to? The new Russian Beast, fresh from Chechnya? An Arab Sand Dragon? The two strongest in Asia, the Japanese Dragon and the

Bombay Serpent, would have nothing to do with him. Would they? Now there's an interesting thought. Lots of potential there. But he'd need to move fast.

Suddenly, he heard the waitress laugh, and he spun around to see her standing there, reading his book.

My book.

"What's the big deal, I just wanted to look," said the woman, noticing his eyes. "I don't have anything to do around here. What's wrong with you?"

"Wrong with me?" said Visser, his lips trembling.

"This is not scary," said the woman. "It's just random notes and . . . and poetry. Poetry about snakes. Is that what you write?" She was bewildered.

"Not snakes," said Visser through clenched yellowish teeth. "Serpents. Dragons."

Nothing seemed funny to the woman anymore.

The other two customers looked over, alarmed.

Visser rose. Now he towered over the woman, seven feet tall, his skin rippling as heat waves passed through him, and her jaw dropped as she realized she was staring at a black-and-white Beast with eyes like yellow marbles.

"True poetry is not written in ink," said the Ice Dragon, "but in fire."

And he set the woman ablaze in the colors of good and evil, a black-and-white fire that matched his own skin, and the fire leapt into the air and carried her up to the ceiling, dropped her ashes in a split-second, and then spread to the photographers, one burned away in white fire, the other burned away in black.

> "Burn a little hope, today, snuff out a little light.
> Ebony doesn't burn, my friend, it only turns to white.
> Die, die, and learn to like it, child. . . .
> It only stings a little while, it's really very mild."

His Serpentine mind was humming.

But he found himself abruptly disappointed, for the fire he had made was turning to ice. It *behaved* like fire, flickering and moving about, but it was ice, no doubt about it. He had no control. The ice-fire stopped its quivering, the sharp spires of ice stilled, and the moving mass of crystalline flames ceased their crunching, breaking passage. The Serpent was left alone with frost-filled walls and ceiling.

His fire had gone cold.

Gloomily, he watched the rest of his TV show in the frigid ruins.

Then he left the little café in the mountains and he headed for the sea to set his plans in motion.

Chapter 9

T

THE LONELINESS
OF A GREAT SHIP

SIMON ST. GEORGE AND his father had found
their way to the middle of the Atlantic
Ocean where the globe had shown Alaythia,
but there had been no sign of her. Simon began to
have serious doubts they would find her even with
the tracer device, because they could never quite
catch up.

"If she took a plane, she would be in China by
now," commented Simon.

"Yes, but if she took a boat," said Aldric, "she
would be closer to the ocean, and she'd have a better
chance of sensing the Black Dragon. He may very well
be on the sea, on the move."

Simon frowned, considering the predicament.

They were at the table in the galley, and the stove

began belching black smoke. Aldric cursed and tried to save his stew. Nearly everything they cooked went bad now; it was as if the ship were punishing them for losing Alaythia.

The ship itself seemed lonely without her. At night it made howling noises with the wind in its sails, and the rigging clanged rhythmically, as if calling out to her.

Simon and Aldric knew exactly how the old ship felt.

To stave off the emptiness—Aldric could spend entire days not talking at all—Simon had begun writing letters to Emily back in Ebony Hollow, though he knew he'd never send them; and if he did, she'd never read them. There were too many details in them about Dragonsigns, about Dragonhunting; they would have sounded insane to her, but he kept trying to find a way to make the dark world he knew seem *reasonable*.

The ship felt like the most desolate place on earth, and the only thing that filled it up was the thought of Emily. He had started talking to her in his head. He knew he was thinking about her mainly because he had no real friends, but it was a useful way to kill time, and he figured it honed his skills for talking to people his own age. He worried that Emily might be in danger if a stray Serpent still seeking Alaythia somehow found its way to New England. He worried that he and his father wouldn't find Alaythia, or that they'd find her dead, and then he feared that even *thinking* about it could make it happen. There was always something to worry about.

His stomach churned that night as he began a new letter.

"I think I'm getting an ulcer," he muttered and looked over at Fenwick on the floor. "I wish you could talk," he added, lying in the dim light of his bunk built into the ship's wall. The fox stared back with no particular expression.

Fenwick would have no sympathy for him. Fenwick had no worries. He was strong.

"Never mind. I'm glad you can't talk," said Simon, feeling chastised.

Then he heard his father clanging around in his room, sparring with no one, brandishing his sword. These days, Aldric never seemed to sleep. He blamed himself for everything, and Simon wished things would go back to the way they were in the old days—when Simon got blamed for everything.

After awhile, Aldric came out of his room and into the hall where Simon's bunk was. Simon stood staring, afraid he was in trouble.

Gruffly, Aldric handed Simon a bottle of Irish

ginger ale. "Here. Drink with me."

And that was all he said.

Simon looked at him, holding the warm bottle in his hand.

"I was thinking we might talk," his father said sharply.

Simon just stared.

"Well, go on, then, open it," Aldric said, and Simon pried off the bottle cap. He stood there awkwardly.

The time passed like sandpaper over skin, the two of them in the hall, saying nothing, the ship rocking gently.

Aldric was in another world altogether. Staring at his bottle, he didn't look at Simon. The silence stretched on between them, and Simon shifted on his feet. Aldric still wasn't saying anything. And then finally his father, grunting some indecipherable apology or explanation, pulled out his pipe and just walked away, returning to his room. His door clanked shut.

Simon remained unmoving.

He looked at the bottle in his hand, the top of it staring back, like the eye of some odd animal.

"Okay," Simon said quietly to himself. He sat on his bunk. Then he lay down and waited for something to happen.

He heard Aldric go up on deck. Maybe the night air would cool him down.

Fenwick padded over to Simon slowly, and nuzzled Simon's hand with his snout. He seemed to want to cheer him up. It took a moment to realize the fox wanted him to move.

He got up and followed Fenwick down the hall, past the cold night air streaming from the hatchway above, all the way to the end, to Aldric's quarters. Simon almost never went in there.

The fox nudged the door open. Feeling a nervous heat in his stomach, Simon hesitated, but Fenwick scurried into the stateroom. Simon figured he could always claim that he was just getting the fox out of there.

The room was a mess, the way it always was before Alaythia had come along. Tunics and coats lay in a pile, old scrolls, spellbooks and travel guides were sprayed out everywhere. Weapons were unsheathed; the chest of international money lay open with currency stuffed in crudely; and an out-of-place notebook computer of Alaythia's was left in the corner, probably from Aldric's anger at not being able to make it work.

Fenwick climbed onto the bed, with its wool blanket and animal pelts—a Viking's idea of comfort—and poked at a bookshelf.

Looking back to be sure Aldric wasn't coming, Simon moved to examine it.

Fenwick knocked open a small door in the bookshelf, revealing a stack of old photographs. Surprised at this secret cache, Simon took them out, and felt a stab of guilt as he stared down at his mother's face.

There were pictures of Maradine and Aldric from a long time ago; stacks of them.

His heart raced with excitement. The past stared back at him.

In black-and-white or faded color, pictures from all over the world.

Aldric was young, in his twenties or thirties, his face more rounded and less hardened. He looked a lot like Simon, and he was handsome. Maradine was smiling, sometimes laughing, bright-eyed and long-haired and strong—and bearing more than a passing resemblance to Alaythia.

He'd seen pictures of her, but never so many. He knew she had lived on a ranch, and she was often pictured next to a horse, one Simon hadn't seen before. She was his mother, and he felt somehow the images should have told him *more*, and that he should have felt more. It was strange. What stirred his emotions was the man in the photos.

Aldric. He was the same in many ways. Tough gaze, clenched jaw, ill at ease in front of a camera.

Still, in a few pictures, he looked calm, satisfied, happy.

Simon looked to Fenwick. Why did he want him to see this? *Is this how you cheer me up?* he thought.

The fox's eyes flashed and turned black, and Simon was seeing the animal's memory. It was the strongest feeling Fenwick had ever sent to him. Simon's surroundings faded away, and he now felt himself on the ship in a different time and place. What he saw amazed him.

In that moment, Aldric St. George was a young man. He was on the deck with Maradine, and they were dancing slowly; he was spinning her around. It was night, and there were a thousand stars, and he was singing an Irish tune, low and murmured. Simon couldn't believe it—his father was actually singing, and it was good. He sounded just the way Simon would have expected, but he had never heard him before, not ever.

He knew then that his mother had died because of her feelings, that was how the Creature was able to find her. But there was no sadness in the knowing, there was just a bright night before him, and his mother spinning, her long hair swinging about.

He smiled, hearing his father sing. He was there, with them both. He wanted to laugh, and then it was gone. Everything vanished.

He was in the creaking ship with Fenwick staring back at him.

It was then he realized the only picture in the room that Aldric had on display was one of Ebony Hollow: he and his father . . . and Alaythia.

If he didn't get her back, he wouldn't get his father back; not fully, not ever. He shoved the pictures back where they belonged and got out of there as quickly as he could.

Chapter 10

⚜

THE TIGER DRAGON

THE BLACK DRAGON OF PEKING had unleashed a never-before-known hatred among Serpent-kind. It was common knowledge that he had helped the Dragonkillers and been instrumental in burying the Queen of Serpents.

Many had died in the Grand Battle of the Serpent Queen, and the remaining Dragons were now trying to take over their territories. The entire Serpentine world had been thrown into disarray, the hierarchies demolished; all over the map, Serpents were fighting for new turf.

There were new avenues opening up in crime, terrorism, business, and military dictatorships, and as always with these things, there were some who grasped the opportunities better than others.

One such creature was the Dragon of Bombay.

She was a Tiger Dragon, bearing a shapely, female, humanesque form with a thin set of huge transparent wings, useless wings. They stretched down her back, pretty and striped, like a fashion accessory, like a mink coat or some other insolent, useless thing.

In fact, fashion was her domain. In her human manifestation, she had made herself look like a beautiful East Indian model, so beautiful she had been on the cover of countless magazines, appearing as a young woman with mocha-cinnamon skin, a tall frame, high cheekbones, sleepy eyes with long black lashes, and a lanky body. You couldn't quite tell where she came from or how old she was. She had used her looks to earn a small fortune on the catwalk, some years back, before an ugly argument with an American model had caused her to lose her temper—and she had torched the Manhattan girl in a New York minute.

Several more of these arguments, usually over boys, resulted in more deaths—and dodging the police had made the whole thing hardly worthwhile.

She decided to move into manufacturing, using sweatshop labor. Little girls and boys, and incredibly poor men and women were chained to sewing machines for long hours so she could make millions selling high fashion at shocking prices.

She had a formula. In the factories there was an ivory sculpture with a giant tiger's eye painted on it on every floor. The eyes hypnotized the workers. The workers never complained.

Each tiger's-eye sculpture had a pupil, like a giant pearl, which moved back and forth with a very slow, eerie clicking. At the same time, the sculptures gave off a low hum, like a growl, that would grow louder whenever the workers showed the slightest rebellion. Then the laborers would grow weak, uncertain, and decide not to challenge their masters.

The Tiger Dragon could not decide which was better, the pain and suffering of her sweatshops (which gave her so very much joy), or the thought that millions of girls had seen her in magazines and starved themselves to look like her. She probably preferred her factories; so much agony to feed on, all in one place.

The sweatshops lay beneath her magnificent, modern palace in Bombay.

Her palace was itself a factory, home to the darkest suffering of all. The workers' pain floated up to her and gave her strength to begin each day.

The Tiger Dragon, whose name was Issindra, came from a family that had ruled over the ancient jungle lands of India, watching as Bombay grew around their domain over the centuries. Through all the squabbles—and she had of course killed the rest of her family by now—Issindra had kept their palace complex intact. In fact, her bedchamber remained a part of the prehistoric wild, with great trees and plants of the forest shooting out of the ground and wrapping around the indoor support columns, as well as her furniture, the bed, the desk, everything. It was like sleeping in an overgrown greenhouse.

She tended this dense garden with sorcery, lovingly protecting its legendary secrets, which were special and fearsome even to the Serpentine world. The power of the palace, hidden in its heart, was kept safe under her watch.

Issindra was now feeling that a nation with a billion people was far too small a place for someone so great as she.

She licked her tiger-striped skin, reflecting.

It would be too much to say that she wanted to be Queen of Serpents herself. She would be content with simply expanding her empire—an empire that encompassed every form of smuggling known to man. This included a very good trade in exotic animals: stolen elephants, rhino, giraffe, zebra, birds, lions, and, of course, tigers, all for private owners, who usually cooked them up and ate them, no matter how rare, as well as a fairly good business in tea exports (her tea was rotten; it made a person feel spiteful and jealous and mean).

The tigers she kept close to her, roaming about her lazy, opulent palace. They could often be found beside her in a giant canopy bed—until she sold them off, and once in a while she would allow the animals to eat one of her workers alive, just for fun.

That is, if she didn't eat the workers herself. She'd been picking at a piece of human meat that had been stuck in one of her teeth since yesterday, and was reconsidering whether the flesh was really worth the bother. She worked at the fat, greasy tidbit with her tongue, squeezing juice from it, and decided it was.

Her entire palace was built to accommodate the tigers, which moved through hollow passages, so that at any time, a worker might hear the tigers moving behind the walls or above them, in the ceilings, sniffing or growling. The beams and columns of the structure creaked as they passed, tigers roaming, padding heavily on the wood floors. A careless seamstress might peek into a hole in the wall by her workspace and find a giant feline staring back. Issindra loved how unsettling all this would seem to a human.

Still, it wasn't nearly enough.

For her to be happy, she needed more. Already she had criminal enterprises sprouting up throughout Africa. The Tall Dragons were newly dead, others were being moved out by her growing operations, and China was yielding nice profits, too. But business was moving too slowly, and Issindra had begun thinking about moving in on the other big fish in the sea.

She had begun to daydream about the Serpent of Japan.

This was no accident. Issindra had begun receiving correspondence from another ambitious Serpent who had felt Japan was weak and ready for the taking. He was a smart old Pyrothrax, one of the oldest out there. He would give her information about the entire Serpent world, and all he wanted in return was a safe haven—and knowledge of the secret to her palace, its strange power, so that he could put the complete past of the Indian Serpents into his insane little history book.

It was not a bad bargain, she thought.

Yes, the Ice Dragon was turning out to be a wonderful spy and ally.

Just the other day, he'd sent the loveliest note:

Issindra,
Thought of you today as I destroyed a couple of nuns. I know how bothersome do-gooders are to you. They left me with the most interesting verses in my head—a good murder always brings on poetry. Have a look:
"Insect me, and I'll butterfly you.
Flay the meaning, fool the fool.
This is the night. I painted it in blood. It used to

mean something, now it's a fiddler in a moonlit field.
With no moon and no one to play for.

   It's candy canes melting twelve hours after
Christmas.

   It is the rat in the trap, waiting for the meaning of
his life to come to him at the end of his breathing, but
it will not come. Not the breathing, but the meaning. I
was
referring to
   The meaning."

Issindra smiled. The old darling. He had no idea how senile he was.

Obviously, she would never consider him proper material for a mate. Recently Issindra had begun looking for a partner. She didn't actually want a mate; a mate would only bring her tremendous jealousy. What she wanted was children—a brood that she could teach, or at the very least, a Serpentine daughter to talk to.

There were times that this longing caused her to peer into local homes, to see an ordinary mother and daughter, with their nauseating, simple happiness. Here is the mother brushing the hair of the daughter, here is the meager dinner the family shares so nicely. . . .

She killed the families she watched; every one of them. But it always brought a tear to her eyes.

Someday she would have this simple joy, the pleasure of home life.

It was typical of Dragon females to desire odd companionship. Like many others, the Tiger Dragon had fallen in love with her own fire, spinning out flames to chat with on many a cold evening, but the fire-figure often became jealous and out of control. The Tiger Dragon's fire-figures had burned anyone who came near her—even her employees. The flames became frightfully intense, scorching the Tiger Dragon's own body before she at last regained control of it. Now her blaze refused to speak to her, becoming obedient but silent, what Serpents called a dead fire. She felt totally isolated these days.

Fire was always a dangerous companion.

As for children, the Ice Serpent alone would be of no help to her. It wasn't that he was too old (that was an advantage, he'd die soon), but that he was from an erratic bloodline. He himself had told her that. The Ice Serpents had always been mad—more mad than any other bloodline—obsessively curious, recording microscopic details of the past that served no purpose and brought no power. The Ice Dragon had come from a long line of weak Serpents who had each committed suicide after creating offspring who had the same indecent flaw.

No. For a mate she would need someone more

reliable. The Ice Serpent had even admitted it in one of his letters, and he agreed with her that children would serve to expand her power, if she could find a suitable mate.

Perhaps if she could trick the right Serpent into falling for her, then, after linking tails in the lovechant, she could promptly eat the father and never have to deal with him again.

The Ice Serpent would not do. She would have to look elsewhere.

Perhaps . . . to Japan.

Chapter 11

SHOWDOWN AT SEA

THE SEARCH FOR ALAYTHIA was now in its ninth day without any luck. Fenwick the fox was all atwitter this morning, rushing about the ship's living area with great excitement, but Simon, with sleep-encrusted eyes, was trying to ignore him, investigating the refrigerator and cupboards for a quick breakfast.

Having a British father had a definite downside. Simon combed through boxes of plain crackers, unsalted potato chips, jars of mincemeat and potted meat, bottled gravy, oatmeal (but good luck finding any sugar around here), canned kippers, onions in a weird fluid, and something called digestives in an ugly plain brown box.

There were fresh eggs, because they had hens

below, but Simon was getting tired of them.

English people hate food, he decided. Suddenly Fenwick bit his arm in frustration. "Ow!" yelped Simon, and turned to see the fox had retreated back, clawing at the metal globe.

"What's he off about?" said Aldric, entering with a drowsy squint.

"He's gone insane 'cause there's nothing to eat but rubbish and balderdash," Simon complained mockingly, and Aldric narrowed his eyes.

"Is he pointing at something?" Aldric asked sleepily, trying to peer around the crazed animal.

"It looks like it's straight ahead," Simon said, pointing at the tiny blinking light on the globe. *Alaythia.* "She must've slowed. We've closed in on her overnight."

He looked at his father.

"The question is *why* has she slowed," mumbled Aldric, coming to life quickly, heading to the ladder.

"Do you have to go straight to the dark side of everything?" said Simon, the pit of his stomach already reacting as he climbed up after him.

Above decks, there was nothing but clear, blue skies and an empty stretch of ocean. And then Simon saw the sun glinting on a little patch of ocean very far ahead. A silver spike that, after a moment, began to look very much like a ship.

It was some kind of small, old yacht, and it was drifting aimlessly.

Aldric hit a switch at the mainmast. All the sails on the Ship with No Name slapped outward, and the vessel sped toward the white yacht.

They reached it before Simon was really ready. Though fully armed with crossbow and sword, Simon was not prepared for a confrontation with the Black Dragon. The old Dragon was capable of anything, even if he'd been friendly at one time.

"Let me go aboard first," Simon said, realizing there was no other choice. "If he's friendly, I should be the one to make contact."

"Out of the question, Simon, we don't know what's on that ship."

"He'll see you as an enemy, Dad. If you go in, you might lose it and shoot him before we even know if we can trust him."

"We can't trust him. He's a Serpent," Aldric said.

"That's exactly why I have to go," said Simon, but he still did not forge ahead without Aldric's say-so. He'd at least learned that much.

The yacht came in closer. No one on deck. The time for a decision was now.

Aldric looked at Simon, and nodded reluctantly.

Simon leapt aboard the other vessel with Fenwick following close behind. Aldric gave him a head start of a few seconds, roping his ship to the other, and then followed.

Simon pushed open the cabin door.

Dark. Silent. It betrayed no life within.

Down he went, quickly, for he knew his father wouldn't give him much time.

There was a sudden sickly smell of death, and Simon held his hand over his nose to block it out.

So his sword was not ready.

The Thing came at him, ripping out of the darkness; just snarls and rage and fangs. Simon fell back as the Creature charged, and his armor was caved in at the chest by the power of its force. He was thrown against the doorframe, the growling of the beast was ear-splitting, its moves vicious and unrelenting, and Simon could only hit at the Serpent's back with his sword; he couldn't get in a slashing blow.

Simon felt a strike to his head. He saw his own blood slap onto his arm.

Throttled by the Dragon, Simon saw in a blur that Aldric was behind him—but his father vanished from view as Simon was pulled into the blackness of the cabin.

It was all glinting teeth and fierce amber eyes, and body blows and hisses, until Simon was able to kick back away from the Serpent. Aldric was now slashing furiously, his sword thudding and cutting in the darkness.

Simon slipped on a slick fluid beneath his feet, and he hoped it wasn't Dragonblood, because that could burn nearly as bad as fire. He couldn't find an opening to attack without endangering Aldric.

As he crawled toward a sliver of daylight at the cabin door, he heard the angry cries of the Dragon and the grunting of his father in intense battle behind him.

When he looked back, he could see something on the floor was glinting and glowing sporadically. Dragonblood. As Simon kicked open the door to let light flood in, he saw his own hands were burned from the fireblood, though he felt no pain yet.

No, he thought. *The fire's turning to ice in my hand!*

He had enough light now. He could see something of the beast, and for a moment, it did look like the Black Dragon—with black flesh and a stooped body—but it turned, and Simon saw its other side was as white as snow.

And he saw his chance at a shot.

He let loose a bolt with his crossbow that struck perfectly at the Dragon's arm. It yelped and leapt backward, deeper into the darkness.

Now Aldric took a step back in retreat.

It was quiet for a heartbeat.

"It's not him!" shouted Simon.

Then who? thought Aldric and Simon at the same

time. This was no idle question. If you didn't know the enemy, you didn't know which deathspell to use—and you couldn't let the beast know that. Simon had already said too much.

Aldric began to advance. If he didn't, the Dragon would sense weakness and pounce. Simon went in, behind his father this time, his sword tightly controlled, arms alert in readiness.

The flickering blood lit the cabin dimly so they could see a maze of papers and books up ahead, stacks of them. The Thing could be hiding anywhere.

"Where in God's name is he?" said Aldric. They had gotten deep into the ship.

"If he had her," whispered Simon, "he would use her as a hostage."

Wouldn't he?

"Unless she's dead," said Aldric grimly, and he threw aside a stack of burning books to see the black-and-white Serpent huddled in the corner like a pathetic rat.

It hissed and leapt forward, surprising Simon. The Creature went straight for the boy, knocked him to the ground, and galloped up the stairs to the deck.

Aldric was a flash in the darkness, following him.

Simon got up with difficulty, his armor weighing him down, and he pushed himself up the stairs, feeling the strain in his legs.

In the clear daylight, Aldric was slashing at the tired beast, his blade glinting in the sun, until the weakened Thing fell back, toppling over the side of the ship into the sea.

Simon ran to join Aldric, watching as the Dragon sank and was carried away by the tide. The instant it fell, a veiled fireblast emanated from below, and chunks of Dragonflesh boiled up and mottled the waves.

The fatty globules floated about, and Aldric hurriedly grabbed a net to fish some of the remains out of the water.

"What happened?" asked Simon, leaning against the rail, exhausted.

"He was old," said Aldric breathlessly, pulling aboard a piece of the smoldering Dragonflesh. "Very old. Maybe his heart gave out. I'm not sure. He could've killed himself rather than face us."

"Didn't seem so old to me," said Simon, wiping blood from the gash on his cheek.

"You cornered him," said Aldric. He took hold of a hot chunk from the net, then dropped it. "The question is, who was he?"

Simon had an instant to recognize that half the ship was painted black, the other white, right down the middle. Weird.

"Is she here or not?" asked Simon and he turned to go into the cabin.

"Wait, wait. If she's there . . . you may not want to see it."

"Then neither will you," said Simon firmly, and he went below, his father behind him.

The Ice Dragon swam down into the depths of the ocean. He had taken from his ship a pouch where he stored the dead flesh of his father (a sentimental item, long held in his collection) that would float to the surface and fool the idiotic hunters. He cursed the humans for making him leave it behind.

He blew forth a fireball to roll up to the surface.

It would've convinced anyone.

Still, he was in a foul mood. He had already failed to kill the Black Dragon, he had failed to capture the Magician, and it was all he could do to stay alive against the hunters. If his latest plan didn't come together, he would die a forgotten, withered pile of wormflesh.

Exhausted, he moved his black-and-white body farther into the deep, traveling past sharks drawn to the area by the commotion.

One of the sharks snapped at him in exploration, and the tired Ice Dragon spat fire at it, burning the predator fish in a splendid display of undersea heat and flame.

He was old, but he was still a Dragon.

Chapter 12

THE CONTENTS OF ONE ABANDONED DRAGONSHIP

SIMON HELD A FLASHLIGHT as Aldric went back into the stinking, rotting cabin of the Dragon's ship. Fenwick scurried around at the doorway, either in warning or in fear, Simon wasn't sure which.

Aldric stamped out the remaining flames, which seemed to hiss back at him, weakly; an old Dragon's fire. Oddly, the quelled fire suddenly turned to ice, crackling underfoot.

Simon noted the interior and everything in it was painted black or white but it was too dark to appreciate the strangeness of it.

The flashlight beam found no trace of Alaythia. Instead, the dripping, smelly, uncomfortably warm cabin held only stacks of books and papers massed on desks and chairs.

Simon glanced over some of the pages. His eyes met a demented scrawl of runic letters and shapes—the language of the Dragons—but written hastily, in a disorderly weave.

"Simon, move forward, I need the light," Aldric instructed, and Simon hurried with him down a set of stairs into the hold.

They came upon a wooden door, but like everything else, falling apart and covered in the odor of death and decay. Aldric kicked it in, and a new wave of unpleasant, long-trapped-in smells floated out like eager ghosts.

"She isn't here, either," said Aldric. He had sensed it immediately, though Simon's flashlight soon proved it to be true.

What lay before them amazed them both.

The ship's hold was filled with even more books, a Serpent's library of hundreds, maybe thousands, of old volumes, and stacks of yet more documents and scrolls. Pages floated in the brown water that covered the floor, and some of the walls were coated in Dragonscript.

"He was insane," whispered Simon, as he looked over an open book filled with the same symbol over and over again. Another book nearby was filled with numbers, running on and on, packed tightly together on the pages.

"Where is she?" cried Aldric, batting around at the walls, hoping for a hidden compartment. "We detected her, so where is she?"

"We've been through the ship, top to bottom," answered Simon, feeling the same disappointment. "What's going on? Was she ever here?"

Aldric leaned back on a column of books, and gave himself a chance to think. "She could've been here, she could've found this Dragon in her journeys, and tagged his ship. The tracer signal is here, somewhere."

"Then what happened to her?"

Aldric shook his head, uncertain. "This beast seems fond of writing—maybe there's a ship's log somewhere in this nightmare," he said, and headed up top for the controls of the vessel.

When they reached the black-and-white control room, sure enough, there was a ship's log. Nine volumes in all.

It was written in a hodgepodge of languages, including Dragonscript, Latin, ancient Greek, Italian, German, Flemish, French, and English.

Frustrated, Aldric threw some of the books against the ship's wall, and stepped outside to fume.

In the quiet, Simon began to read, though he had picked up only very little of the Dragontongue from Alaythia. Still, some of the words were clear to him, and he eventually realized where the ship's log ended. As the ship lolled in the water, Simon tried to make out the last few days of events, and he lost track of time.

When he reached the end of the Dragon's journal, he was unsure if hours had passed, or minutes. His head felt funny, and he suddenly wondered if the log might be working an enchantment into his brain, the Serpent reaching into his mind . . .

But what he found had made the risk well worth it.

"Dad . . ." he said. "Dad, you need to see this. . . "

The Ice Dragon was not a true Water Dragon, and the ocean was tiring him badly. His heart worked painfully to keep him swimming forward. Ice was forming on the surface wherever he went.

The sea was making him even colder than usual. He had trouble focusing. All he could think of was the fame he'd win, if he could pull it off. *It wasn't enough to kill the Hunters*. He had a grander plan now. Two powerful Dragons, the Japanese and the Tiger Serpent, brought together in wedlock *to continue the species*, with him as the matchmaker; the savior of his own kind.

He would bring them together carefully. Of course, it would be nice if the Ice Serpent could father a new tribe himself, but at his age, that was out of the question. He'd have to be content with playing king-maker, or queenmaker, as the case might be. The Hunters would simply die in the process. For that alone, he would be a legend.

Everything depended on whether the Tiger Dragon and the Japanese Dragon could set aside their differences. Only time would tell.

He searched his elderly mind for a spell that would serve him, and he remembered an ancient one for seeking land. He uttered the chant in Dragontongue, and his black-and-white body shot forward, magically covering miles of ocean in seconds. He emerged, exhausted, on a remote island—an abandoned U.S. Navy training post—where several natives on the beach stared at him as he came out of the water in the only guise he could manage, though a well-dressed Swiss professor was almost as strange as Serpentskin would have been. Ice formed on the beach below his shoes.

"Is there a ship about here I could hire?" he asked.

As the Ship with No Name chafed against the Serpent vessel, Simon was rambling, eager to show Aldric what he'd found, while a black-and-white television next to the controls buzzed endlessly with an old detective show.

"He was hunting me," said Simon, pointing to the

Ice Dragon's journal. "It says here, 'the Black Dragon had encountered the St. George boy and kept him secret, and had been watching him over the years, hoping he would have a use.'" There were other words Simon couldn't decipher, and then, "'the threat this new Dragonhunter poses cannot be underestimated. I take it upon myself to eliminate him.'" Simon glanced at his father questioningly. "Whoever this Serpent was, we didn't find him by accident."

"Swiss," said Aldric. "I found him in the Book of Saint George. He's an Ice Serpent from Zurich. But I have my doubts that he's dead, Simon. We didn't see his death. It's possible he could have survived and gone somewhere to regain strength."

"Then he might come back," Simon said with growing alarm. He handed Aldric the logbook and looked out to sea warily.

Aldric examined the book and said, "Wait. Look here. It says, 'He has occupied Asia, and was recently helped in his hiding by the Black Dragon, this boy.' Then it says, 'the Black Dragon kept the St. George boy safe from a distance, using spells to help him from time to time, because the boy might someday be of use to him.' Well, it says a lot of other tripe I don't understand, but that's the point of it, isn't it?"

Simon was reading desperately, trying to take in the mixture of languages.

"That's what it says," Aldric insisted. "It says, 'this St. George boy has occupied Asia, and few European Dragons have heard of him. The boy has killed as many as sixteen Serpents.'" Aldric repeated, "The boy occupied Asia."

"Asia?"

"Simon, he wasn't pursuing you at all. This says he was hunting a St. George child . . . who lives in *Asia*."

Chapter 13

THE UNKNOWN ST. GEORGE

A FULL DAY PASSED ON the leaking, fetid Dragonship. The St. Georges spent hours feverishly reading the Ice Dragon's deranged manuscripts and books, which went back years.

"Who *is* this person?" Simon asked.

"We know he's a boy," said Aldric, "but there's little else we can say for certain."

"We can't find the page where this all starts, this is driving me crazy. Where does he come from? Who is this other St. George?"

Aldric rubbed his growing beard, deep in thought, and looked at Simon. "To answer that question, we have to figure out where the boy is first. It's clear the Ice Dragon wants the boy dead. If I'm right that this Ice Dragon is still alive, he'll still go after the child. The boy is unprotected."

"Wait a minute," Simon said, "What about Alaythia? We can't just leave her and go following this trail to who knows where."

"This trail could lead to Alaythia. The signal hasn't changed and she was certainly aboard. If she learned about this boy, she might be headed to the same place."

"Dad, she may not know anything about it. She may never have been here." Simon considered it. "Could the Ice Dragon have drawn us out here? I mean, he knows so much about us, and the way we work . . ."

"Far more than we know of him," Aldric said in disgust.

Simon moved to the open door of the Dragon vessel. "So what do we do? Even if he is setting us up for something, which way do we go? She's still out there, somewhere. Look at Fenwick, he can sense her."

Across from them the fox was scurrying up and down the deck of the Ship with No Name, giving a grunting signal, impatient.

"Something's not right with him," Aldric agreed, and moved to the yacht's railing. Following the fox's gaze, Aldric looked down, where embedded at the side of the vessel was a glistening arrow.

"She *was* here," Aldric said, leaning over the rail. "Alaythia fought this Serpent." He pulled the arrow loose, and allowed Simon to see the tiny tracer-device pin at its head.

"He got to her." Simon's voice quavered.

"She fought him off, Simon. She got free."

Simon wasn't completely buying it yet. "What happened to her ship? He could've sunk it with her onboard."

Aldric smiled. "She got out of here. She knows how to take care of herself; this arrow proves it. And this boy, whoever he is, we're talking about a new Dragonhunter, a new force to fight alongside us."

Simon looked skeptical. Leaving Alaythia out there was not the plan.

"Alaythia's probably already on her way there," Aldric stressed.

"This is a lot of guessing." Simon frowned. He knew they had to find the missing boy. Alaythia could take care of herself if need be, but some kid who might not know what a Serpent is wouldn't stand a chance. "Where do we even start? Where is this other St. George? All we know is Asia. . . ."

They had already studied the navigation maps and every piece of information they could find. They went back to their ship and consulted the Books of Saint George and the most obscure parchments of the Dragonhunters for clues. It wasn't until Aldric took the time to stare at the Ice Dragon's attack plans in his journal, over and over, that things came together.

"I *know* this place," he murmured.

Simon looked over his shoulder. His father was staring at an historical drawing of a house, a big one with an Asian roof design, the place the St. George kid was supposed to be. It was a clipping from some architecture journal. "You know it?"

"I've been there," said Aldric. He moved across the cabin, throwing aside scrolls and papers to get to the White Book of Saint George.

"Well, Dad, where is it? *What* is it?"

"I don't know for certain, it was. . . . We were hunting something. . . . I've been to that place . . ." his voice trailed off as he combed through the text, but he looked at the pages as if they were suddenly terribly unfamiliar. Simon took the book from him gently.

"Forget this. It's not helping," Simon said quietly. "Where did you see this place?"

"It's like a dream, Simon, I don't remember it well. . . ."

"Was it a long time ago? What do you remember?"

"Rain."

"Rain? Is that it?"

Simon could see his father's eyes alive with old memories and abandoned emotions. "We needed shelter," he said. "We had been attacked. We were cursing the fact we needed a Magician, someone who could interpret Dragonrunes, someone to speak the language, but there was no one with us. And there was . . ."

Staring off, Aldric began mumbling something about the Asian house, a teardrop-shaped jade statue at its door.

"Simon, you remember before I came to take you from that school of yours? You remember me talking about my brother?"

Simon nodded, seeing Aldric was having trouble finding words.

"My brother, Ormand, was with me, we went to this place," Aldric said, tapping the drawing. "We were hunting a Dragon . . . and we ended up there for the night. I remember the innkeeper, and Ormand and I went on to attack the Dragon the next day."

"Where is it?"

"Kyoto," he said, his eyes gleaming, and before Simon could remember exactly where that was, Aldric added, "Ancient capital of Japan."

A course was set. Aldric cut loose the Dragon's vessel, setting it afire to ensure nothing inside that ship would ever trouble the sea again. If the Ice Serpent wanted to be remembered through his writings, Aldric would do him no favors.

As the flames swallowed its deck, the ship crawled with strange figures *inside* the fire . . . firelings, creatures spawned from Serpent flames. The sight of them always made Simon tremble. Aldric had salvaged some of the African Dragons' fire, in torches kept safe in chambers on his ship, and their yellow-and-black fires were serving him well now.

Several of the firespawns—mere silhouettes of men, flickering and billowing in the ocean wind—began climbing the cabin as the Dragon ship began to list in the waves. The firelings screeched at Simon as their brothers were swallowed by the sea and turned to a toxic yellow steam, fighting to survive in the tide.

Their screams of rage were slung across the air, an unearthly wailing that sounded like a massacre of thousands of seagulls.

Get us out of here, Dad, thought Simon. *Get us out faster.*

The Ship with No Name began to leave the firelings behind. They were now headed to Kyoto to stop the Ice Dragon from killing the St. George boy, whoever he was. As the tide threw salt water in his face, Simon's mind flipped through the possibilities. *Who was this boy? Where had he come from?*

Aldric had always said that Simon was the last of the bloodline, the last Dragonhunter on earth. Now the idea his father could have *lied* to him began to tangle itself in Simon's thoughts. He knew his mother had died when he was a toddler, but almost nothing else. The look Aldric had on his face as he remembered the Japanese mansion was a look of guilt, as if deep down Aldric had always known the truth, but was only just now accepting it. *Could Aldric have had a son with some woman in Japan—someone he forgot about—a woman he left behind? Was it even possible?* Anger simmered in Simon's mind. *Of course it was possible; anyone who could leave his son at a boys' school when he's only two years old is capable of anything.* But Simon realized he could have been reading too much into his father's expression. After all, this was an incredible discovery. It was surely a shock to Aldric as well.

He couldn't have had another son.

Could he?

His reverie was broken by Aldric stepping nearby to watch the Swiss yacht burning on the ocean in the distance.

"Ugly thing, firelife," said Aldric, "You'd better man the guns in case they manage to get this far." But when he looked at Simon, he could see he was paying little attention. "Something *else* on your mind?"

"What?" Simon was looking at his face trying not to show any emotion at all.

"Alaythia's fine, if that's your worry. And we'll find out about that boy soon enough, so don't go off daydreaming when I need you." Then Aldric seemed to realize something. "Oh. Thinking of that girl again, were you?"

Simon let him believe it.

"She must be something special," Aldric observed. "She's safe back home, you know. Why is it you never tell me anything about her?"

Simon didn't say anything, and Aldric nodded. "Well, I can listen. That's something I can do, isn't it? Doesn't take much skill, does it?"

He was really trying to be a normal father; it was almost touching. Still, Simon couldn't let go of the idea Aldric might have another son somewhere. He told himself he was being crazy.

Simon looked out to sea.

In the distance, the firespawns were clinging to the mast of the sinking ship, fighting each other for life.

The wails and screaming of the yellow-black firelings merged with the ocean noise, and all the bodies began to drop and roll into the sea, creating a swirl of flame and chaos, sizzling and hissing and steaming. The blaze spread over the ocean and then was abruptly sucked back into a single flame—yellow and black—that died on the water with a distant sigh, the embers drifting about with a whispering *psss psss psss*, a final note of implacable fury.

Simon could only stare.

This kind of anger dies slowly.

Chapter 14

⚜

THE DRAGON OF JAPAN

THE JAPANESE DRAGON LOVED ORDER.

He used order to create suffering. Orderly deaths in train accidents, orderly deaths in factory mishaps, orderly deaths in automobile crashes, and so on. To the Dragon of Japan, death and suffering were beautiful, and to achieve these results with careful, deliberate, regimented planning was his highest aspiration.

The Dragon of Japan enjoyed tea made from the blood of Japanese people. If the tea were made from any other type of person, he would know it, and he would be angry.

The Dragon of Japan did not like to feel anger. He worked hard to create a calm, serene, meditative state, all the better to enjoy the dying and misery with which he surrounded himself.

Equilibrium was the watchword of his life. To never grow too pleased, nor too unhappy, to always keep all feelings in perfect balance—that was the highest state of being.

Equilibrium.

He was known among the Dragons as Najikko. In Dragontogue, it meant Master of the Healing Power of Death.

Of this, he was indeed master. In his human guise, the Serpent of Japan looked like a young, pleasant-faced Asian doctor, who wore bright blue contact lenses in his eyes and a tailored suit on his trim body. He was a man who put people at ease as soon as they met him. He always had candy for the children, a firm handshake for the men, and a warm smile for the women.

He was a plastic surgeon.

He was terrible at his work. He could be counted on to make awful mistakes, slashes and slips and slices and slivers, but no one ever sued him or stopped him from practicing medicine. No matter how much he fouled up people's faces and bodies with his wretched surgeries, the patient always left feeling sad, but satisfied; miserable, but calm; and almost no one ever complained.

If they did—if they were strong enough to resist

his enchantments—they were eliminated by the doctor's "associates," cruel men and women who were skilled at painful assassinations. Not quick. Not clean. But painful.

His medical practice had begun many years ago when he realized he could treat burn victims who had been harmed in his fires, and could take even more joy from their suffering.

Dr. Najikko, as he styled himself, was not content with the agonies he could create in just one hospital. He was the head of a massive medical corporation called Murdikai, which operated hospitals in twenty-seven countries, most of them in Asia. In these hospitals, death rates were extraordinarily high. People checked in complaining of a sore throat and a cough, nothing serious, really—and they were never heard from again.

Their organs were heard from again, however. Dr. Najikko extracted from dying patients their hearts, lungs, livers, kidneys, and so on, to secretly sell to people who needed transplants. He would sell the organs and make huge sums of money, and then the people who received the transplants usually died anyway.

Dr. Najikko, the Serpent of Japan, had no fondness for humans.

One day, a long time ago, a human had attacked

Najikko and badly injured his leg. It was injured so badly, in fact, that he did not have a leg; he now has a golden *artificial* leg attached to his body. You could see it only when he was in his Dragon form; otherwise, he looked like a normal man, unspoiled, handsome. The injury, however, was a constant reminder of the dangers of human beings, and when he felt anger rise in him, the gold-plated leg would glow with the heat of fire beneath it.

For Najikko, the best part about being a doctor was the ability to cause injuries like his own.

He considered the false leg to be his only blemish. His Serpent body was gold-silver, and armored like a rhinoceros, with a black pattern on it that looked like randomly scribbled biohazard signs spread all over his skin. His Dragon head was small and sharp, with horns at the top, a twisted fist of spikes he often made use of.

Najikko lived in Tokyo, in a penthouse above a hospital, so that the pain of the sick and dying would always be there, close by, to give him strength. Except for a parlor to receive guests, his house was not really a house at all, but a series of enchanted operating rooms that were in use. His chairs and couches and appliances and such were placed nearby operating tables, while ancient medical instruments—hooks and syringes, axes and saws—decorated the rooms.

Paintings of medical procedures were carefully placed on the walls, to bring a feeling of serenity and quiet happiness to him any time he looked upon them.

As he wandered alone from room to room, his tail sliding behind him, he could hear the low moaning and pleading of some of his patients, who were supposed to be in real operating rooms, but who instead had been secretly brought up here for a brief stay by the hospital staff who directly served the good doctor.

As he casually picked up his tea from the sterile steel kitchen, Najikko clicked a button, and one male patient (in his forties, nonsmoker, businessman, complaining of troubled breathing) was given far too much medicine, and quickly passed away.

He pulled back from the sense of joy that flooded him. Equilibrium always. That was the key. Mustn't allow the unclean rise of emotion get the better of him.

He complimented himself on his discipline, when the sight of a newcomer to the room shattered his quietude. It was a beetle. An amber-gold beetle that crawled out from under a steel lamp.

The Japanese Dragon stared in disgust.

An insect. Impossible. In his sterile, *perfectly* clean dominion.

Unacceptable.

The Dragon clicked his metal claws on the metal

floor, following the beetle and trying not to grow too irritated. The insect moved quickly, pittering on tiny feet that the Serpent's sensitive ears could not help but hear, circling wildly around a steel armchair, its miniscule mind locked in terror.

Down came the Dragon's gold foot, and his clean environment was satisfactorily stained with beetle guts.

Najikko's Serpent heart did not permit glee, but it was tempted.

And then came a second ticking of beetle legs.

More than one, this time.

Then more, and more.

Najikko turned and saw on the steel floor a small swarm of clicking, wandering golden beetles emerging from under his stove—a veritable invasion. His eyes narrowed. This was a clean environment. Sterile means sterile. Nothing germ-ridden, nothing unwanted, nothing earthy and out of his control.

Calm. Equilibrium.

This was the dilemma of being Serpentine. Wherever he went, nature found him and grew perverse, no matter what he did to stop it, and insects were the most common and vile of the effects. It took enormous effort and concentration to keep the pests away. One's success at this was a measure of power.

Disgusting things, he thought, and with great precision, he fired a small blast of flame into the swarming beetles, and turned them into a smearing mark of black ash on his perfect floor. A mess.

Control the anger, he rebuked himself. *They are nothing, less than nothing. You are lord over their pathetic lives as you are lord of your own emotions. You are perfection,* he told himself, *perfecting itself.*

He washed the ash away with a flick of a switch, as clean water was shot out of automatic nozzles he'd installed everywhere, and the liquid carried the beetles away down a drain in the floor. A last beetle crawled up out of the drain, but Najikko crushed it with his foot.

Repulsed, he cleaned his claw, scraping off the bug guts.

He turned and moved away from the kitchen area before anything else could compromise his good feelings, his equilibrium repaired. A Tibetan monk would have been impressed.

In fact, Najikko felt a surge of power as he surveyed the city from his penthouse. The afternoon view was spectacular. Earlier in the day, he had used his magic to cause an airplane crash on a major roadway. He could see the chaos from his home, rescuers and wounded, helicopters and hubbub. It was good for business at the hospital, and it gave him a wonderful sense of calm.

He could hear in the background Asian melodies played on the cello of the great performer Yo-Yo Ma, gliding from a stereo near the plastic display skeletons in the living room. The music soothed his nerves.

The Japanese Serpent watched the rescue efforts unfolding, clicking his feet, and in his state of relaxation he allowed himself to enjoy the thought that he could now safely be considered a king. *The Japanese King of Serpents.* Indeed, he controlled nearly all of Asia, and had made inroads throughout the world.

If only he had someone to share it all with.

Here was a new and nagging discomfort to his serenity: loneliness. Was there a solution? Beyond the city, there was a new rival to his criminal territories, a new enemy by the name of Issindra, that tigerlike Bombay Serpent. She was the other power on this side of the world. Her men had begun blowing up the shipments belonging to his illegal medical syndicate. She was angling for a fight.

And for the second time in weeks, a strange notion came to him.

Perhaps after he'd defeated her, he could make her his slave.

Chapter 15

HOW THE OTHER HALF LIVES

SIMON ST. GEORGE HAD entered a world of confusion.

He knew nothing of Japan, or its language, or its customs, and he was still reeling from the shock that there was another person on Earth who shared the Dragonhunter's blood.

The life of this person could be in danger, and they had to move quickly. Aldric had been able to retrace his footsteps from his previous journey here, but his memory remained vague and cloudy. At least it had led them here.

Simon and Aldric stood in armor, cloaked by their long trenchcoats, and kept watch over a Japanese home, an art deco house spread over a generous space in the overgrown city of Kyoto. It was made of dark wood with narrow slit windows, a three-tiered cake of a building with an Oriental roof design. He couldn't imagine how Aldric could forget the place. It was odd and pretty, but it didn't feel secure enough—the boy could be in there, and the Ice Dragon might still be after him.

It was morning, and mist pulled itself from the ground and shrouded the home.

Suddenly, there was a motion behind the frosted glass of one of the high windows. Simon tensed.

"Doesn't look like any struggle's taking place," whispered Aldric.

The two waited, crouched in an alleyway near a temple that looked to be a thousand years old or more.

Another car pulled up to the Asian mansion, a long black 1950s sedan, custom-made from the look of it, unlike any Simon had ever seen. From out of the car came a stocky Japanese man in a suit, and from out of the house came a small boy with a black satchel, who bowed to the driver.

Simon couldn't see the boy well at this distance, but another figure soon joined him, his mother, still in her bathrobe. She hugged him and kissed him on the top of his head.

"It's her," said Aldric quietly to himself.

The driver opened the door, and the boy—a little

kid, younger than Simon surely—got in. The sedan sped away into the mist.

"Come on!" said Aldric, and he dashed back for their rented Citröen—it was old, too. They had gotten it from a shady guy with the only car rental shop open at three A.M. It was loaded with their Dragonhunting equipment, and one very temperamental fox, who growled in fear as the car surged forward.

Simon could never stand Aldric's driving. His heart rattled inside him as Aldric hit the gas harder and the car swooped into the mist, chasing the boy's sedan.

Seemed like a spoiled little brat, thought Simon. *Gets a fancy car to take him to school every morning, his mom waiting on him hand and foot. It was clear which St. George boy had gotten the raw deal, and it wasn't this little jerk.*

"I can hardly see in this fog," muttered Aldric.

"If you go any faster," Simon sighed, "they're going to know they're being followed."

"Don't lecture me."

"But you're not doing it right."

"When you get your license, you can do the driving," his father grumbled.

"That day ain't coming fast enough," complained Simon, and the car hit an unexpected bump, shutting them both up. Aldric had hopped a curb as he trailed the other sedan in a turn.

"Where is he going?" Aldric asked himself aloud.

"It's morning, it's Tuesday," said Simon. "He's going to school. Normal kids go to school on week-days, it's something that happens all over the world."

"How do you know?"

"I remember being normal."

The heavy fog was still misting the windows, but it gave Aldric's car some cover.

"Don't go so fast," Simon advised again. "You don't want to crash into the kid." *But* I *do*, thought Simon. *A small concussion,* he reasoned, *just a slight one, to even the score a little bit. Rich little punk.*

The boy's sedan passed into a clearing at the edge of the city, revealing a startling sight: a huge windmill lay ahead in the middle of a rice field, its propellers spinning softly and tossing back mist, and its tower crowned with a pagoda-style building.

It was one of the oddest things Simon had ever seen. Then the sedan stopped to let the boy out, and he joined many other children who were walking in a line to get into the giant windmill. They all wore dark clothes, had the same dark satchels in their hands; single file, orderly and perfect.

The huge windmill was a schoolhouse.

"You have got to be joking," Simon said. His father had taken him out of the Lighthouse School, and somehow, on the other side of the world, the other St.

George was going to a Windmill School?

"The Windmill School for Gifted Children," Aldric read aloud, seeing the English words on the building, beneath Japanese symbols.

"*Gifted,*" said Simon disdainfully.

Aldric shook his head in disbelief.

"Are we going to warn him?" said Simon.

Aldric looked nervous. "I . . . I'm . . ."

"Are we going to tell him who we are, who he is?" Simon asked.

Muttering in his usual way, Aldric just opened the door and stepped out. Simon let him take a few steps before joining him, curiosity winning out over anger, and the two walked into the mist. Their car disappeared behind them, but the spinning windmill pushed away the fog so the children were easily seen.

I feel like some kind of Dragonhunting stalker, thought Simon. *What are we even going to say to him? We don't speak Japanese; we're going to sound like aliens.*

They were closing in, amid the rushing mist, as more children joined the line, their parents watching them go.

Simon hoped he and Aldric looked unthreatening. They hadn't yet reached the boy when Aldric spoke to him. "Uh, excuse me, there, if I might have a word," said Aldric, sounding like a butler, all polished-up consonants and proper English manners.

Oh, this kid gets the special treatment, thought Simon. *"If I might have a word."* Yeah. *Here's a word for you. . . .*

The boy kept walking toward the school. When Aldric called hello again, the other children helpfully tapped the boy on the back.

He turned around, and Simon was startled to see a kid who looked half-Japanese and half–St. George.

"I wonder if we could talk to you for just one quick moment," said Aldric, his face clearly showing the same surprise that Simon felt.

"A moment? Before school?" asked the boy, puzzled.

The Japanese boy spoke English.

Of course. Gifted, thought Simon.

"May I ask who you might be?" he said, but there wasn't an ounce of suspicion in him. He had the most innocent, nicest face imaginable. He looked like he wanted to be helpful to *them.*

"We think you could be in terrible danger," said Aldric, getting closer. "This may be an emergency. I think it's better if we don't talk out in the open."

At the door of the Windmill School, a female teacher looked up, and walked toward them.

"What possible trouble could there be . . ." started the boy, "out here?"

Suddenly, Aldric was smashed from behind by a powerful blow. He tumbled against a fence, and

Simon turned to see a group of several big Japanese men rushing forward.

The first one did not hesitate to toss Simon to the ground with a push so hard it knocked the wind out of him.

Aldric rose quickly to find one of the men had a gun. In response, Aldric fired a tiny dart from the miniature crossbow mounted on his wrist, and the arrow flew from his sleeve and slammed into the attacker. The gunman howled, and his shot went awry, stinging the back of the windmill. Instantly, the giant fan began swinging violently fast—something had gone wrong with its motor—and a shock of wind swept over them.

Children screamed and ran, and Simon watched the spectacle of Aldric in an elaborate fistfight with five men in black suits, the swirling white mist around them a stark background.

Simon rushed one man, who was as big as a small tree, and grabbed him by the neck as the attacker lunged for the other St. George boy. He hung on grimly.

Aldric was having a rough time of it. Simon had never seen him struggle so hard with Dragon henchmen before, but he had one thug clasped by the head, a crossbow to his face.

Then the man somehow flipped Aldric in a move

Simon could not believe, and Simon himself was whirled around, as the attacker sent him flying into the field.

With the mist rushing by like galloping white horses, the Japanese men swept up the mystery boy and threw him in an already moving sedan—the boy's own.

"Come on, come on!" yelled Aldric, running after the sedan, firing his crossbow at it. "GET THE CAR!"

Simon ran for their Citröen, and hopped in, driving crazily for his father, his inexperience at the wheel quite obvious. He soon caught up with Aldric running like a madman down the misty road.

Aldric jumped in the passenger side, and spurred Simon on, shouting.

Simon smacked the gas pedal, swallowing hard in fear, and watched the mist racing past, as the car burned rubber in pursuit. For a moment, there was no sign of anything, and then—*BAM!!*—Simon slammed his car into the mystery boy's moving sedan, which accelerated out of the collision.

"I didn't mean it, I didn't mean it," Simon was saying, but immediately, the attackers leaned out of the sedan's windows and began firing.

Bullets swam past the old Citröen.

Fenwick the fox gave a squeal, scurrying over Simon's head and scratching him with his tiny claws, before rolling himself into a tiny ball in the backseat.

Aldric was leaning out of the speeding car—"Faster, Simon!"—as he shot arrows into the sedan. The metal squealed. The arrows dug in. But the car sped on, to no effect.

The white haze swirled around the two racing cars, and Simon began to see the world that was taking shape around him. They were headed back to the heart of the city. *The heart of the city, where there were more buildings, and people, and cars . . .*

He yelped in shock.

His car barely missed plowing into two monks and a cyclist in white. As Aldric reloaded his crossbow—barking orders to Simon to miss this, miss that, speed up, slow down—the two cars roared past an intersection where scores of people were crossing the street. The pedestrians scattered off, yowling as the cars exchanged fire.

"They're not hitting a thing," said Aldric, confused.

"Close enough," said Simon, as part of the windshield cracked from a bullet.

"Warning shots," muttered Aldric, but he fired again at the sedan, his arrow shattering the rear taillight.

Simon was veering too wildly to help Aldric very much—he hadn't practiced driving nearly enough back home, and this was an emergency. Terrified, he meant to hit the brakes as a rickety little train rushed toward him from the right, but instead he hit the gas, and was nailed back to the seat. Simon rocketed past the train.

"Nice manuever. We're still on them," said Aldric.

Simon had no thoughts in his head. His heart was beating too loud to hear anything.

His legs had trouble reaching the pedals, so the car sputtered a bit, until Simon arched his back and plunged his foot down on the accelerator, losing his view for a moment as the car roared forward and closed the gap with the enemy.

Then the other sedan took a turn, and darted down into a tunnel, with Simon following. But the tunnel closed up behind him, and Simon had the awful feeling he'd just driven into a trap.

Chapter 16

CULTURE CLASH

THE CARS RUSHED DOWN the tunnel. There was just enough light to see the sedan up ahead. It was as if they'd stumbled on a secret passage.

Suddenly, the cars emerged in a giant underground circle, and Simon's car scratched the concrete edge of a wall, sending sparks flying as it took the curve. The circle was completely different from the tunnel—it was well-lit, with square, painted lanterns, wooden sides, and a wooden floor, all surrounding a beautiful exotic tree.

The other sedan stopped. Simon slammed on his brakes.

Aldric leapt out, but Simon was still too rattled to move. He watched from the car as Aldric confronted the attackers. The mystery boy was taken by one man and whisked up an ornate pagoda elevator that disappeared into the wooden ceiling. This left four assailants.

Aldric had his sword out, and Simon hurried out of the car to follow suit.

Their enemies brought out swords of their own. Samurai swords.

Aldric held off three of the attackers while Simon swung his sword at another one, who quickly disarmed him with a move of his Samurai sword, and turned away, as Simon fell to the ground.

Not so fast, thought Simon, and he tossed a silver dagger at the attacker. It stuck into the man's sword arm, just as he was preparing to slash at Aldric. The man looked back with surprise, but did not seem to be in pain. He pulled loose the dagger.

Aldric was atop the Citröen, surrounded on three sides by assassins.

"No one has to die," warned Aldric. "You can give me the boy you took, and leave with your lives."

The large man who had fought Simon now spoke in Japanese to the others, who lowered their swords, bewildered.

"The boy we took . . . ?" the man said, in good English.

Simon could see Aldric was just as baffled. "Where is he?" demanded Aldric. "We're here to protect the boy."

"So are we," said the man.

Aldric lowered his sword.

The Japanese leader moved back slowly, and lifted Simon off the ground, light as a feather, and pushed him forward, toward Aldric. Simon could see now that the man was fairly young, younger than Aldric, and had a strong face, without the dull eyes of a Dragon henchman. *Too intelligent,* Simon thought.

"*We* protect the boy," the leader said, "and you appeared to be doing him harm."

Aldric jumped off the roof of the car to stand by his son. The others fell close around their leader, still tense.

"Nothing of the sort. We had reason to believe the boy would be under attack," said Aldric.

"Under attack by who?"

"A Serpent, if you need to know," said Aldric, and the word got a reaction. These men knew what he was talking about.

"And how is it you know of the men-Serpents?"

Aldric blinked. "How is it *you* know of the men-Serpents?"

Simon looked at his father. He looked at the tall Japanese leader. He couldn't believe what he was hearing.

Tea was served.

Simon and Aldric stood uneasily on one side of

the room, examining mysterious Japanese screens and sparsely placed bonsai trees. Through long, thin windows Simon could see their cars in the underground circle below, and Fenwick down there scratching at the windshield.

"It's customary to sit," said the Japanese leader, who had joined his comrades on the floor. They had not disarmed. There were no furnishings; only cushions provided any comfort. It wasn't like the elegant home they'd observed this morning, with its antique chairs Simon had seen through the windows.

"I'll stand, thank you," said Aldric. "And I'd like an answer to my question. If you don't work for a Serpent, who do you work for?"

The Japanese leader looked at his partners. "Self-employed," he said.

Aldric took a deep breath. "Like to play at riddles, do you?"

"No," said the leader, and he kept his eyes on his friends and away from Aldric. "I watch others play at riddles."

One of the largest of the men, an overweight, imposing fellow, looked for an instant like he might laugh. Simon was sure of it.

The humor left no question who was in control here. All of the men were dressed in similar black suits. They looked impressively relaxed, as if they could fight off a surprise attack from a resting position. They were all very muscular, inert but intense, like a row of sharpened knives.

"If you're trying to get my attention, you surely have," Aldric continued. "No one knows of the Serpent ways except me and my son, and I have great interest in knowing how it is you're familiar with the Creatures. If I can't get an answer freely, I may force it from you."

The leader frowned. *I'd like to see that*, he seemed to say, and Simon felt a bit worried. "The time for gnashing teeth is over. Would I offer you tea if I wanted to continue this fight?"

Aldric eyed him distrustfully. "I assume you want to know what it is we know," he said. "We are from the Order of the Dragonhunter, and we hunt this evil you speak of, wherever we find it. We follow the code of the Books of Saint George, and beyond that, I don't think you need to know anything else."

"Your names," said the Japanese leader.

"Ah, well," said Aldric. "Aldric St. George. This is my son, Simon St. George."

"Taro Yamada," said the leader, introducing himself "Good to have you back."

Aldric seemed taken aback, but kept his cool. "You are familiar with me . . . ?"

"Somewhat," said Taro. "I am certainly familiar with your messes."

Simon could see his father had no clue what all this meant. Then he noticed a dim figure behind one of the screens, but the shadow seemed to step away, its shape dissolving. Was the boy back there?

"Sir, the one who should be explaining himself," continued Taro, "is you."

"I told you. I was hunting a Serpent. I thought the boy was in jeopardy."

"Which Serpent?"

"It is a killer from Zurich."

Taro looked to the others, who turned grim. "A second Serpent? In Japan?"

"We're not sure." Simon broke in. "We may have killed him at sea."

"*May* have killed him?" Taro grunted. "You mean you may have let him go?"

Aldric bristled. "We don't often make mistakes. This one's clever. And he had a great deal of information about the boy you protect."

"Kyoshi."

Aldric nodded, recognizing an offer of kindness in the giving of the boy's name. "He may still be in danger from the Zurich beast. We'd like to see to it he's kept safe. We'd like to know . . . where such a boy comes from."

At this, Taro looked startled, though he quickly hid it. And then to everyone's surprise, the boy stepped out from behind one of the opaque, painted screens. "You mean you don't know?" asked the boy, in English.

"Kyoshi," scolded Taro, and the other men leapt into action, moving around the boy protectively. "You were to stay out of the way."

Simon looked at the boy, who seemed ashamed at disobeying Taro, but his eyes were filled with curiosity. Simon could see him well now. He took him to be about eleven years old.

Taro stood, and frowned again at Aldric. "Meet your nephew," he said.

Nephew?

It was a most interesting morning. It seemed the Japanese side of the Order had some things to learn as well—they acted surprised to be unknown to the St. Georges. Simon's head was filled with wonder at their remarkable situation.

They'd been led to a second room in the secret base, dark and filled with Japanese scrolls. As the leader Taro spoke, and Kyoshi watched from the side, Aldric and Simon stood surrounded by the other men.

"You are not alone in hunting the Serpent," said Taro, and he hit a switch. The room lit up, with gleaming Samurai swords, suits of armor, rifles and spears, and devices Simon had never seen before.

"The Asian Order of the Serpentkillers has existed for centuries, though its origin is unknown. We may even have crossed paths before. Certainly we knew of your Hunters since your Medieval Age, when someone from the European ranks pursued a Dragon here and required help. It is said this partnership was highly difficult, but little else is known. The Hunters always protected the island, and I am the logical extension of that great cause."

Simon passed a quick glance over the other warriors. Their eyes were active with thought, and gentle when they found Simon's gaze, but certainly bore no respect for him, a mere boy. They obviously understood English, but they were content to let Taro alone do the talking.

"The first Samurai of this secret group were men of valiant honor, who let nothing be known of their work. Our world fell out of touch with yours. The strict adherence to our code of purification meant that anyone who discovered us was brought into the fold, or eliminated by death. I can tell you these early times were filled with treachery, and our oral history tells of many betrayals by foreigners coming into our formation. But we have heard from no one in your Order for many, many years."

He regarded Aldric for a second, tapping a steel claw-like weapon on a display table. "And we have had no need of support outside of ourselves."

Like the men, Kyoshi said nothing, standing completely still. It took effort to notice him in the room, in his black school uniform, leaning against the dark wooden wall.

Taro indicated the scrolls on the table. "The deathspells of the Asian Serpents are recorded here, some translated from the European spellbooks, some original. We are the caretakers of these works, which were once maintained by monks, who have all passed away."

"What are these?" asked Simon, drawn to several tiny silver bullets, warm to the touch.

Taro clicked his tongue. "I'm telling our life story. It doesn't interest you?" Annoyed, he took the bullets from Simon and replaced them in a case. "The bullets contain serpentfire. The fire is held in check by an ancient Magician-forged metal. Same with the swords, same with the arrows, which I'll thank you not to touch. The tamefire is the safest way we have of killing the Serpents."

"Tame . . ." pondered Simon. "I've never heard of tamed fire."

Taro looked weary. "The word is . . . well, a bit *hopeful*. The fire is a necessity. Using Dragonfire against the enemy is superior to deathspells—though the fire rarely behaves as intended."

"You were saying?" prompted Aldric. "How did we get from medieval Japan to today?"

Taro took the interruption with a slight smile. "People here in Japan passed down the work of the Hunt to their children, and their children's children, and we five here are the last of them. We are the remnants of the Samurai in the Modern Age."

There was no boasting in the way he said it.

"Although, without a true leader, we are more aptly called *ronin*," he added. "Not that we are waiting for anyone to fill the job."

"But how do you . . ." Simon spoke up again without asking permission, and saw Taro's surprise. "How do you hunt the things? You can't see them, can you?"

Taro looked to Aldric, perturbed, perhaps. "For a good, long time, this was a great difficulty. We followed the codes given to us in the old scrolls. We hunted in the dark, of course, looking for the Dragonsigns, the wrinkles and creases in nature, the storms, the pestilence, the anger and hopelessness that grows around such animals. When we thought we'd found one, we watched. If the Thing was seen to spread evil, a decision would be made, and we would cut him down."

"You must've done a pretty good job." Simon said. "We haven't noticed much evidence of Dragons in this part of the world."

Aldric gave him a look. "Well, you know the reason for that, Simon. For centuries, we only had one of the Saint George books. It made little mention of Asian Serpents." He turned to explain this to Taro, who seemed disdainful of arguing in front of strangers. "It's our own ancient collected knowledge. It wasn't until we recaptured the White Book of Saint George that we learned there were so many here, and others whose ancestors must have left this region a long time ago, like the Dragon of Zurich," he added.

"Strange that a Serpent from so distant a place would take interest in Kyoshi now," said Taro, "since we keep to ourselves. But if he were not with us, we'd be lost. Kyoshi is our guide, you see. Long ago we found him. He was on television, on the news, after a terrible fire here in Kyoto. He was ranting about having seen a Serpent-like man who had started the inferno. He was a very small child back then. We were tracking the beast, and naturally, we came to the boy. He had seen . . . what we could never see."

"You . . . see them, too?" asked Simon solemnly. Kyoshi looked at him, nodding.

Taro glanced down with pride. "We had searched for such a person for centuries . . . and there he was."

Kyoshi nodded again, serious, looking the very picture of obedience.

"Yeah," muttered Simon, looking at Kyoshi questioningly. "There he was. I just don't get where he came from."

Taro seemed embarrassed. "We might better answer that question with more comfort, back at our house," he said.

Aldric nodded, as his eyes moved toward the tree nearest him. The bonsai was twisting, its branches seemingly alive, as it shriveled and bent low, the earth around it now spitting forth little worms.

"I think," said Aldric, "the Ice Dragon may be making an appearance after all. . . ."

Chapter 17

⚔

A Traveler to the Orient

Unbeknownst to the Dragonhunters, Visser, the Ice Serpent, was sitting in a nearby teahouse, enjoying the unfolding of the morning and the soft movement of the light as the sun rose higher.

It was not as entertaining as *Columbo*, but his television was gone.

Shivering from the cold, he shaved some frost off his hands onto the floor.

There had been an earthquake or two earlier, which he had accidentally caused, his magic spilling out of him in old age with no rhyme or reason, but he felt certain the Dragonhunters hadn't noticed it. At the time, they were battling one another in speeding cars and wouldn't even have felt the tremors. And the fog could be reasoned away as well.

True, his presence was causing the bonsai trees in the Japanese café to crack and twist strangely, but the St. Georges and their Asian counterparts were in their secret base far below him, and Visser felt it unlikely his magic had strayed so far down. He prided himself on his elaborate knowledge of *them*, but he was certain they had no awareness of *him*.

A black beetle crawled out of his teacup, and he quickly scarfed it down before anyone noticed. The Japanese woman at the other end of the café looked at him strangely, and for a moment he thought he might have to torch the place, but she went back into the kitchen and left him in peace.

He rolled the beetle around in his mouth, and after a moment, other insects and worms wriggled up from his stomach and gently over his throat to tickle his tongue, playing about, creeping sweetly and nicely. They wrapped themselves over each other, and rubbed their little feet and tiny antennae over his teeth. *Everyone warm and happy in there*, he thought. *Each elegant, crawling thing a shade of perfect black or white*.

Thus satisfied, he turned his attention to the street, waiting for the Samurai to emerge with the St. Georges. There were many little wheels spinning in his plan, and he wanted to keep track of them all. *This is how we do it, my little friends*, he thought, addressing his insects. *First we bring the Hunters together, and then we bring the two strongest Dragons, and then we watch the humans die in the most poetic possible way. We've created a beautiful Dragon alliance in the process.* Two powerful Dragon Houses would unite, and he would be the mastermind of it all. *The matchmaker.* He would be remembered for the renewal of his entire *species.* Who knew how long it had been since the last Dragon was born?

He was growing impatient. *The irritating Japanese with all their ceremonies. They must be holding things up.*

With his quivering, frosty hands, the Ice Dragon lifted from his pocket a small rat, a useful tool of Serpents, and he set it down to run outside toward a crack in the street. Then he reached out with his mind, and tried to see through the rat's eyes as it descended underground to a tunnel. The Ice Dragon was weak, and the sorcery more difficult than he expected, but in a few moments, he could make out the meeting of the Dragonhunters, and he heard them speaking of . . . him.

Then the rat seemed to get caught, wriggling in some kind of narrow space, and Visser sighed. *My luck as usual. I'll have to see to this myself.*

"This Ice Dragon may be following us." Taro looked at Aldric with disdain. "But you've made things even more dangerous," he said. "You forced us to come here, and possibly expose our hiding place, after that scene you caused at the school."

Kyoshi looked as if he wanted to be somewhere else. He placed a well-manicured finger over his lips, regarding Simon's shoes as if they were marked with fascinating hieroglyphics.

"You might have been less obtrusive," continued Taro.

Aldric raised his voice, "We were trying to be open and forthright—"

As they chattered on, Simon watched as the boy pulled a little paper swan from his pocket, and then pulled a smaller swan out of the larger one. Gazing playfully, but without a smile, in a funny little move, he made the smaller swan look as though it had been eaten by the larger one, hiding it in his hand.

The other men were watching, finely attuned to the boy, but Taro and Aldric were still arguing. "Would it not have been better to speak at a different time, with less of an audience?" Taro asked.

Aldric gave him a scathing look, pointing to a white rat wriggling in a crack at the wall near Taro's feet. "Audience?"

"A spy," said Taro, and he pulled out his pistol.

"Too late," said Aldric. The rat was gone.

"How long was it there?" asked Simon.

"Too long," said Aldric, looking around in alarm. "The Thing's found us."

Simon turned in fear as the awful crackle-sound of a fire slipped into the room.

There was a shuffling beyond the wall—the Dragon had scuttled away, but he'd left a gift.

Shapes were moving behind the Japanese screens, and all of the Samurai drew their guns, protecting Kyoshi in their center. The boy folded his arms, trying to be calm, and watched, with no attempt to fight for himself.

The shapes behind the screens now burned with light. They had been embers that had glided in from cracks in the wall and had come together to form men made of fire.

"Firespawn," said Aldric, as Taro called out, "Embermen."

The shapes were stooped and very thin, made of ashes and ember, not at all the threatening fire-monstrosities that had eaten the ship at sea, but rather, the work of a tired old Dragon almost devoid of power.

But harmless they were not.

The screens began to burn, as the shapes clawed their way through, fiery skeletal hands ripping the beautiful Japanese screen-paintings of flowers and ancient scenes.

"*Reeeek? Reeeck?*" cried the old firelings incomprehensibly, in creaking voices of sizzle and hiss and dying sparks.

Withered, drooping faces made of ash, and flickering with half-dying light, began emerging from the ruined sitting room. *"Youth . . . death . . ."* uttered the first embered face, and the second echoed, *"Youth death, youth death . . ."*

Hungrily, these old men of fire lunged for Kyoshi—young, weak, and without a weapon. Simon instinctively stepped in the way, even as the Samurai moved in.

"Youth-death, youth-death—burn burn burn burn—"

There were eight of the fire-wretches, and Aldric slashed two of them apart almost instantly, but their ashen bodies collapsed into pools of fire, spreading, as if gaining strength somehow from Aldric's anger. Simon buried his sword in another rippling piece of fire-flesh, but as the Creature recoiled, the fire drew itself up the blade and singed his hand.

He cried out and dropped his sword—which another firespawn promptly snatched, and swung the sword, aflame, at Simon's head. He ducked, as Taro fired a barrage of gunfire into the old fireling.

"Your swords!" cried Aldric. "You must use your swords!" He swung his own at a sprinkler plug in the ceiling, and water showered down upon them, but it only slowed the wraithlike creatures' momentum for a moment.

Throwing Kyoshi behind him, Taro continued

shooting, and his bullets passed through the groping firelings. They were cowed only a little by the show of force, but the shots broke apart a huge ceramic planter filled with water. The liquid spilled around the feet of the firelings, bringing a sibilant hushing of ash and water. But the firelings simply stumbled forward, spreading fire as they came.

Aldric leapt over a pool of flame to head toward the elevator, calling for his son, but Simon did not join him. Taro and the Samurai were headed out a back way with Kyoshi—and the last one out, the big man, looked back at Simon as if he were crazy for not coming. Simon figured they knew a safer exit and, sweeping up his fallen sword, he rushed after them. Aldric stared, a moment's hurt at not being followed, and then charged back across the flames to Simon.

The Creatures were still crawling toward him, writhing on the watery ground, pulling themselves forward, as Simon ducked down a stairway after Taro.

Aldric followed, and the flames took the stairway behind them, as everyone rushed into the circle to their cars.

Aldric could see the damage to Taro's armored sedan. Arrows stabbed into it everywhere. "You can take ours," he shouted over the fire.

Taro looked at the forlorn Citröen, and instead, pushed Kyoshi into his own car.

"I've seen your driving," he said, and his sedan quickly tore away.

Simon slashed a stray fireling that was trying to get the sword back from him. Aldric kicked the wounded firespawn back, and the emberman burst into a small explosion, setting the giant tree afire.

Simon leapt into the driver's seat of the Citröen, shoving Fenwick out of the way, but Aldric pushed him aside. "But I got us here," cried Simon.

"You're too cautious!" yelled Aldric, and he laid on the accelerator so hard Simon nearly flew into the backseat. The Citröen raced around the burning circle, and Simon watched flames lapping at the car windows. Fenwick screamed a high-pitched wail, and the car flew through the fiery wall, down the tunnel.

Flames parted from the front windshield, turning to an icy frost, and Simon could see Taro's black sedan racing up the tunnel ramp and back onto the streets of Kyoto.

Simon shot a look back. The fire was disappearing under a shower of frost!

Now, up ahead, Simon could see an old man, alone on the street. He blurred into the Ice Dragon of Zurich, turning the corner, appearing as a stooped, ugly black-and-white Serpent.

"There! He's there!" called Simon, but Aldric had already seen it, turning the steering wheel to follow him, right behind Taro.

The Citröen took the turn, but the old Serpent was gone.

But the Creature had cast a spell that sent rows and rows of riderless motorcycles roaring out of a dealer's shop. There must've been fifty high-speed motorcycles rushing straight for them.

With the same pitch as Fenwick, Simon screamed.

Squealing, Taro's car veered so it was side by side with Aldric's.

The motorcycles zoomed toward the cars, a huge flock of them, one of them speeding directly *over* Simon's car, its wheels leaving a black smear on the windshield, as it rolled over the battered roof and clattered away.

Other bikes were smashed apart as the cars banged into them, one after another.

The whir of the motorcycle engines was like a mad, growling beast. Aldric didn't even stop, smashing through the bikes, tossing them aside. In his armored sedan, Taro drove onward, too, but curved off onto an empty walkway.

The motorcycles they passed were now swooping around to chase them. Simon looked back, and saw the motorcycles pursuing, smashing and clattering against the cars relentlessly.

But Aldric stayed on course, never losing focus.

Simon saw the old Serpent duck into an alley. The cars took the curve after him, and found a very unattractive dead end.

Taro and Aldric hit the brakes. The cars screeched in agony, tires burning with resentment, brakes begging for mercy, as Aldric's car spun sideways and smacked into a wall, where Taro's screeching car crashed into it seconds later.

Next, a speeding troop of runaway motorcycles rushed in, crashing, toppling, flying, clattering, and piling up in a horrid sculpture of destruction.

Aldric tore his way out of the Citröen's ragtop convertible roof.

With Fenwick chattering in fear behind him, Simon joined his father on the street, as Taro and the others roamed the dead end in shock. Suddenly it seemed obvious where the Dragon had gone.

Aldric's eyes narrowed at the exact moment Taro spied the same thing—a flicker of motion high up on one of the buildings nearby. The Ice Dragon was going over.

Stalactites formed on the building and ice rained down on the Hunters.

Aldric started to climb a fire escape, but the Samurai were running around the outside of the building with Kyoshi in the middle of them. Simon again followed their lead. He looked back to see Aldric changing his mind and coming after him.

Around the corner was a busy street clogged with traffic and people, and an old man weaving his way among them, trying to get away.

Simon again saw a blur turn into a tail-whipping beast, running off into the crowd.

"There!" shouted Aldric, rushing past, and they ran after the Dragon. Firing their guns was out of the question—too many non-combatants. So they and the Samurai chased on and on, waiting for a clear shot, with Taro and his men falling behind while trying to keep Kyoshi in their midst.

The Ice Dragon fled, his black-and-white body a vivid optical shock as it slipped in and out of a population who saw him only as a doddering old man. Simon caught up to his father, and they gained fast on the old Dragon, even with his head start. But the Ice Serpent turned another corner, to a wide boulevard with traffic coming at him head-on. Simon saw the Dragon scurry down on all fours, crawling under the speeding cars and trucks—amazingly—sliding on his belly like an iguana, and missing any injury.

Simon almost stopped with surprise, seeing the two-toned demon scuttling fast under the rushing autos, a huge torrent of motion coming straight at the Dragonhunters. Aldric yanked Simon aside, out of the path of the speeding cars, and the two continued their chase alongside the traffic, with Taro and the Samurai coming up behind.

Suddenly the Ice Serpent was hit in the shoulder, a glancing blow from a rushing car. The beast tumbled under a parked truck, and Simon and Aldric saw their chance to catch him.

They split up, Aldric taking the front, Simon the side, and both bent down to take aim under the truck.

For one second, Simon stared into the ugly yellow eyes of the monster that had ripped into him in the putrid hold of his ship—

But the Thing was about to descend into a sewer, and, without thinking, Simon grabbed its fat, squirming tail. His fist clenched around the soft, wrinkled flesh, and he held it tight. It wasn't going anywhere.

Or so he thought. It broke loose from its tail like a lizard, and dived into the sewer hole, leaving Simon holding what looked like a long snake. The tail wiggled and shook and looped around his neck, strangling him, but Aldric batted at it until it stopped. It fell to the ground and instantly burned into black ash and blew away in the wind.

The Samurai had just caught up, gathering around the truck, but the Serpent had blown a fire up from the manhole. Quickly, Taro pulled at Kyoshi's collar, like a cat, getting further back, and everyone fell in behind them, even Simon and Aldric, fearing the spread of the fire.

"Where does that hole lead?" cried Aldric, staring back at the fiery opening.

"It leads to pain," said Taro.

The surreal, black-and-white fire swept upward, and everyone fell further back.

The truck exploded, split down the middle in ebony fire and snowy flames that immediately turned to ice, crystals stabbing out and lifting the truck's pieces, glassy spikes rolling forward down the street, ice that mimicked flames.

Chapter 18

LIGHT WITHOUT HEAT

"WE'VE LOST HIM," GROWLED Taro, and he stared at Aldric as if it were somehow his fault.

The ice-fire fascinated Simon, but the others seemed more concerned about its results.

"I am very disappointed in the St. George abilities," Taro mumbled to the men.

They spent a good deal of time circling the area, but there was no trace of the Ice Serpent, neither in ripples in nature, nor in the moods of the ordinary Japanese people, who didn't like being stared at by strangers.

Giving up the chase, they went for safety to Kyoshi's mansion home, where Aldric and Simon had seen him leave for school that morning. It was indeed different from the secret training base Simon had seen before—not a place for battle preparation, but rather, a welcoming residence decorated with Japanese art and comfortably furnished. Aldric seemed to know the way to the parlor, and he kept muttering to himself, looking at everything as if it were familiar from some cloudy memory, until Fenwick bumped his leg, snapping him out of it.

None too pleased to see a fox prowling in his house, Taro slumped in a wide leather chair, in an elegant club-like living room adorned with Asian artifacts and paintings of warriors.

"Our fortress is destroyed," he said. "The tree went up in flames. . . . We could not even manage to save that . . ."

"Of all things to worry about . . ." Aldric looked at him. "What's another old tree?"

Taro stared at his teacup, clearly trying to hide his anger. "It was where the Order was founded. Ages ago. It had great significance. The underground fortress had to be built around it, and the tree grew without light. It was all that was left of an original Samurai fortress where great Magicians once lived. Have you never had a connection to a tree before?"

Simon thought his father might laugh. "A tree," Aldric repeated. "No. Can't say that I have."

Simon noted the Samurai seemed to have a deep connection to nature; every room was ornamented with plants and flowers, painstakingly arranged and presented. He leaned on a wooden tree planter, watching his father try to get comfortable on an Oriental settee, and then he stared at the floor, thinking, as Fenwick nuzzled up to him.

"Why did he wait until that moment?" said Simon. "The Ice Dragon could have attacked at any time, but he wanted to see what we were up to. Don't you think? He wanted to eavesdrop."

Taro looked at Simon, and again Simon felt small, like a little kid. Maybe the Samurai was just offended that a boy was allowed to speak at all.

"We, of course, are a fascinating group," said Taro. "I'm sure he couldn't take his eyes off us. We're a collection of the greatest Warriors on Earth, who couldn't capture a sniveling, elderly Serpent, himself incapable of creating more than a single blast of fire, which melted into ice."

"I'm serious," Simon insisted. "Look at the attack he made on us, it was everything he had—and he didn't have a chance. So why did he bother?"

"This one," said Taro, referring to Simon, "does not understand such arrogance."

"Oh, I think he's seen arrogance before." One of the older Samurai chuckled, throwing a glance to Aldric. They'd picked up on Aldric's blustery manner right away.

The largest Samurai, the heavyset man, said something in Japanese, and quiet laughter followed. Simon looked at Kyoshi, who buried a grin.

"What's that?" asked Aldric, distrustful.

Taro translated with a smile. "He said next time you might not run directly *into* traffic. In Japan, at high speeds, cars are known to . . . smash people."

The huge, smiling man ran a fist into his other hand, dangling two of his fingers in imitation of a running man, giving the impression of a car hitting a person, as if he were explaining this simple fact to a three-year-old.

The Samurai snickered again. It didn't seem all that funny to Simon.

Nor to Aldric. "Must've lost something in translation," he said. "And I wouldn't mind if we finished the history lesson about you blokes, top to bottom. If I'm going to be made a fool of, I'd like to know by whom."

"Was he in danger?" said a voice.

Aldric turned, and Simon saw his reaction. Aldric looked as if he might recognize the woman who had quietly appeared behind them. Simon was struck by her beauty. A Japanese woman in a sharply tailored black blazer and skirt, her long dark hair tied up behind her head, she had an expression of tired sadness.

"My mother," said Kyoshi. "Sachiko."

The woman bowed slightly, and turned to Taro. "Tell me now, was he in danger?" She repeated her question.

Taro's eyes went to Kyoshi, who looked nervous, and sidestepped the issue. "He never left our sight," he answered. It put the woman only slightly at ease.

"This is Aldric St. George, and his son, Simon," said Kyoshi.

Sachiko nodded. "I know who they are," she said. "Please be welcomed, gentlemen. Were there proper introductions? Have we . . . told them about ourselves?"

Taro looked embarrassed. "We were tracking one of the Things, there was no time to—"

"Leave it to men to forget such simple manners," said Sachiko, with just the slightest touch of fire in her voice. "Let's set that straight, shall we? This . . . is Akira." The fiercest looking warrior, his head shaven, his face stony and cold, stood and bowed. "This is Mamoru." The hefty one lifted his bulky frame and bowed with a jolly smile. "Kisho, and Toyo," said the woman, and the other two warriors bowed; one small and lean, the other fit and capable, but older, with graying hair.

"And my husband, Taro."

Simon looked to Taro, who bowed again, as if he'd never met him before. *Such formality in this place*, Simon thought.

"Would it be impolite for me to say that I did not expect to see you again?" the woman asked, with a smile that made the question seem like a delicate joke.

"You have the better of me, I'm afraid," answered Aldric. "I'm not altogether sure that I know you . . ."

"My face is not familiar?"

Aldric paused. "I wouldn't say that . . . but I can't quite place it. I'm sorry. I ought to have remembered someone so beautiful."

Taro cleared his throat, as if Aldric's attempt at gallantry had caused him to choke.

"I feared you might forget . . ." said Sachiko, and her snowy face looked nervous. "And Ormand as well, I should think."

"My brother Ormand has passed away. He was killed just over a year ago. In battle."

Sachiko looked at him blankly.

"But I don't remember him speaking of you," Aldric added. Simon wanted to wince at his bluntness.

"I suppose," said Sachiko, swallowing hard, "it's pointless to chat before getting to such intimate matters, and as I recall, niceties are not your forte anyway. Ormand is the father of my son Kyoshi. That much you have learned?"

"I hadn't known before . . . I'm still not sure I can believe . . ." Aldric's voice trailed off. Simon and Aldric both looked at Kyoshi.

Aldric said quietly, "It's hard to get your mind round it, isn't it? I must say I don't see much of his father in him . . ."

"*I'm* his father," Taro retorted.

Simon could see Aldric looking apologetic, but Sachiko said quietly, "Taro has been here with us since Kyoshi was five years old. He is the only father he's ever known."

"Forgive me," said Aldric. "But it's hard for me to believe that Ormand St. George would leave behind his own son. That's not my brother's way."

"He never knew he had a son," answered Sachiko, in such a low tone Simon had to lean forward to listen. "When you came here, the first time, so many years ago, you and your brother stayed not for one night, but for three months." Aldric looked quizzical as she went on. "You were recovering from serious wounds, and the Dragon you pursued was cunning and hard to find. It took time for you to track him. In that time, Ormand and I became very close." Simon saw Taro look distastefully at Aldric as she said this. "To your surprise, as I recall, I was able to help you in locating this Serpent. I have certain strengths as well. You see, I have a . . . I don't know what to call it, a divine gift, I suppose. All my life I have had dreams that foretold the future, and at emotional times, I found I could even move objects across a room, using only my will . . . a strange power . . . something my mother called 'elemental wishes.' You and your brother gave me a different name: Magician."

Simon was a bit startled. The hearty and eccentric Alaythia was the only Magician he had ever known, and this delicate Asian woman somehow did not look the part to him.

"I found the Serpent for you by looking into a still-water pond. Through the use of meditation, over many weeks, I saw reflected in the waters the den of the Dragon beneath the Earth, but that is not where you found him. He came for us. As Ormand and I drifted in a boat in a pond not far from here, I sat staring into the water, searching for something that would lead us to him. And out of the sky, the Thing attacked. He nearly killed us all. A terrible fire burned blue on the pond's surface, in broad daylight . . . bright, vicious . . . We swam beneath it for a long time, until we found our way out. You and Ormand decided to pursue him, and I made a fateful decision: to erase your memory of this place. I wanted this so badly, as painful as it was, and so the mist I called to your mind swept away the images in your head. Your emotions, though, are strong, and I think they kept a little piece of my world in your memory."

"I could swear," said Aldric, "that I had spent only a night here."

Sachiko smiled, with some pride, Simon thought.

"But why do it?" Simon asked her.

Sachiko's eyes moved away from them. "I learned much from your brother, Aldric," she answered. "And one of the things I learned was that when a Magician falls in love with a Knight, they cause a stirring, so to speak, in the waters of life. . . . They cannot disguise their emotions, and these feelings are like lifting a shield from your arm. The Dragons begin to feel your presence. They want to find you, they need to . . ."

The pictures in Simon's mind's eye floated immediately to Alaythia, and his fear for her grew as he listened.

"I could accept my own death," said Sachiko in a steely voice. "But not your brother's."

"So you wiped our memories clean, and sent us on our way," Aldric said, his brow furrowed, as Simon figured he was trying to retrieve a trace of this history that had vanished from him. Her power must be considerable to have worked so strongly.

"Then my son was born, and he began to show signs of knowing," Sachiko went on. "He was a St. George, and there was no denying it . . . though I tried. I did not want him in jeopardy. Time passed, and jeopardy came to us, despite my efforts. The Things perhaps sensed my love for my child. So . . . then . . . that was when Taro found us. He brought some warmth to us, he gave us a new life . . ." She smiled at Taro and he looked away. "And a sense of safety, if you can have it in this world. But to call Ormand back would've been out of the question. I could not face him. He would not remember me. And my life had changed."

Her voice had hardened with resolve.

"Your situation with Ormand," said Aldric carefully, "that kind of difficulty is what started us on this journey. There is a woman out there who works with us. She has a power such as you have, and she believes she puts us in danger from the Serpents. I've started to think maybe you and Taro, and the others . . . might help us with this problem."

She nodded. "Hiding such emotion is a difficult magic, but possible. I didn't know that then."

"She's lost," said Simon. "She's out there somewhere in Asia, looking for the Black Dragon. She thinks he can help us. She's out there alone; we have to get her back."

Taro cut him off. "We have our own work to do. This entire business has interrupted one of our most important operations."

"What?" snapped Simon. "What's so important?"

"We are to destroy once and for all the worst Serpent I have ever known."

Chapter 19

Heat Without Light

"HE IS THE SERPENT of Japan. Najikko Mok Voko. Death-Doctor. Demon-Snake," Taro explained. "He has moved throughout the island of Japan for many, many years, taunting us right here in our own land, and we have never been able to bring him down. Earthquakes. Tsunamis. Sickness. Accidents. It is mass death that he is after. He always slips free of us; eight times we have met, and eight times he has slithered out of our hands. The last time we fought, he left Akira with a severe memento . . ."

The seething, sharp-faced Samurai presented his arm, to reveal terrible scarring. Simon tried not to wince.

Taro continued, barely able to contain his anger. "In many burned buildings, in cities across Japan, the

Dragon leaves behind Samurai armor, a sword or a helmet—badly scorched, as a warning to us. He humiliates us. We've missed him too many times to let him go now. We believe we've found him, settled in Tokyo. You see, Toyo here has been having trouble with his heart . . ."

"Don't tell them that," complained the eldest Samurai.

"And he needed a hospital," Taro continued. "Kyoshi went there, and saw in one of the hallways the Serpent, walking among the sick. He disguises himself as a surgeon."

"I understand," said Aldric. "But if you can help me find Alaythia, she could be of great assistance. There is already the Ice Serpent moving among the people here, and we now have the possibility of facing two Serpents at once. I think it may have been the Ice Serpent's plan all along—to force us to confront both of them at once. They could then wipe out all the Dragonhunters in one fell swoop. We need to find Alaythia. We need all the help we can get."

"We never needed help before," said Akira, angrily.

"Haven't you?" said Aldric.

"I've seen nothing to suggest you will actually *be* of any help," Taro said, looking down at the floor. "You are reckless and unthoughtful in your every move."

Aldric shook his head, saying, "The boy is still learning, but he has great skill."

"I was speaking of the older St. George," said Taro. "But the boy is equally careless."

Aldric's hands tightened. "I'll thank you to watch your words about my son," he said. "And you might look at me when you're talking to me."

Taro met Aldric's gaze. "You and your son have given away our secret sanctuary. The Ice Dragon knows of us, and may spread word everywhere. Your Saint George heritage is well-known to us from our scrolls, but you seem to have no greater abilities than our own—you did not manage to save the underground fortress of our ancestors."

"No one could've saved that—" Simon protested.

"And your younger does not know his place," said Taro, refusing to look at Simon. "I'm sure he's a very fine boy, but this is a business for men."

"My boy keeps his own mind."

"Then let him keep it to himself," said Taro, and Simon blushed. "We have trained good and hard, and long studied our chances, and we have decided to move on the Tokyo Dragon immediately. That is our plan and we will follow it."

"Change the plan," said Aldric.

"We follow the plan." Taro's voice grew louder. "Always."

"If we leave Alaythia out there any longer . . ." said Aldric. "I fear the worst. She's gone to find the Black Dragon herself. He is old. We don't know his mind. If we lose her, then *you* lose an ally. You could use her—she's powerful."

"If we leave the Dragon of Tokyo alive any longer," said old Toyo, breaking in, "then more people suffer and are tormented by his twisted magic. He keeps hundreds of people in his grip at all times. He uses his hospital as an immense torture chamber."

"And if you die in the attack," said Aldric, "then I have no one to assist me in finding Alaythia. To attack two Dragons—which is what we will probably face—is bloody foolish."

"We have no time for searching her out," said Akira, sounding fierce. "You may need us. But we, I think, do not need *you*."

"Well . . . now . . . perhaps we do," said Mamoru, smiling. "I think perhaps we have need of each other, if we could see eye to eye. What's your thinking on this, Kisho?"

"There are two ways to see it. We might succeed only together, or we might just get in each other's way," said Kisho.

"He is very wise," Mamoru whispered to Simon.

"He didn't say *anything*," muttered Simon in disbelief.

Aldric grumbled. "Who am I supposed to be talking to? Who makes the bloody decisions around here, anyway?"

"We all make them," said Taro. "Together."

"Well, that's your problem right there," said Aldric sharply.

"It has worked for us for ages," answered Taro.

Sachiko moved in between them. "Kyoshi, why don't you show Simon your room?"

Kyoshi nodded, and quickly took Simon's hand. Simon shrugged it off, a bit annoyed, but started to follow him nonetheless. Fenwick trailed behind them, his bushy tail nearly knocking over a potted plant.

"Your plan won't work anyway," Aldric said, almost pleading. "It relies on one Dragon, doesn't it? What if there are two? Indeed, what if we are walking into a trap with *many*? I've been through that—what happens to your plan then?"

"We have watched this one many days," said Taro, "and there is no sign of an unlikely partnership with the Ice Dragon. We will attack each, one by one."

"What are you saying here, you've 'watched him'? You mean you let this Creature go when you knew he was there?"

"We had to be sure. We had to form careful plans, and wait for the right time."

"Then wait a little longer. And do it right."

Simon waited at the end of the room, though he could see Kyoshi wanted to move on before they got into trouble.

"Your feelings for this woman cloud your judgment," said Akira.

Aldric glared at him. "You don't know my feelings. And you don't want to."

Sachiko smiled and indicated a door. "Let us take a walk in the garden, Aldric, and let them speak privately. They understand, I'm sure," she said, eyeing Taro, "that the woman is very important to you, and therefore to all of us. We will work to find a compromise."

Aldric let her lead him outside, while Simon was pulled down the hall to Kyoshi's room.

It was just like Simon's room at home.

Simon entered in amazement. Small Samurai figures lined the shelf just like the little knights Simon had kept since childhood. The same comic books he collected were stacked on the bedstand, exactly as they were in his room. Games that Simon liked to play were laid alongside his favorite music, and the bookshelves had Japanese versions of Simon's best-loved stories, right down to the Ray Bradbury collections and Tolkien rip-offs that were his guilty pleasure.

Fenwick skittered to a corner, as something large and white thumped down from above the door and landed on the bed. It was some kind of monster cat, thought Simon.

"It's a bobcat," said Kyoshi, and helped the creature down from the bed. "His name is Katana. It's the name for a Samurai sword. My mother brought him back from a trip to America."

Simon stared at Kyoshi. Fenwick stared at the bobcat.

This is getting too weird, thought Simon.

"Does he . . . do anything?" Simon indicated the bobcat.

Kyoshi considered. "Not anything you would really notice."

Simon smirked. The kid was keeping secrets.

"I keep a stash of food in here," said Kyoshi, "for when I get sent to my room. Do you like Smoochers?"

Simon looked at him. It was his favorite candy.

He took the pack Kyoshi was offering, and watched as Kyoshi sat on the bed with his pet. Simon's eyes took in the huge stash of candy in Kyoshi's desk.

"Do you get sent to your room a lot?" Simon asked him.

"No," said Kyoshi, "I get sent to my room as a reward for finishing my work, so I can come in here and play. The candy I get when I receive good grades in school."

"A lot of candy," Simon noted.

Kyoshi shrugged.

"So, do people call you Key for short?"

"No."

"Well, can I call you Key for short?"

The boy shrugged again.

"So, um, Key, how old are you . . . like, eleven?" Simon asked him.

"Twelve," the boy answered, obviously hurt. He crossed his small arms across his chest.

"This looks a lot like my room," said Simon, changing the subject. "Except you don't have any swords on the wall."

"I can't have swords," Key answered.

"No swords?"

"They're sharp."

"That's why they're good."

"I can't have daggers or darts. Or arrows, either."

"Why? Arrows are the best."

"They can kill people."

"That's the coolest part!"

"My father doesn't like me to have sharp things, or dangerous things, or fast things, or things that are too intense, or things that encourage me to play rough."

"What *do* you get to do?"

"He will let me play with girls," he answered simply.

Simon smiled, and Key added, "Mother doesn't like the girls so much."

"Key, you're twelve years old," Simon said. "Why am I totally sure she has nothing to worry about?"

Key looked at him with a serious face. "Oh, she should."

He gave a half-smile and Simon started laughing.

Meanwhile, in the study, the Samurai were getting no further in their talks. The discussion went on for an hour. Aldric, sitting on a bench outside, could see them through a window.

"What are they doing in there? How much longer can they go on?" Aldric complained.

"Try to be calm," Sachiko said with amusement. "Enjoy the garden—it's meant for tranquility—or else my grandfather got rich on silk for nothing."

Aldric looked at the Japanese garden, and felt nothing but emptiness and worry.

"Taro will consider your feelings strongly." She reassured him. "There is an idea we have, it is called *ameru*. Do you know it? It's hard to explain, but it's a very strong sense of . . . helpfulness, you could say. The word, to be literal, means the fierce love a mother has for her child, but it stands for more . . . it runs through the whole society, it signifies the notion that taking care of others brings the highest joy to yourself.

Do you see? What I mean to say is, the others will weigh very heavily the risk of leaving your friend Alaythia out there alone."

"You said she was important to me. It's more than that. I don't think I can handle the boy without her. Or much of anything else . . ." Aldric's voice drifted off. "She makes things understandable to me."

They sat in silence. Tranquility never came, but Aldric enjoyed the pretense of it.

"Do you have a girlfriend?" asked Simon.

Key nodded, always with that serious face. "I have a few."

"A few?"

"We go to gaming places. We go bicycle riding sometimes . . . if my father is satisfied we're not riding near cliffs or mountains or traffic or . . ."

"How do you end up getting more than one girl-friend?"

"Around here, smartness counts for a lot," said Key, moving his chesspieces around idly.

"Oh."

"And it's not as if I'm a dog."

It took a moment for Simon to realize he was joking.

"We go in groups," Key said. "I get along better with girls."

"What about you?" said Key. "Do you have a girl-friend?"

"That's kind of personal, isn't it?" said Simon. Key still didn't laugh, but he seemed amused, and Simon added, "Yes, I have a girlfriend. I think."

"You think?"

"Yeah, okay, I don't exactly have her *yet*. Give me some time."

They laughed, and Key used an umbrella tip to throw open a small wooden trunk at the end of the bed.

"What's that?" asked Simon.

"My . . . *yoroi*. My armor," said Key. "I never get to wear it."

Simon could hear the longing in his voice. The armor was shiny and black, with a gold emblem on the helmet.

"I have also two *katana*. Sharp and beautiful. My father keeps them locked away, but Mamoru has shown them to me. I have also the throwing knives for boys, *kozuka*, but I never get to touch them. Do you know what this is?" He held up a little carving of a coiled Dragon. "You know it? Netsuke art?"

"I've heard of that."

"You have?"

"Comic books."

Key nodded. "It's ivory. Do you want to see? Feel it. It represents the good force within Dragons, it's sort of . . . the promise that they'll bring good luck if they can turn against their natures. Hard to imagine, really."

"No," Simon said, taking it in hand. "Not in the right situation. I knew one once. Doesn't make any sense, but he saved my life. The Black Dragon."

"The Peking?" said Key, to Simon's surprise. "He is named in our works. The scrolls tell of a time when the Dragons here helped the harvest. Food grew in abundance wherever Serpents lived. I have never known if that was an accident of their powers, or if they kept people well-fed just so they could draw on human misery."

"Yeah, well, understanding them is kind of a waste of time, isn't it?"

Key took his time to answer, as he had with every question. "I read a lot," Key finally said. "From the ancient libraries. The lore is not clear. There are many old stories of the helpfulness of the Serpent. Probably the legends come from some truth about them. . . ."

"My favorite legends are about the dead ones."

Key stayed silent again, and Simon began to feel like everything *anyone* said would be analyzed by the boy. "I would hope to find a Dragon like this one that helped you, but there is good reason for the Samurai order," Key said, his voice filled with bleak understanding. "I lead them where they need to go," he went on. "I find the Serpent, and I have the armor to fight . . . but I cannot."

"I've done that," said Simon. "And I'm not sure you really want to."

"Yes. I do," Key answered, his eyes still on the armor.

"Well, if you ask me, it doesn't make sense to keep a support fighter out of this when we're so short-changed on people as it is." Simon's words rang true to Key, he could tell. "It seems a shame not to get some use out of that armor.

"Key," Simon added. "If I have anything to say about it, you're going to get some use out of that armor."

The Samurai continued their discussion into the afternoon. Sachiko brought trays of lunch to Aldric and Simon, who had joined him outside in the garden. Key went back inside with his mother, so Simon and Aldric were left alone to wait. Munching on his fish with displeasure, Aldric complained bitterly about Japanese slowness.

"They can't seem to get hold of the idea that Alaythia is urgently needed, right here, right now," mumbled Aldric. "I'm afraid they think women are for decoration."

"We'll find out what they think," Simon responded, and he looked toward the manicured bushes, where Fenwick was just pushing his way out. The fox growled in alarm at an antique archway, where Simon realized the bobcat had been watching them. The cat hopped away as Fenwick nuzzled Simon's knee.

"You didn't leave him to *spy* on them, now, did you?" Aldric asked with scorn.

Simon ignored him. His eyes met Fenwick's darkening pupils, and he could see what the fox had observed. "They think we're too pushy, too loud, and that you're lying about all the things you've done," he said, reading Fenwick's eavesdropping. It was better than a spy camera; he heard their words in his head, a mixture of English and Japanese, the kind of hodgepodge mix-speech Simon was used to hearing around the world more and more these days. "Dad, they don't think they can trust us."

"They can't, apparently," Aldric chided his son, and he rose to go in.

Simon stood in embarrassment as Aldric broke in to their discussion inside the mansion. "This has got to end," he said loudly. "There's too much to be done." Seeing the commotion, Key tried to get Simon to come back to his room away from the argument, but ended up nervously following Simon to a good place for listening in.

"Eavesdropping is not allowed," said Key, not looking like he meant it.

"It isn't?" asked Simon, staring at the bobcat in Key's arms. So the bobcat *did* have a use, after all.

"Well, you did not say anything interesting," Key mumbled. Simon half-grinned, and the boys turned toward the meeting to watch. The irony was instantly obvious to both of them; the Dragons could never end their disagreements long enough to dominate humankind, and here were the Hunters fighting just as pigheadedly.

"We are decided." Taro was addressing Aldric.

"*Are* you?" asked the Englishman, irritated. "I suppose my viewpoint didn't much matter. So what's your choice to be?"

"We have decided we will discuss this decision in private, firstly."

Unreal. They decided not to decide, apparently. Simon sighed.

But Aldric turned angry. "You will choose *now*," he said, "there is no more time for discussion."

"If you want a decision now," said Taro, "you will not like it."

The other Samurai came up behind him, forming a wall.

"The Dragon of Tokyo will die," said Taro. "And then we will see to this woman, Alaythia."

Aldric looked at Simon. There was no understanding these people.

Chapter 20

NEVER GO TO TOKYO
WITHOUT A SWORD

TOKYO SEEMED A NEON blur as the armored black sedan breezed down the boulevard, Taro in the driver's seat, Sachiko beside him. The other Japanese men, with baffling efficiency, had found room somehow beside them and in the next row.

Simon and Aldric sat in the very rear of the car, crammed in beside Key and Mamoru. Aldric had never looked so uncomfortable, with his shoulders pinched, knees pushed together, and a stern expression on his face.

Simon hadn't said a word on the journey. The rice fields and country houses were long gone, replaced by the high, anonymous, knifelike buildings of Tokyo. Kyoto had buildings that were sheets of glass and steel, too, but it had elegant structures laid among them, and wraparound greenery. Crowded as it was, Kyoto was modest compared to the fast-forward bustle and the sheer functionality of Tokyo. This city was like a socket with highrise batteries sticking out of it, powering a giant toy that did nothing but make light and noise and push figures pointlessly and hurriedly around.

Watching the street's giant television screens looming over him, Simon felt powerless. Taro had insisted both Fenwick and Key's bobcat were left behind in the Kyoto mansion, and Simon was sure it was just to show who was in control. He wanted to glare at the man, but didn't have the nerve.

The bargain Taro left them was simple: the St. Georges would give their support to the attack on the Japanese Serpent, and *then* the search for Alaythia would continue.

Simon and Aldric had fought about it. "We can go off on our own," Simon had argued, trying to keep his voice down. "We can find her without them."

"Leave them to fight alone?" Aldric responded. "How would you feel if they did that to us?"

Simon had stammered, fumbling for an answer.

"They could die in the attack, and we would have that on our conscience," Aldric went on. "Alaythia would want us to measure up to their sense of honor. Can we agree?"

It had struck Simon for the first time that his

father was not going to act without his approval, and so they had agreed on how to answer Taro together.

Aldric took the deal. Now he simmered beside Simon, but everyone knew they needed Sachiko and her magic to help find Alaythia. And if, as Aldric feared, the Ice Dragon was somehow involved in all this, the attack in Tokyo might lead them *to* Alaythia.

So the Hunt went forward.

Najikko, the Japanese Serpent, listened to the painful murmuring of the sleeping patients in his living room, and his Serpentine eyes closed in meditation. His silver, glistening chest swelled with energy, and his gold-armored muscles relaxed, as he felt himself quell the fire within.

Equilibrium, he thought. *Calm. Empty all wasteful emotion.*

Earlier, he had been upset by the insistent tapping of several spiders on his sterile steel table, and had been forced to crush them with his hands. The spider innards had stained his skin, and he'd been trying to get his long nails clean for hours, interrupting the more important mental business before him.

Deep in concentration, he reached out and took hold of a scroll that lay on the table before him. The scroll had come from the treasures in the Black Dragon's former lair in Peking; many Serpents had raided those quarters, but the Japanese Serpent had been first, and reaped the rewards. The spell on this scroll was highly valuable.

There. It was coming to him. The final piece of sorcery was coming together in his mind, like a complex mathematical problem finally solved after months of labor.

Let the Dragonhunters come, if they did.

His weapon was nearly ready.

The hospital was a forty-story highrise of sleek glass, brightly lit and draped with huge flags of the Murdikai Corporation symbol: two Serpents entwined on a staff, spitting fire. To Aldric, it was madness to attack something that so resembled a fortress; foolish to strike at a Dragon in its own den if there was another way. They could wait for an easier chance to strike, he told the Samurai, but no one listened. A plan is a plan.

So here they were. Aldric and Simon were irritated to find themselves given only a backup role in the assault. They were shunted to the side, holed up on another highrise next to the hospital, watching from the top of a hotel as Key and the Samurai observed the Dragon's lair from a nearby roof.

Key held binoculars. His job was to confirm the Serpent was in its lair. With his own binoculars, Simon glanced over to check that Key was safe. The kid was still dressed in his school uniform. Taro had told him there'd be no need for armor, that he wouldn't get that close to the Dragon.

Right. And he talked about our *arrogance,* Simon thought resentfully. He turned and peered at the top floor of the hospital across the street.

He saw what appeared to be an operating suite, but huge, and decorated and furnished like a home, though almost everything was made of brushed steel. Sleeping patients stirred in their beds, and now Simon could see, in the operating room's center, a crouching, silver-gold shape, sitting with its back to the window, its tail rising and falling calmly, rhythmically.

"It's there," said Simon, and Aldric took the binoculars to see for himself.

The Thing had made a kind of private hospital in his penthouse apartment, a place where the homeless, no doubt, and people without families—patients he could quietly remove from the lower floors without much trouble—were kept in constant slumber. The Dragon could draw strength from their anguish, keeping them under his own watchful eye, away from nurses or anyone who might ease their pain.

From the roof of an office building across the street from the hospital, the Samurai signaled with a flashlight that they were ready. They had been calming themselves, their heads bent in meditation. Before they had headed to Tokyo, Key had remarked that Taro could never be brought out of a meditative trance once he entered it. His focus was that sharp. Aldric found the whole thing ludicrous, and he was eager to see the Samurai taking action.

Simon and Aldric raised their crossbows. "We should be in this," grumbled Aldric, watching as the Samurai fired grappling hooks into the hospital building, and *flew* over to it, their bodies nothing more than dark forms in the night.

They were like hawks, made out of darkness, hidden from glory.

Simon could see Sachiko and Key watching from their vantage point. Sachiko was in a dark pantsuit and black coat that concealed her tight-fitting armor, but Key looked painfully vulnerable.

Simon turned back to keep his sight on the Tokyo Dragon.

But the Dragon was gone.

It wasn't in its place anymore.

Frantic, Simon moved the telescope sight on his crossbow all around, searching for the shape of the Dragon inside the penthouse. He let out a breath of panic, and Aldric responded with a grunt. They'd worked together long enough; Simon knew what he meant, *quiet, not a word, stay on task.*

The Samurai had swooped toward the hospital,

one by one, zipping across their cables over the street, their hands clutched to speeding devices on the lines. They landed in silence, and clawed up onto the roof. The penthouse lay before them.

Simon could still see no sign of the Serpent.

Desperately, he wanted to warn Taro, but if he broke the radio silence, it might be heard by the Serpent in the penthouse.

Simon and Aldric stood poised, waiting for a target. *Where was he?*

The assault was in motion. In the Samurai went, loping through the rooftop doorway. It looked like Akira was first, guarding Taro's entry. Lastly, Simon could see the giant Mamoru step in, immediately moving to help patients, who stretched out their hands to him, once he lowered the helmet visor so they could see his face. For an instant, Simon was jolted by Mamoru's concern for them, and felt a stab of fear, thinking the big man looked extremely vulnerable to attack.

The others were swarming the operating suite, but Simon could not get a fix on the Serpent. His stomach burned with anxiety.

"This is crazy. If he's gone invisible . . ." worried Simon aloud. "They won't see him."

"I can't believe I agreed to this—" Aldric said, an edge of fear in his voice.

Suddenly, Simon saw a flash in his scope. Something fell from the ceiling onto Mamoru. *Something was there.*

Simon tried desperately for a better view.

His scope found Mamoru. The Serpent had caught him.

It threw him about, its silver-gold skin flashing in the light.

Simon stared in horror. "Holy . . ."

"Quiet." Aldric was fixing for a shot.

Taro had turned, realizing what was happening, and leapt toward the Serpent, slashing at the beast. Mamoru shouted in pain, and Taro buried his blade in the metallic Creature, once, twice, and again. Then Simon heard a click, an arrow spitting forth. Aldric had fired a shot. The arrow whisked over the street. Hit the Serpent. It reared up. Its eye filled Simon's scope. It was furious.

Simon fired.

Click. Hiss. The arrow launched.

"Aaaaaaahh!"

It smacked into Taro's armor just as the Dragon ducked its head.

"No . . . no, no . . ." said Simon.

"No . . . no! No!" said Aldric.

Taro howled, grabbing the bolt that had struck through to his arm.

Aldric cursed and aimed for the Dragon again, as the other Samurai—who had been searching the penthouse—rushed back in, striking by sword, to protect Taro.

The Serpent knocked into Taro and leapt up again to the ceiling, latching on supernaturally, crying out angrily and hissing. The Samurai pulled loose their pistols and began blasting up at the Creature—the room a shock of white muzzle flashes—but it would not be vanquished. It speedily clawed on all fours across the ceiling, slipping past a modern, angular steel chandelier, and finally tumbled behind a comatose man's bed.

"He hides behind innocent people . . ." growled Aldric.

"Get him, get him," Simon murmured helplessly.

But then something occurred to him.

His vision was being blocked by an irritating horde of moths, fluttering in his way. Too many of them to be a coincidence. And Simon knew this doesn't happen when the Creature is far from you. This kind of effect happens when a Dragon is close, nearly upon you . . .

Simon looked around, trying to figure out where the beast was. . . .

Then his eyes found Key on the rooftop next door. Something was rippling in the air, a mirage, forming behind Key.

It wasn't in the hospital—the Dragon had slipped invisibly to the roof!

"Dad!"

Simon watched through the scope of his crossbow as Key was pulled back by the Dragon taking form, coming from behind to snatch the boy by the neck. Sachiko was thrown down as the Serpent moved back against the wall, trying to figure out its next move.

Its disguising magic fell away, and all could see the beast for what it was.

Aldric fired a shot, and the arrow sliced the wall near the Serpent's head.

It hissed and barked in the night.

Simon waited for his shot, his heart pounding. Key could die.

He fired.

The bolt went whishing past the Dragon and the boy, and soared off into the darkness; useless, wasted.

But Key would not die this night—Sachiko rose and began slashing at the Serpent with metal gauntlets, studded with silver spikes that whirred and clicked and spun. The motorized spikes could not cut the Dragon's armor, but the attack was so shocking it caused him to fall back.

His hold on Key let up just enough for Key to kick himself free, and as the Dragon lunged for him again, the creature was nailed by a barrage of arrow-fire from the Samurai across the street.

Rit—rit—rit—rit—! A dozen arrows expertly sliced the air and jabbed into the Serpent, who recoiled against the wall, with nowhere to run.

Taro was shouting something in Japanese, threatening the beast.

Sachiko pulled her son out of the way, and drew her own sword. To Simon's surprise, Sachiko began attacking, driving the Serpent away from Key.

She was calling something out, a spell of sorts, as her sword clanged against the Serpent's armor. Suddenly there seemed to be half a dozen more of her—six different Sachikos, attacking the Dragon by sword in the night!

The Serpent seemed stunned, falling back near the ledge. The images of Sachiko were illusions—striking but causing no harm. Still, the Dragon couldn't get a fix on which was the real thing, as Sachiko kept moving, her sword hacking at him fiercely.

Aldric leapt to the other building. Simon knew his legs weren't as strong, but in his adrenaline rush, he let go of logic and made the jump right behind Aldric. The two Knights landed on the rooftop just as the Japanese Serpent gave a tremendous roar. Throwing out its arms in a spinning motion, leaping into the air, it sent out a wave of light in a wide circle, forcing all of the Sachiko images to fall back to the ground and over the ledge.

Sachiko herself cried out, as her illusions withered and wisped away, destroyed in a painful flash.

Her son threw himself over her, and Aldric pulled his sword, its gleam catching the Serpent's attention.

"You've found each other," hissed the Serpent hatefully. "Knight and Samurai. The two worlds united."

"Leave the boy," warned Aldric.

"And you'll spare my life?" The Dragon tilted its spikey crowned head. "This one dies, as do you all."

"I don't fear your fire," said Aldric. Simon knew the tactic. A Dragon spends all his fire at close range, and a blow to its neck will send the flames rolling back inside the beast.

"You shall see my fire's strength," threatened the Dragon. "But I shall choose the time—not you."

It leapt from the building and began clawing its way down the outside of the highrise, from hopelessly high up, the busy street of ant-sized lights speeding down below, so far beneath him it made Simon sick. The Dragon did not fly; it was wingless, with wide blades where wings should be, but it went down the sleek glass building in great leaping arcs with shocking speed.

Simon turned to Key, and Sachiko looked up at him, "Watch my son," she said, and without warning, she dived over the ledge, soaring down toward the Dragon.

She had jumped off the building with no protection whatsoever.

Simon gasped. He'd never seen such courage in his life. His heart flew into his throat. He wanted to scream.

She flew down the side of the building, down the grid of lights, diving like an Olympic athlete, hands in a sharp point, and flew downward, downward, and slammed into the Creature.

Windows shattered, and the two tumbled over each other, falling down through darkness and light, somersaulting in the air, together in a snarl of fangs and blades, until at last they hit onto a ledge at the middle of the building.

Aldric gasped, looking for a way down. Suddenly, the Samurai unhooked their cables from the penthouse across the way, and all of them swung back toward the Dragon. They were swooping over the street, as their lines hurtled them toward the Dragon and Sachiko. They swarmed across and down the side of the building like wasps, as Sachiko slashed at the Dragon with her whirring gloves.

Aldric had a moment of hesitation; he seemed to be in awe of their speed. Then the Knight grabbed one of the Samurai's lines, and began climbing down himself.

Hanging on the same line, Taro looked up at him.

"NO!" he cried. "It can't handle your weight!"

Too late. The line's hook started cracking on its mount, and Simon and Key ran to get hold of it, but too late.

"Oh, no!" they shouted at the same time.

Cut loose, Taro and Aldric tumbled down, falling past Sachiko and the embattled Dragon, landing on a balcony just below them.

"What wonders I could do with that face," Aldric heard the Dragon say, his claw brushing Sachiko's cheek.

Sachiko leapt backward, tossing herself to a nearby balcony, like a film running in reverse. Simon just stared.

Suddenly—with Sachiko out of the way—the Serpent began taking bullet fire from the Samurai clinging to the side of the building. At the same time, directly below the Dragon, Aldric was firing silver darts from the mini-crossbow guns on his wrists. Bullets and darts were clanging against the building, everyone trying to avoid friendly fire. Taro threw several silver throwing stars that lodged in the Serpent's hide, but there was still no bringing down the beast.

Fearsomely silent, the Dragon shattered his way into the office building, escaping them. In a heartbeat, all of the Samurai and Sachiko lunged after it. Aldric looked up at Simon, but after checking for the boys' safety, he, too, barreled in.

Up high on the building, Simon grabbed Key and pulled him along. "Come on."

"We are not to interfere," said Key. "We have a duty to stay alive. We'll be going right into the fight—"

"Into the kill, you mean," said Simon—optimistically—and he dragged Key toward a service door to pursue the Dragon.

Chapter 21

⚜

BEWARE OF FALLING SERPENTS

THE JAPANESE SERPENT TUMBLED through glass into the office building, where a shocked late-night worker stared up at him from a desk covered in coffee cups.

At first, the Dragon looked like a well-dressed young citizen who had somehow fallen out of the sky and through his window. But as the worker watched, the intruder took a quick moment to catch his breath, and suddenly arrows began to appear on his body. The Serpent's cloaking magic was wearing thin from pain, his true form quickly becoming visible: a full-fledged Dragon, silver and gold, and armored with natural plating, arrows sticking out of its arms, its back, its side.

Just as abruptly, a group of black-clad Samurai

tore through the shattered glass wall, along with a woman armed with a set of mechanical claws that whirred with little spinning daggers, jutting out from all angles.

The office worker nearly fainted as he saw the Serpent back away from the human attackers, and clutch its arms over its chest. It chanted in a half-Japanese nonsensical speech, an insane language, but its words seemed to cause the room to quake.

Shards of glass on the floor rose up and swirled into little tornadoes that began cutting at the human soldiers. But the woman threw out her arm—hissing in speech as fantastically strange as the Serpent's—and the glass shards twirling viciously around the room came together and formed into the vague shapes of men.

The jagged, glass-shard figures began to take swings at the Dragon, slashing at his armor. The Dragon threw them back with some kind of magic, but two of them flung themselves upon its back, shattering and stabbing tiny shards into its thick hide.

Furious, the Dragon roared, and rushed the innocent office worker, throwing him back toward the glass men. The glass figures collapsed around the worker, giving no serious cuts. But getting the man out of harm's way slowed the warriors down.

Aldric had joined them from behind, slipping on

the glass as he entered through the cracked exterior wall, the way they'd all gotten in. Now he saw his target escaping.

The Serpent rampaged through empty offices, knocking through cheap cubicle walls in the blue dimness of fluorescent lights, as Aldric and the Samurai pursued it, firing whenever they could get a shot.

Taking the lead, Aldric sent a bolt directly into an unprotected spot on its wounded back, and the Dragon wailed, racing on its thin Serpentine legs— one real, one made of metal—clattering over glass and plastic as it threw down anything in its path.

The wound immediately began leaking fireblood in a dazzling spray of light, streaming from the back of the Creature.

The flying blood burned Aldric as he ran through it, chasing the beast charging through the offices.

It howled in fury and blew off the elevator doors up ahead, and as Aldric got there, he could see the elevator was gone—the Dragon was climbing up an empty dark shaft, firelight from his wound sprinkling down in a cascade.

Sachiko and the other Samurai clattered up around Aldric.

"This was not the plan," Taro said breathlessly.

"Never make plans," said Aldric, hoisting himself into the elevator shaft. "Waste of time."

He began climbing after the beast in the dying light created by its dim, flickering wound.

Then, up above the Dragon, he saw a set of elevator doors forced open with a dagger, and staring down at him were his own son and Kyoshi.

"SIMON!" roared Aldric.

"I knew it—I heard it in here," said Simon triumphantly, but instantly his glee turned to horror. The beast was rising fast, climbing, all jaws and claws and flaming blood.

"GET OUT!" Taro cried to Simon, as the Samurai poured into the shaft.

From above, Simon had an instant to see the look of fear on Sachiko's face as she realized the danger to her son. He threw Key back away from the elevator shaft just as the Dragon clambered up behind him, onto a floor of office cubicles. The Thing swiped at Key's leg. Simon's heart was rioting. He and Key ran for it, but the Dragon leapt upon them both, throwing them down together, its arms blocking them in.

Its huge metallic head came down upon them, yellow eyes wild with triumph, jaws bared to show silver-gold fangs. Glaring, the creature muttered in Japanese.

Simon was frozen, watching the jaws of the Dragon moving in hateful rhythm.

Key understood the Dragon was cursing them in

Japanese for causing him to lose his temper, for forcing him to fall out of order with the harmony of the universe. The Thing was angry for being angry.

Down in the elevator shaft, Aldric led the others up in a furious climb up the cables. Suddenly everything lurched strangely, and a black mass began falling toward them.

The elevator was working.

It was coming down upon them. Fast. Very fast. The car was nearly upon them—Aldric put on a burst of speed, and he and Taro tumbled to safety. They landed on the same floor as the Dragon.

Aldric looked back, fearing Sachiko and the others behind him would be hit and carried down by the elevator car, but there was no more time to think. The Dragon turned its head and smiled—pinning Simon and Key to the floor.

"Don't move," said Aldric, in shock.

"We can't . . ." Simon moaned.

"*Back*," the Dragon spat. "And he may live. My quarrel is with the one who took my leg . . ." The beast moved his eyes toward Taro.

"Aldric, don't," Taro warned.

"You took my leg," the beast hissed back. "I'll take your *son*."

Simon couldn't reach the Dragon's chest, couldn't use the deathspell.

The Creature sliced the air with his silver-gold tail, hissing in Serpentspeak.

Taro spoke to it in Japanese, trying to provoke a move, but the Serpent didn't take the bait. It held Simon and Key to the ground as the Dragonhunters slowly approached.

A puddle of fireblood had leaked on the floor, burning Key's knee as it dripped.

"It wants us to lay down our arms," said Taro, translating the Dragonspeak.

"Madness," said Aldric.

"He means it," said Taro, throwing down his sword. "It does not make idle threats, not this one . . ."

"I'll not give up my sword," said Aldric, eyes hardened.

"No choice," said Taro.

"Not for you, maybe," said Aldric, and his eyes locked on Simon's. Aldric could see Simon still held the dagger he'd used on the elevator doors.

As the Dragon snarled, Simon seized the moment and shoved the silver dagger into the Creature's side. The Dragon howled, rearing back for an instant, and Aldric was suddenly there, attacking with sword, again and again.

The Serpent threw him off, but Simon rolled free. Key remained in place, however, and the Dragon dived for him. Simon had nothing to fight with, but

Taro stepped over him, sweeping up his Samurai sword with incredible quickness, and stabbing the Serpent again.

The Dragon hurtled Taro backward against a wall, and now stood blocking the path to the two boys.

Key pulled at Simon's jacket, and the two rushed away. The Dragon spun, and ran at them, its head bowed, its crown of spikes lowered. But Key threw his body at Simon, pushing him out of its way, running clear at the last moment. The Dragon ran into the glass wall and shattered it, then fell, arcing downward in the sky, slowing himself the last thirty feet, landing directly upon a speeding car.

Clinging to the roof of the car, the Dragon was driven off into the night.

Aldric ran to the open wall and watched as the Serpent was carried away, silver-gold tail slashing. The driver must've been terrified, gunning the engine, because the car was quickly gone from sight.

The battle would end here.

"I can't get to him now." Sachiko sighed, arriving to see the Dragon escape.

"It's not for you to do." Aldric looked at her in disbelief, and then back to the Samurai. "You let your women fight?"

"Why wouldn't we?" Mamoru replied incredulously.

Everyone waited for Aldric to answer, but he didn't. Simon thought him jealous; he'd always called Alaythia too vital for combat.

"Am I in trouble?" asked Key, getting up from the wreckage of the office.

No one answered. Instead, everyone looked at Simon.

Chapter 22

THE DOCTOR IS OUT

TARO STOOD OVER SIMON. The Samurai had part of Simon's broken arrow pointing out of his arm. "I have something that belongs to you," Taro said through gritted teeth.

Simon felt terrible. Words completely failed him.

Sachiko went to him, and pulled loose the arrow's barb, as Taro yelled out in pain. Almost instantly, however, a tiny blast of light from Sachiko's hand stemmed the blood, and the wound began healing under her touch. Simon got the feeling from Taro's look that it still hurt, nonetheless.

"You were to stay put," Sachiko said to Key, her worry evident.

Taro looked at Simon. "And you were to watch him."

"There's no time for blame," said Aldric, though he shot Simon a hard look. "We have to be after it."

"We will be after it," Taro answered, still smoldering at Simon. "But there's plenty of time for blame."

"Come now, he can't have gone far—" Aldric said.

Taro resisted. "The Dragon is gone. We must go to its den. We'll figure out where it would run."

"What are you talking about?" said Aldric. "We can still catch the Creature! He fell out of the sky. There are people who saw *something*, they can tell us where he went—"

"Stop. We will make our own decision."

"Could be good to go now, could be waste of time," Kisho considered.

"Bloody brilliant," said Aldric. "With this kind of decision-making, we'll be as old as Toyo before we get the beast!"

Toyo stared at him indignantly.

"Stop this," said Sachiko. "We're losing time."

Taro took a deep breath. "We should go back to the hospital and see the den now; find out what we can about the Creature. Then we will go after it. Agreed?"

The Japanese all nodded together, and then marched past Aldric and Simon.

"You're going to leave it out there wild?" Aldric protested.

"The police will be coming," said Sachiko, not stopping. "If we want to see the den, we must be quick."

Simon and Aldric went with the others, having no desire to burn any more bridges by going off on their own. The Dragon would wait.

On the street, small groups of people started to gather. Windows were shattered, alarms were ringing. Cops would be here any minute.

Among those gathered in the street was a very old gentleman with a goatee, dressed in black and white with a dirty trenchcoat. He was shivering as if it were twenty below zero. Ice was dripping from his flesh, melting, trailing down the inside of his coat and pooling at his feet. Dead flies floated there, specks of black in the glistening puddle.

He'd watched the Hunters all night. He wasn't through yet.

He knew he was too weak now to kill them all at once; he would have to watch them, and wait for a new opportunity.

While people stared up at the cracked windows, the Hunters moved unnoticed into the hospital, up an elevator, and slipped to the penthouse as many of the hospital staff evacuated down stairways.

Simon held his breath as a security guard hurrying to the top floor stopped to question them, but

Aldric knocked him out and dragged him to a maintenance closet.

In the penthouse, the Samurai speedily cleaned up their equipment from the battle. Bullets and arrows were picked out of the walls. There'd be no trace of them. Weakly, the patients in the penthouse stirred, barely conscious, under spells and drowning in their drugs. But already sirens were blaring in the city, and Sachiko had to lock the penthouse doors from any prying medics who wanted to see what all the clatter had been about. Simon saw her seal the locks shut with a burning touch of her finger.

"It will take a few moments for the other security men to respond," said Toyo. "They are mostly retired police, elderly, and are concentrated on the first floor. There are two glass elevators connected to this room, but we've now destroyed the code system to operate them. I would guess the guards will take a freight elevator, and they must pass through a busy emergency ward to get to that elevator. It will let them off outside that door, around an L-shaped corridor they are unfamiliar with. We'll have a few minutes."

Simon couldn't help but admire the old man's memory of the blueprints. Key seemed disturbed there wouldn't be enough time, and began poking around a set of controls that looked like a fire alarm to Simon.

Taro and Mamoru quickly checked the drugged

patients in the Dragon's den, as the other Dragonhunters looked for clues to where the Serpent had
gone. Oddly, though, one of the Samurai kept piling
blankets on a weak patient in a very solemn, methodical way, one after the other, too many to be helpful.
Simon stared at him for a moment.

"Kisho can be unusual," Key whispered hurriedly,
looking over. "He's not quite right."

"What do you mean by that?"

They were in a hurry, but Key seemed to want
Simon to know this. "Long ago, a Dragon tried mind-
reading him to find our base, tearing into his memories. He didn't give us away, but he came out of it
forgetful, confused."

But Kisho's odd sympathy had stirred one of the
sick men.

"Weapon . . ." the patient said in Japanese.
"Najikko . . . has weapon . . ."

The words rattled Simon as Key translated them.

"What weapon?" Taro started asking. "What does
he have?"

Suddenly the room felt desperate, as the sirens
outside closed in on the hospital.

The patient reached out a shaking hand, and
pointed to an old medical cabinet, huge and imperi-
ous, with rusted handles on its aged wood. It was
unique in the brushed-steel environment, and

Sachiko was already moving over to it with suspicion, chanting an unlocking spell.

Inside, an ancient scroll lay, unrolled, Dragon symbols glowing red, as if by some mysterious energy.

"The Old Power of the Asian Dragons," said Sachiko. "The Serpent has found it."

The Samurai looked up at her from around the room.

"What do you mean?" asked Simon.

"Perhaps the children should not know this," Taro said.

"Simon is a fighter with the rest of us," Aldric answered. "I'll not have secrets from him."

"It is a legendary weapon of the Black Times," said Sachiko. "It was said to be the work of two wedlocked Serpents, weaving their powers together."

"If it ever existed," said Taro. "That spell is most likely a legend. I think you're mistaken about what you've found there. It's just a history scroll. I've never known the Dragons of Asia to work together any more than the others, now or in the past. They work together about as well as we do." He smiled faintly.

"But if it *is* true, Taro . . ." Sachiko whispered, and her eyes went to her son.

"What *is* it?" Aldric asked, testily. They were speaking in English, but so quietly he hardly understood a word.

The sirens were wailing outside the hospital, time was slipping away.

"No one really knows," said Taro. "Only that it kills many, and that it kills fast. And that the Dragons who used it lost control of it quickly, and died in its fury."

"Not a mystery anymore. It is a formula for intensifying Dragon flames," said Sachiko, who had been studying the scroll.

Taro stared at her. *"Intensifying them?"*

"If the Dragon has perfected this spell," Sachiko continued, "he's made his fire ten times more powerful. Ten times more unpredictable, no doubt. He may even fear his own creation slipping out of control. This is no ordinary adversary."

There was a hurried rapping at the door. Security. The police.

"Well, we've lost him now," said Aldric. "Before we track him, we'll need Alaythia with us—"

"No time," Taro snapped.

The door began banging loudly. The police were going to break their way in.

"We'll have to go out that way . . ." Taro moved toward the balcony.

"Or we could use the elevator," said Key, and he pointed to the big glass elevators connected to the penthouse from the outside. "I fixed the wires so they don't go through the code panel."

Everyone looked at him. Taro frowned. "You did not get permission."

"Efficiency is no substitute for obedience," interjected Mamoru, trying to look stern.

So much for quick thinking, thought Simon.

"Take the scroll," ordered Taro, and Sachiko swept it up quickly, as everyone moved away from the doors.

Suddenly, a clatter of claws at the balcony caused Simon to stop in his tracks.

The Dragon of Japan had returned.

Its eyes caught sight of the scroll in Sachiko's hands.

"Thieving from me? From *me*?" screeched the Dragon, and it slashed a claw at Toyo, who was closest. Simon took note of how fast the old man moved out of the way.

The Dragon let out a growling guttural sound—*krrrrrr*—building up fire in its throat.

"Changed my mind. Efficiency is good," said Mamoru, and he shoved Key toward the glass elevator.

Aldric pushed Simon to follow them.

The doors slid shut.

The Samurai swung their shields into position, bracing for the Serpentfire blast.

But it did not come. The Dragon regained control, and leapt instead for the glass elevator from the outside. The boys were just launching down the side of the building—alone.

"NO—" cried Aldric, and he dived at the elevator. But the boys fell out of view.

The glass elevator glided down, along the outside edge of the building, giving a view of the traffic many stories below. Inside the glass capsule, Simon and Key cringed, realizing how high up they were.

"Go, go, go," begged Simon. He saw lights blurring past him as they fell, very fast. But not fast enough. There was a clatter above them. Something was coming.

From up above, Aldric saw the Dragon rushing like a bull for them, galloping down the exterior of the building, an unnatural force of nature, gathering speed in a run.

Meanwhile, inside the hospital, everyone flew into action. "Not another elevator," Taro groaned, as he and Sachiko ran for the remaining one. Aldric and the Samurai leapt in behind them, the doors shutting all of them into one elevator.

Outside, the Dragon was sprinting after the boys, leaping now, hurtling, crashing onto the lift.

In the packed elevator above the ruckus, Aldric cracked part of the glass, the wind blowing against him, and watched the boys' lift sliding fast down the highrise, the Japanese Serpent clinging to its roof.

"We're not fast enough. How do we get down there?" said Taro.

Sachiko started to leap down, but Aldric pulled her back. "No. Not again. Too much risk," he told her. "Wait for a clear shot." The lift was a fast one, it fell quickly after the boys. Aldric could see them getting closer through the glass walls.

In Simon's elevator, the drop was sheer terror. The Dragon had now clawed downward, clinging to the side of the shooting elevator, its jaws gaping, silver-gold teeth scraping the glass.

Key screamed, and Simon threw the boy behind him for safety. But there were no weapons. There'd be no fight. They'd be torn apart, pure and simple.

He'd left everything in the building above—his sword, shield, and bow. For a second he thought, *Dad's going to kill me.*

Simon looked up. The elevator with all the warriors was trailing him. Aldric had smashed open its glass, and was firing barbs at the Dragon from his wrist-device. None of them hit, but his father was there, his father was coming, his father would help him.

The Dragon snarled, smashing in the glass, its head caving in part of Simon's elevator, its jaws snapping at them.

His father was useless.

Taro and the Samurai broke open more of the glass around them, and began firing pistols at the Dragon from above. Every shot connected. The Dragon seemed dazed, scarcely able to cling to the falling elevator.

Then—to Simon's shock—the Dragon let go, and tumbled down, dropping four stories to the ground. The Creature landed on its wicked legs like a cat, and scampered across a night-lit street to a train on a platform.

"He's going to get away," said Key, staring down.

"No, he's not," said Simon. He was filled with adrenaline and anger. When they hit the ground, Simon pulled Key out of the elevator and sprinted for the train platform. He knew the Hunters would follow him.

Ahead, the Dragon was just slipping inside the doors of a train.

Simon and Key ran aboard, at a car far behind the Dragon's. Simon could hear Aldric yelling behind him as the doors slid shut.

He and Key took a deep breath, looking at each other in fear, scanning the empty train cars ahead.

Suddenly Aldric was banging for Simon from outside the car, furious, yelling, but the train's speakers were drowning him out, barking something in

Japanese, and Key was saying, "Sit down!" The train was taking off; the outside doors were locked. Aldric was forced to grab hold from the exterior, as behind him, the Samurai leapt forward, clinging to the rear of the train farther back, unable to get in.

The thing was, it wasn't an ordinary train. It was a bullet train.

It reached two hundred miles per hour in a matter of minutes.

Chapter 23

BULLETS ON A BULLET TRAIN

THE BULLET TRAIN WAS in violent motion. Simon tried desperately to open the doors of the train for Aldric, who was clinging to the side, his hair blowing wildly, his face contorted from the wind speed, his trench coat flying off into the night.

But the train was far too well made. The doors weren't budging. *Stupid Japanese perfection!* thought Simon. *Couldn't they at least screw up when they made the doors?*

Simon could see the other Samurai outside the train, behind Aldric. But the electronic lock on Aldric's door wouldn't break, despite Simon's kicking it furiously.

Persistence paid off. Finally, with Key helping, Simon somehow got the doors open, but Key was nearly sucked out of the train in the draft. Aldric pushed Key back in as he tumbled into the car with a thud, turning immediately to help Taro inside. The other Samurai were already angrily clawing into the car on their own, some of them breaking open other doors. They had clung to the train with small suction-cup devices, which now shriveled away like little black balloons and were pocketed. *Ingenious*, thought Simon.

Sachiko pulled Key away from Simon. *"I will watch you now,"* she said to her son, and turned to Taro, *"Get him."*

Taro turned to leave the car and look for the Dragon, and the Samurai rushed forward with him. Aldric gave Simon a look of severe annoyance, but this was no time for arguing. The two followed the Samurai up ahead, moving through the unlocked doors.

The train seemed empty, evidently it was the last one of the night.

Simon passed into a new car, its sleek, white padded benches offering plenty of places to hide. The Samurai in their black armor and helmets moved in cautiously. Akira first, Mamoru last, same as in the hospital raid.

Down the narrow aisle they went, and as they entered the next car, they came upon a little boy dressed in a school uniform, apparently very late in getting home and looking absolutely terrified.

"Is it in here . . . ?" Taro asked very quietly, in Japanese.

The terrified boy nodded.

"Where?" he asked, but the boy could not answer, he was shaking from fear.

Taro tried to see where the boy's eyes were indicating.

Suddenly, the speakers began barking again with an official, automated voice.

"What's it say?" asked Simon. He and Aldric could only see glimpses of the boy between the armored backs of the Samurai.

Taro didn't answer, between trying to keep his eyes on the boy and turning very slowly at the same time, to see where in the car the Dragon was hiding.

The speakers were barking again.

"It says," Mamoru translated. "New train. Automated."

Simon stared. "There's no one else on here? No one's running this?"

Mamoru listened to the speakers. "This is a test run, for engineering trial, not open to the public."

"Why?" Simon asked.

"It says they're testing new and higher speeds," he answered.

"Higher speeds? Faster than *this*?" said Simon.

"If it's not open to the public," said Kisho, "then what is *he* doing here?"

As he said it, Taro's eyes searched the train and came to rest again . . . on the schoolboy.

The boy suddenly began crying, he said he was lost, he was coming back from his uncle's, he was late. Mamoru was translating all of this as best he could.

Wanting a better look, Simon climbed on one of the benches—and saw the child's voice coming from none other than the Japanese Dragon.

"Look out!" screamed Simon, but the Creature knew the game was up. They all watched as the little boy opened up a mouthful of silver-gold teeth. Taro raised his sword, and the cornered boy broke apart like colored mist, to reveal the angry Dragon. It opened its jaws and let loose its fire.

Taro howled and stumbled back, turning away from the fire, and the flames broke over him and spread to the roof of the train, a dazzling silver-gold blaze brighter than any Simon had ever seen.

Aldric fell back, and the Samurai went with him. The fire scattered off Taro's armor and splashed the train in quivering flames of silver and gold, like metal that had learned to dance. The silvery fire grew forward, while the golden flames licked backward, and the Dragon escaped ahead through the burning train.

Protected by the blaze, the Serpent screeched back at them in Japanese and Serpentine, cursing them for making him spend his fire. And then it was gone, darting through the veil of burning liquid silver and the rising smoke in the car.

Some of the Samurai used their pistols—Kisho and Toyo were expert shots—but the Dragon had vanished, and the fire forced the men back.

Simon and the others raced back through the train as the fire quickly spread. They barreled into the last car, and Taro smashed the doors closed, but the fire would only be stayed for a moment. Simon saw Sachiko eyeing him with a look that said, *that fire is your fault, isn't it?* Her distrust was palpable.

Simon felt awful.

The train lurched forward even faster, and everyone was thrown around to the ground, against the walls of the car, or into the thick glass of the windows.

The fire burst the windows at the door to the next car and began stabbing into theirs. Simon looked outside, searching for escape. A city was shooting past, glazing his vision in a kaleidoscope of lights.

"We have to get off," declared Aldric.

"We can't get off," said Taro. "It's going three hundred miles an hour!"

"Then we have to get clear of the fire," said Aldric, trying to batter down the exit doors. "Your plan didn't cover this; we have to improvise."

Taro wiped sweat from his brow. "We left the plan a long time ago."

The fire was now eating up the car ahead, and Simon could feel its terrific heat leaking through the doors.

With a crash, Aldric splintered the glass of the side exit doors. The wind whipped furiously into the car.

"Faster than three hundred," Key said quietly.

Aldric looked at Sachiko. "Can you do anything with the armor?" he asked her. Alaythia could touch the runic symbols on their armor and give flight to its owner, but Sachiko shook her head; clearly it was a talent she didn't have.

Aldric looked desperate.

"We can hold out against the fire," said Mamoru. "The armor will repel it."

"That won't work for Key," Simon said angrily to the heavyset man. Key looked back in fear.

"I meant we'd enclose him in a circle, protect him with *our* armor," Mamoru retorted. "The alarms are sounding, someone will try to stop the train."

Aldric looked at him doubtfully. Not much of a solution. The fire was already burning the car up ahead quite brutally; their armor might last a minute, two, not more than five, tops.

"Tell the optimist he can stay with the car," Aldric

said to Simon. "I'm getting off."

Simon nodded, trying not to show his panic. "How?"

Aldric shattered more windows with his sword, and the force of the wind socked the car harder.

He yanked Mamoru's crossbow out of his hands and fired into the floor of the train. The arrow had a long cable attached to it.

"Get your own! That one's mine!" Mamoru said.

"You don't want the job," said Aldric.

He's going to . . . what? Simon thought. *This is suicide.*

Taro fired his arrow into the floor as well, and nodded to Aldric. Now they would be securely fastened to the bullet train as they moved outside.

The two approached the doors.

Tokyo sped past them with heart-battering acceleration.

"What are you doing?" cried Akira, baffled.

"Uncoupling the cars!" shouted Aldric.

Sachiko stared. "What?"

"I'm going to crawl outside and uncouple this car from the train!"

"Won't work," cried Akira. "I know train. You'll never uncouple them!"

"We have to try," said Taro.

Aldric was gripping hard to the cable on his crossbow. But the power of the wind was nearly unbearable.

Now the gold-tinted fire in the car up ahead held a new surprise: the Japanese Dragon was *outside* the train, returning out of the flames. He appeared at the broken window—attacking!

Aldric was hit first, a claw to the face.

He lost his footing.

He flew back into the train car, thwacking against the Samurai, several of whom were thrown down at once. For a second, they were distracted from Taro, perched at the window.

Rocked by the wind, Simon saw Taro furiously battling the Dragon on the side of the train. But Taro had only one arm free; he had to keep a grip on the cable that held him to the car. It was impossible, yet Simon saw Taro slam his armored fist onto the Dragon's crown of spikes, and *fling the beast over the side of the bullet train.*

At four hundred miles an hour, even a Dragon goes splat.

It does not die, however. No deathspell, no death. And its own fire will not harm a Dragon. In a situation like this, death will not occur.

Something else happens.

And what Simon witnessed, staring from the bullet train, he would never forget.

The Dragon was raked off the train, slipping from the side with a whoosh of air. It collided spectacularly with a giant neon advertisement and sprayed the night with sparks.

After the sparks came the fire. The Dragon was blown apart, gold and silver flames cascading out in a jaw-dropping glory of an explosion. Pieces of Dragon rained down, disappearing as the bullet train furiously, relentlessly blurred its way onward.

Aldric and the Samurai recovered, rushing to get to Taro at the open window.

They were too late. Taro had let go.

He flew back into the night. Gone.

The thought crossed Simon's mind—*he sacrificed himself, so we wouldn't die trying to save him*—but as he looked out the window, he realized Taro had fallen into a waterway near the train.

"Go!" screamed Sachiko.

Simon stared. "We'll hit too hard!"

"I will soften the fall," she cried.

"You can do that?"

"I think so."

"What?"

"Never had to help so many before!"

The Samurai were launching like paratroopers, so Simon took it on faith, and leapt into the night. Aldric shouted to him, amazed at his trust, and then jumped out after him.

Simon could see his father for a moment, then

Sachiko jumping with Key's hand locked in hers. Falling through the air, Simon saw for a split second that the fire had grown all the way to the front of the train. The whole bullet train was now a silver-gold worm of light, gliding dazzlingly out of the city of Tokyo.

Then Simon smacked into black water and wondered whether Sachiko's magic had done them any good at all. The water felt very, very much like cement.

But he was alive; he knew her spell had worked.

A moment later, Simon poked his head out of the cold Tokyo Bay waters.

He watched the bullet train speed on without them, a fiery missile in the night, until it derailed, colliding with a *second bullet train headed the opposite way* in a tremendous explosion.

Simon gasped, treading water. The Samurai were burbling up around him in the night, and Sachiko's powers must've aided them, or their armor surely would've pulled them down.

Aldric was helping Key onto the bank, and looked at Sachiko. "Your son, he needs to be ready for this kind of thing. You can't keep evil away from him, don't you understand that? You don't protect him by keeping him out of the fight—you do it by preparing him *for* the fight."

Sachiko climbed onto the bank as gracefully as can be imagined. "I do not know you so well," she told Aldric. "But I am going to guess you are not the best one in the world for giving parenting advice."

Simon got onto land beside Key, who was paying no attention to the argument, instead staring off at the destruction of the trains far ahead.

Black, twisted metal wreckage flickered with distant light.

Tokyo had a disaster on its hands.

Chapter 24

TRICKS OF THE TRADE

SOMEWHERE OUT IN THE burning Tokyo night, the ragged pieces of the Japanese Serpent had fallen onto a quiet street. Silver flames crawled over the building high above the Serpent's torn-apart body, and golden flames harassed the lower floors.

The Dragon's metallic scales and armored hide lay broken apart in hideous chunks, strewn across the concrete, burning, and lifeless.

The Dragon of Japan was destroyed.

Momentarily.

It felt nothing for a time. No thought. No emotion. Like the deepest of slumbers. And then its mind—still in one piece—began to work again. For a moment, the Creature enjoyed the emptiness, the lack of feeling, that it was experiencing. Feeling nothing was, after all, the Dragon's favorite feeling of all.

This idea was the center of his philosophy. Keep emotions bundled so tight they cannot breathe. No anger unbalanced him; no delight awaited disappointment. He felt only the calm and the quiet of sensory deprivation, and no words came into his mind except one.

Equilibrium.

Several men who lived in apartments near the blaze came out to see what had happened, and they watched in utter confusion as the fleshy armored chunks on the ground slowly grew long worm-like golden tendrils. The thin, slithery things grew from every part of the Dragon's wriggling hide, and they moved across the pavement, dragging the separate parts of the Dragon with them. Then the tendrils grew together, wrapping themselves tightly, and began pulling the beast back into one finished body.

It was not a quick process. Some of the men ran away, and some felt ill. This was an old magic at work, a force within all Dragons, bred into them since time began. When the Dragon finally rose, he was not quite fully put-together. There were gaps in his body, and his arms and legs were connected only loosely by golden wires. Equilibrium was out of the question.

Like a Serpentine scarecrow, the Dragon limped away from the fire.

The first emotion that came to him was desire—a desire to get away.

The second emotion was rage.

Simon and Aldric could do nothing to stop the silver-gold fire erupting on the outskirts of Tokyo. Firefighters were hurrying in. As helicopters soared overhead and the wailing of sirens filled the air, Simon felt the Samurai staring at him, blaming him for forcing the confrontation on the bullet train, and he wanted to die. He felt the burning in his stomach returning, his adrenaline surge now fading, and the twisted excitement of battle wearing off. *They don't trust me. And they probably shouldn't,* he was thinking. *Sachiko hates me for almost getting her son killed. He's not ready for any of this. Dad just keeps trying to defend me, and it's pathetic. I wish he'd just stop.*

"He did the best he could," Aldric was saying to Taro. "He's just a boy."

"Then he shouldn't be interfering in battle," retorted Taro, and he began walking away, headed for the area where the Dragon had fallen.

"That's your mistake," Sachiko offered Aldric. "I never wanted my boy to face this. *I* remember what happened the first time you came here. I made a vow. Never."

"You could show some gratitude," Aldric retorted.

"Or is that not a Japanese trait? You'd all be burned to a crisp right now if it weren't for us."

This remark did not go over well. Taro turned to look at him. "He filled me full of holes," he said, motioning to Simon, "and you served no good purpose except flailing around like a badly managed kite."

"A kite?" Aldric snorted.

"Yes," said Mamoru. "What is the English word for reckless angry fool with two left feet?"

"There is no word for that."

"Well. We'll call that an *Aldric*."

Mamoru and the others kept walking, and Aldric looked ready to attack them with his sword. "It's not funny," he mumbled, looking at Simon. "It's not one whit funny."

"You ought to listen more. Did it ever occur to you," Aldric said angrily to the others, "that our side of the Order has been more successful at this, judging from the long list of Asian Dragons out there?"

"Did it ever occur to you that Asian Dragons might be harder to kill?" Taro said over his shoulder, and this seemed to shut Aldric up completely.

They walked after the Samurai. Simon noted that Mamoru always managed to keep their spirits up. It seemed Mamoru pushed the others along, physically and mentally, a big, heavy, bowling ball of a man; an armored Buddha, who somehow made everyone feel lighter. His ragged, wolf-growl of a voice had pride in it, though Simon didn't comprehend the words of the song he was singing.

"What do you want? Huh? It's no good to cry and moan," Mamoru was saying to the other men. "We gave the enemy a good, honorable fight, and we'll give him a good, honorable burial . . . in fire. The night is not yet over." Sachiko offered him a weak smile.

Simon had come up beside Key, who looked at him with weary eyes. "There are times Mamoru is helpful. And then times like this. He really does have a lot of skill, if you're in the mood for it. He's even done work as a clown before."

"A *clown*? Did you say a clown?"

"They have to fill up the days between battles somehow. He says it frees his mind from the endless training."

Simon looked over at Mamoru, intrigued.

"He does magic tricks," Key added.

"Not magic," Sachiko corrected him indignantly. "Just tricks."

"He's very good," Key said, with admiration. "He picked up the skill after his wife died. Killed by a Dragon in Osaka. Mamoru learned to do tricks for some children whose parents died in the same attack."

"Quiet," ordered Akira from up front, and Simon and Key lowered their voices to whispers.

"What's his deal? Does he just hate me, or is he like this to everybody?" Simon asked.

"It's not just you. Akira doesn't trust outsiders."

"Great."

"You can't blame him. He's always had problems with foreigners. When he was a kid, a group of Navy men got into a barfight with his father. And they killed him."

"American Navy?"

"Yes."

"What happened?"

"They had no reason. I guess they were drunk. His mother wanted peace, not revenge, so the other Samurai did not go after the killers, and they were never arrested. Akira found out from a witness that these Navy men had tattoos, different ones, on their arms, you know? Akira put the same tattoos on his own skin when he was twelve. Then he left our Order for a time, and he went after them himself and killed them, one by one."

Simon looked at Akira walking ahead in the night, his tense frame full of anger.

"The killers," said Key, "had families. Children. Akira felt so disgusted at what he'd done, he tattooed on his arms the orphans' names."

They were talking quietly, but the mention of these children must've bothered Sachiko; she moved ahead a bit, the wide circle of Samurai still keeping Key safely in the middle.

Simon could see Akira's sword was still drawn, almost defiantly, so anyone might see it, though they hadn't met anyone walking on the road, just a few fast-moving cars.

"His sword has a red grip," Simon said curiously.

"He's very traditional," said Key, "but he made the handle red when his father was killed. A sword is the soul of the Samurai. Akira hates the gun; he says it destroys the 'honesty of the kill.'"

"It does," said Taro, hearing this last bit. "But it is the best way to beat the enemy. At a distance."

Simon looked over at him.

"Are you going to tell all of our little secrets?" Taro asked Key, letting his warning tone linger in the air. The boy gave an ashamed grin, and averted his gaze.

They were so far away from where the Dragon fell that they needed to board a city bus, and they were a dripping, miserable sight. The warriors were able to collapse their helmets for concealment, and Simon again noted the ingenuity of their designs. They looked much like police in riot gear, and the few people on the bus did stare. Before long, the driver announced the bus was being sent to evacuate survivors of the fire, and everyone had to get off, so they resumed walking. Simon was wearing down, even with his resilient St. George blood, and Key looked exhausted.

As they neared the fire, Simon had the distinct impression they were being followed, and when he looked behind them, he saw how nervous Key was. He had a guarded look on his face. *Something's out here. Something's with us.*

By the time they reached the street where the Dragon had been thrown, there was no trace of its remains. The fire it had caused flickered quietly.

They stood at the scene of the Dragon's temporary demise, and things started to click in Simon's head. "Do you see what I'm seeing?" he whispered to Key.

"I've never seen this many rats in one place," said Key, looking up at the ledge of a building. At least forty rats were swarming up there, fighting for position, and many were dropping, falling dead to the street.

"It's at least ten degrees colder on this block than it was back there," said Simon, and Key nodded. The Dragon was here. Somewhere.

The boys looked at their fathers. "Indicate nothing," said Taro to Aldric, and they continued moving along the street, acting as if they had no idea anything was wrong.

Simon moved up beside Aldric. "It's the ledge, up there."

"He isn't there."

"Dad. He is."

Aldric and Taro exchanged looks. "He is shifting his effects," warned Aldric.

"The Serpent places his shadow on the other side of the road," Taro whispered to Key. And then he spun, and fired his crossbow into a parked car across the street. The window shattered. An inhuman cry was heard.

The Samurai and Aldric ran for the car. Simon trailed them. But Key was blocked by his mother.

Simon rushed past the Samurai, their crossbows held at the ready, and looked into the car. A timid old gentleman stared back at him, and the image in Simon's eyes twisted slowly until he realized he was looking at the Ice Serpent of Zurich.

It wasn't the Japanese Serpent at all.

Covered in frost, quivering, his fangs chattering, the old black-and-white Dragon was begging for his life. Its tail had grown back into two thin whips.

Akira pulled him from the car, but it was Aldric who placed a sword at the old Dragon's neck. "What are you doing here?" Aldric demanded. "What's your business with Najikko?"

"This is not what you think," the Ice Creature said in German-accented English, flailing in Akira's grip. "I do not work with the Japanese monster. I can be of help. I am no threat."

"You were threat enough at sea, weren't you, now?" said Aldric.

The old Dragon trembled, stuttering.

"Speak," said Akira.

"Is . . . is . . . is very simple. I only watch Najikko," the Dragon claimed. "I am working toward a history of the Serpentine way. I do no one any harm. You know this," he said, pointing to Aldric. "You find no proof of wrongdoing in my ship, yes? Yes? Only thoughts. Words. I am old. I have nothing to my life but my words."

"They were burned away," Aldric said angrily. "They've gone down with your ship."

The Ice Dragon looked at him sadly, choked with tears. Simon was not sure he felt sympathy for the beast, but its act was convincing, its age and weakness obvious as it stooped lower, cowering.

"Years of work, two hundred years," the Serpent said, sobbing. "I have only a few days worth of writing left to me . . ."

"Enough of that," said Aldric, pulling the Serpent to stand. "Sniveling old miserable thing, we'll take you captive. We'll let you finish your writings. You'll die soon enough anyway, you bloody relic. But I'm warning you, do not lie, or your death comes *now*. What do you know of the Japanese Dragon? What are you doing here?"

"The Japanese Dragon is newly powerful. He has tremendous strength. The ancients' fire, the Terror of the Orient," said the Serpent. "He is going now to his greatest adversary . . ."

"Who?" demanded Taro.

The Serpent hissed, "Issindra."

"What word is this?" Taro asked him, confused.

"It means tigerskin," answered Simon behind him. "It's their name for the Tiger Dragon."

"India," said Aldric. "She is somewhere in India, or was, years ago."

"We have it in the White Book of Saint George," Simon added.

"Where is it now?" ordered Taro, and he ran the tip of his blade into the Serpent's chest lightly. Ice cracked there and shattered to the ground.

The Ice Dragon withered at the threat. "Still in India. The Tiger Serpent can be found in Bombay. She seeks a mating partner with the Japanese Dragon—"

"*What?*" Aldric and Taro spoke in unison.

The Serpent nodded vigorously. "They seek offspring. Alliance. Empire. They will meet in India to set aside their animosity . . ."

Simon was disgusted.

Next to him, Sachiko had withdrawn the Dragon scroll from the inside of her jacket.

"He can't go to India," she said. "The Tiger Dragon

and the Japanese Dragon are from the two most dangerous bloodlines in the Serpent world."

"Yes," hissed the Ice Dragon, his eyes unmistakably pleased.

Taro shoved him back with his swords, "What do you mean?" he asked Sachiko.

"The scroll," she explained, holding it up. "The Terror of the Orient was created long ago by two Dragons joined in wedlock. Their symbols are here, their power together was the most volatile in all of history—"

"Yesss," echoed the Ice Dragon.

"In all the centuries of their existence, no two Serpents have ever done more damage. The last time these two breeds unified, the worst natural disaster in history occurred."

"People thought it was the Krakatoa volcano explosion," sneered the Ice Serpent, "the sky all over the world glowed for a year from the flames, but that many deaths could only be the work of Serpentine magic . . ."

He trailed off, as Sachiko tried to explain. "The Japanese and the Tiger, they're from the same bloodlines as the creators of this scroll." Then she went on excitedly in Japanese, hurriedly speaking to Taro.

"In English!" Aldric protested. "What does all this mean?"

"Their fire would be more intense than any others' in the world," she answered. "These two Serpents cannot be allowed to unify. They are almost mythologically opposite in the enemy lore, their bloodlines are never to be crossed. Even Serpents would fear this alliance. You understand the idea of star-crossed lovers, don't you?"

"I'm beginning to."

"To imagine their offspring—"

"I'd rather not."

Simon turned, hearing voices. They had moved into an alley off the street, but some people were now starting to notice the commotion the Samurai were causing.

"Dad . . ." warned Simon.

"Take him with us," Taro was already saying to Akira. "He could be of value, you agree?"

Akira nodded.

"We don't take Serpent prisoners," Aldric said harshly. Simon looked at his father, surprised.

"We gave him our word," Taro responded.

"What does that mean to him? He'd kill us as soon as look at us."

Sachiko approached, seeing an argument about to develop. "We have to get out of here; we're drawing attention."

"I know his deathspell," said Aldric, not breaking

eye contact with the Dragonman. "Won't take but a moment."

The Ice Serpent squirmed, but Taro moved Aldric back. "We can use him. If you will not keep your word, at least keep your head."

Aldric glared at Taro, and Simon feared he'd fight for the right to destroy the Dragon—but he never had the chance. The Ice Serpent swung both of his tails around the necks of Aldric and Akira, hurtling them back with surprising strength. Taro was kicked backward, as the old Serpent scrambled over him, catching the Samurai by surprise.

No one could believe the elderly Dragon had it in him. It rushed toward Key, who was directly in its path, as Sachiko drew her sword. Simon lunged to protect the boy as well, but the Ice Serpent did not attack. It fled, veering off, down a street protected by the silvery flames left by the Japanese Dragon.

In the escape, the Ice Serpent gave himself no credit, thinking, *pathetic worm-relic, you couldn't even choke up your own fire! Run, or you'll die!* Ice filled his throat instead of flame. Running was his only option, and he had used every ounce of flight in him to chase a bullet train earlier in the night. Only fear gave him strength now.

Simon alone had a clear shot through the smoke, but he hesitated, still in shock, and the flames soon blocked his view of the Dragon as well.

There was no going after him. But his words echoed in Simon's head.

The Dragon was headed for India.

Mating season was about to begin.

Chapter 25

ᛏ

FIRE THAT CAN HIDE

"THIS IS THE REASON we fail," said Taro. "Everyone going off in their own direction! We never made mistakes like this before."

"What could we have done?" asked Simon. "He caught us by surprise. No one knew his strength."

"You," Akira interrupted, "are the worst of them. You are a boy. You fight like a child. You are a danger to us all."

Simon couldn't help getting angry. "*You* don't trust us; we don't trust each other, and *that* is the danger to us all."

"So much insolence," Akira said, glaring at Simon.

"This is the reason," Taro said again, tiredly. "We were caught by surprise because we were fighting amongst ourselves. Everything with the Knight is for his own personal glory."

"Not for the Samurai?" Aldric jabbed.

"No. The Samurai is given to personal sacrifice, not personal glory; not working for himself only, but for all. All of us."

Aldric shook his head. "There's your failing in a nutshell. You need to quit thinking like a pack!"

Some of the Samurai sighed, no one willing to continue the fight.

Aldric turned to Simon and spoke in a low voice, "Ignore them, Simon, you did your best. You have to fail sometimes, it's how you learn."

Hearing Alaythia's words from Aldric's mouth was strange; they didn't fit him right. *Alaythia*, Simon thought. *How I could use you now.*

Simon looked over at Key. But the boy didn't seem to care about their argument; he was staring at something *behind* them.

Simon turned to see what it was.

The fire that the Tokyo Dragon had unleashed on the bullet train had not gone out with the spray of fire hoses. It did not behave like any fire the Dragonhunters had ever seen.

It went directly for human victims, stabbing at them, lifting them in the air on tentacles of flame. The flames moved down the street in a mass, like an octopus, but with dozens of arms, spreading, as if more of these Creatures had grown inside the fire.

The firefighters could hear it taunting them inside their heads, over and over, the words hard to understand, but it seemed to tell them, in whispers, *See the rage I hold. Know this hatred. Know this death.*

Simon and Key could see people in the distance falling, aflame, dying. Victims fell from the elevated train platform like kindling thrown onto a firepit.

"He withheld his true strength," Sachiko observed quietly.

Simon was incredulous. "Withheld it?"

"If he had used all his capability, the result would be far worse."

Simon and Key looked back at the fire in disbelief. This was the Japanese Serpent's power now. What would it be like amplified ten times, and joined with the chaos of another Dragon?

All the Dragonhunters stood helplessly in the street and watched as the metallic flames, in a heap the size of a truck, sunk into the pavement and apparently began rolling underground through the sewer system.

The fire stabbed upward through a building and speared people in several apartments, torching them, as it burrowed through the city.

It was the mind of the phenomenon that was truly terrifying. The firefighters were the first to hear the wailing of the angry blaze in their heads, but soon all of Tokyo could hear the unstoppable screaming of the fire, howling inside their brains, as if all the animals on earth were roaring at once.

"We caused this." Simon grimaced. "We should've stopped that Thing when we could."

"The fire won't go out," Sachiko said, visibly holding back emotion. "It must be one of the tricks he learned from the scroll. I'm afraid we haven't even glimpsed his power."

"How do we stop it?" Aldric asked Sachiko. "There must be some method."

"Kill the Dragon, kill the fire," she answered. "That is what the legends say."

"He never meant to do this," Taro conjectured. "If the Ice Serpent was right, the Japanese Creature didn't target us. He wouldn't want to spend his energy, not to burn his own city. It was just his anger that got the better of him."

Toyo nodded. "He'll still head for the Tiger Dragon. In India."

"Then we'll follow him," said Aldric, startling Simon.

"Dad, what about Alaythia—"

"We can't lose this Creature now," snapped Aldric. "He's got the power of a nuclear bomb in his belly. We've slipped off Alaythia's trail, and there's no sense banging on about it. She can handle herself for a bit longer, Simon. You can see what's out there. It's going to keep killing."

Simon said nothing. Aldric moved on, hungry for battle.

Najikko, the Japanese Dragon, had suffered a setback, to be sure, but he fully believed the Hunters could have no inkling whatsoever about where he was headed. Najikko had told no one; he intended to meet the Tiger Dragon alone. The plan was to pretend he was asking for a truce, a partnership. But once he had her in his sights, he would enslave her. He would destroy her lackeys, her odd collection of wild tigers, and her entire operation in one massive firestorm, thereby leaving a powerful message to any other Serpent who would dare challenge him. *I am the ruler of this new order. If you wish to survive, you will become a servant to me.*

At the moment, he seemed a ruler of nothing but misery. He had managed not to use his true firespell—power spent is power lost—but he'd seriously failed to keep his temper in check and had lost equilibrium, and that caused him only more anger.

The power he now possessed seemed to be alive *even inside him.* His stomach and his heart pulsed with uncomfortable new sensations; his fire wanted out. It wanted to soar and spin and burn. He could hear it growling in him, a kind of atom bomb with a brain of its own, which hungered for killing. It was only his supreme self-control that kept it contained, he reminded himself. *If I use this power, it will drain me. I may never have it again. Keep it in check.*

He still had the appearance of Dr. Najikko, the respectable Japanese surgeon. But it was all generated by illusion, and now even this power was weak, his false leg ill-attached, hanging loosely from little silver wires, like a doll that had been yanked apart. He slumped on a lonely Tokyo bus, feeling drunk with exhaustion and confusion.

Already disgusted with the dirty environment in which he found himself, Dr. Najikko grew more ill at the sight of several beetles that were swarming around his feet and crawling up his legs, but he hadn't the strength to burn them. He had never grown used to the insects, and they seemed to mock his power. He could never be rid of them. One of the beetles had somehow found its way *inside* his false leg, or else Najikko was imagining it; in any case, his irritation at the insect crawling about on his skin made him nearly crazy with anxiety. He shook his leg, trying to get the horrid beetle away from him, and looking all the stranger for it.

He repeated in his head an old Serpentine mantra

for relaxation, but it did him no good.

It made him ill to think that as soon as he was out of this germ pit, this cesspool, he'd be catching a bacteria-swathed airplane to a polluted, festering Bombay. He'd need a bit of time to heal, however, before he could take on the Tiger Dragon with all her trickery.

A single vagabond shared the bus with him, staring at the doctor in disgust and befuddlement. He seemed to wonder if the doctor was a figment of his intoxicated imagination.

Najikko snarled at the man. "What's the matter with you? Never saw a man falling apart before?"

The bum continued to stare. "You need a plastic surgeon," he replied.

The black-and-white Ice Dragon was in an entirely different state of mind. Running half the night, he got out of Tokyo as quickly as possible, and in the form of the old Swiss professor, took a flight to India. His strength was spent as well, but his spirit was overjoyed with the coming possibilities.

Sitting on the plane, surrounded by darkness, a single light above him striking his pretty pages, he filled his journal with observations about the Dragon-hunters. *The collision of East and West is working just as one would expect; they are an angry, badly coordinated troop that*

are more dangerous to themselves than to Dragonkind . . .
The Dragonkillers took the bait, believing everything that I
told them. They have just enough information to fill in the
rest themselves, and will join the grand conflict at just the
right time. What an ending I shall have.

He shivered, both from the chill on his skin and
sheer excitement.

His performance had been masterful; the decoy
papers he'd left on his ship were taken as authentic.
He had had the genuine version of his precious *History
of Serpentkind* sent to him from Zurich, and all sixteen
volumes were now safely tucked into his suitcase.

He was thrilled, snorting a laugh as other sleepy
travelers stirred, moaning their complaints. Everyone
on the jet felt cold and sick, of course, in the presence
of the icy lizard, and the meals had turned to worm-
riddled mush, so there was nothing to eat even if
someone had wanted it. A tide of mosquitoes agitated
the sleepers, and turbulence rocked the airplane all
night.

The Ice Serpent let the mosquitoes feed on his
tongue. They burned into little wispy bits of nothingness.

The airline attendants watched from the end of
the plane as the strange Swiss passenger chortled amid
the humming insects. The creaking of his bones as he
twisted and shifted in his seat made them shudder.

Everyone was wishing he'd try to sleep. But he was writing endlessly. He'd filled a whole journal and started another before they'd gotten even an hour into the flight to Bombay.

Chapter 26

WHERE TIGERS LURK

SIMON SPENT THE PASSAGE to Bombay learning from Key all about his newfound companions. Such a stupid, tragic thing that the St. Georges had been out there alone all this time, with only Alaythia to help guide them. Simon was especially thankful to the Samurai now, since they helped do the chores on the ship and kept Aldric busy talking weaponry. The Samurai had been intrigued by the arsenal aboard the Ship with No Name; the weapons cache had helped convince them to use the vessel for transport.

Most of the weapons were the work of Alaythia, which impressed Sachiko. In the Asian tradition, Magicians were not just trackers and forgers of armor and war-making tools, as it was with the St. George order, but rather, frontline warriors as well. Sachiko also fashioned the Warriors' devices, but her work did not stop there, and while it was true that during a hunt someone always had to stay behind to watch Key, it was not always Sachiko. Key said that her leaving him clashed with Japanese tradition, but his mother wouldn't have it any other way.

Sachiko amazed Aldric and Simon by weaving her own spells into the Ship with No Name, causing it to move with great speed. The vessel was calm, unrattled, and there was nothing on the ocean to mark their progress, but the medieval-looking navigational gauges indicated the miles were dissolving away like time in a dream.

Naturally, Aldric didn't like Sachiko messing around with his ship, but the ship did not seem to resist, and there was no denying her power. They'd be in Bombay by the next day, nearly as fast as a commercial jet.

But it was clear to Simon that Aldric was uncomfortable with so many people aboard, and by sheer numbers, the Japanese seemed to have made the place their own, chattering, bringing out smelly foods, rearranging things to have more room.

Simon avoided his complaints. Key kept him entertained, and his mind off his worries, by telling him bits and pieces about the Samurai's past.

"They are linked to each other," said Key, "according to their special skills. Kisho and Mamoru are the marksmen—the arrow is like a servant to them. Old Toyo has a way with the gun, though he hates it. He sings to it before a battle, low and calm; it's almost scary if you hear it. He knows exactly when he has the split second to reload, and how to keep his shots clear of the others. Akira is best at hand-to-hand combat and good with the sword, too, but my father is the best. And you saw how my mother is, if anyone moves against me. They all work together like the fingers of a hand. At least . . . until you two came into it."

Simon tried to smile.

"They hone all of the skills so anyone can pick up the slack," Key went on.

"They don't talk to me much; I don't feel like I know them," Simon said.

"You're not supposed to. It's a members-only club."

Simon accepted this. "So Akira is the angry one, Kisho is the crazy one, Toyo is the old fart . . ."

"Simon." Key cut him off. "I like you very much. But you have a way of talking that is not . . . polite."

Simon felt instantly ashamed.

"Old Toyo is the eldest, yes, and he's like a grandfather to me," said Key. "And most of what I know of history I learned from him. He would like to give up this work; he thinks it is not in him anymore. It would destroy the honor of so many who came before to surrender his mission. But I *did* hear him say it one time."

Simon nodded, trying to think of what to say. He looked at Fenwick and Katana lying on the galley floor, licking at fallen gravy. "But it's the big guy you're closest to, huh?"

"Mamoru. His name is Mamoru."

"I know. I'm sorry; the names are hard for me to get."

Key looked annoyed. "Mamoru has a giant aquarium in his apartment, the place he kept with his late wife," he said. "Almost the only thing there, except for a really big refrigerator. The refrigerator is this giant thing—as big as him. It's filled with food, most especially frozen fast-food so he can have it anytime. It's his big secret. He loves the fast-food, fried chicken. He used to give me the little toys from the kids' meals as presents, and he still thinks I don't know where he got them."

"Mamoru's a cheap guy?"

"He spends it all on the aquarium. He even keeps Samurai crab in there."

"Samurai crab?"

"You never heard of them? You should see them sometime. They're . . . A long time ago, there was this naval battle, and the soldiers were outnumbered so they sacrificed themselves and leapt into the sea. Their spirits found refuge in the crabs, and they're still there to this day, waiting forever to defend the island. If you look on the backs of these crabs, you still see the faces of the soldiers, or so they say."

Over the journey, Key told more stories about the old ways of the Samurai. "If a warrior was condemned to die," Key said, "the Samurai executioner would have to swing the blade down on his head so that it would not be completely cut off, just *almost* cut off, hanging by a strand of skin at the neck. Very hard to do."

Simon traded him. "In Europe, they used to execute people on the rack. They'd stretch them out really bad, until they broke apart, or they'd be drawn and quartered, where they pull people's arms and legs out and then slice the body into quarters so they die slowly."

"Yes. I know of that," Key replied.

"Also people would come out and have parties watching executions," Simon offered.

"Yes. I know of that," Key replied. "In parts of Asia, it's said that soldiers would cut the eyes out of dead people and lay the eyeballs on their backs, to defile them, so they could not see in the afterlife."

Simon racked his brain for a story as gross as this, but he didn't know nearly as much history as Key did.

"In *seppuku*," Key added, "the warrior commits

ritual suicide, by disemboweling himself. He uses the hara-kiri knife, and severs the skin right below the belly, and the insides just fall out."

"That's twisted."

"It's tradition. For Samurai, the stomach is the center of a person's spirit, not the heart."

"Anyone you know ever do that?" Simon was joking, but Key actually nodded.

"I didn't know him," Key replied. "But there was a soldier before I was born who did this. He had failed to protect Mamoru's wife during a Serpent battle."

Simon was shocked. "Who was it?"

"Akira's cousin. No one asked it of him, but he knew the code. Akira took it very bad. In these times it's very hard to follow the old ways."

"I can sort of see that."

"I have trouble thinking how it should go, everything has changed so much. In the days of old, there was no technology, except the gun, the cannon, the sword. It's so much more now. It makes unity harder. We argue what to hold on to from the old ways. Keeping the group together is the most important thing. For the Warrior to even conceal his weapons, it's improper, but we have to make adjustments for the real world. We don't agree on it. Toyo thinks we've gone too far away from the old code."

The oldest Samurai had just now climbed down

the ladder to enter the room, so Simon and Key quit talking, but when he was out of earshot, Key whispered, "He bends the code, though. His favorite thing is the comedy shows. Not exactly keeping his emotions flat, you know? I hear him laughing late at night in his room."

Taro entered next, and told his son to get to his studies. "*He* can be very funny, too," Key whispered. "But never for me." Key took out a schoolbook and added respectfully, "When the others leave, my father is still in the training chamber for hours, never breaking his concentration."

Simon looked at Taro, who stood across the room, still and watchful, his eyes clouded with worry over what lay ahead.

The Ship with No Name reached the city of Bombay, greeted by palm trees swaying in the hot winds, the hum of motors, the multicolored motion of crowds, the exhausted beauty of an ancient city. Simon followed Aldric and the others down into the stench of the streets, which were truly an assault on the senses. For safety, Aldric paid a group of men to watch the ship.

"Too much money," mumbled Taro.

Aldric glared at him. "This ship was made by my late wife from the undying forests of the Norwegian Hidden Woods. I won't have it torn apart by vandals."

Taro nodded. "Some trees, I see, *are* sacred."

"And I don't need any help managing my money," Aldric added. He was already in a foul mood from the cramped conditions on the journey.

"You gave them enough to buy their own ship."

"I'm quite aware of that, thank you, I'm not an imbecile," said Aldric, but he quietly slipped the rest of their bills to Simon. "You handle the money, Simon."

Simon slipped the cash into his backpack. The pack was too heavy to make off with easily, but he still worried it might be an attractive target for thieves, and guarded it closely.

"Not good," Akira was mumbling. "We should send the boys back. Someone should guard them at the ship. More safe for them, by far." But no one was listening; Sachiko wanted to watch Key personally and she would not be left behind. There was no arguing with her.

The future is going to look a lot like Bombay, Simon thought. Beggars called to him, and smog stirred around them like Dragonsmoke. The world was creaking under the weight of so many people, and it would have so many more people to endure in the years to come. If a place like Bombay could survive, the human race itself could survive.

But Bombay had more than just overpopulation to deal with. The Tiger Dragon was nestled here, thriving on the pain and the sorrows of the city. The question, as always, was where? The city was over-stuffed with sinister and fantastic architecture. Over here, a patch of European buildings were crammed in, as though squeezed together by a giant; over there, dome-capped traditional Indian structures were vying for dignity against apartments thrown up seemingly in a hurry, still wrapped in their scaffolding. Wide boulevards were gobbled by worried crowds, and narrow streets sagged with the sick and exhausted.

Simon watched the people carefully, their faces anxious, wrapped in their own concerns. Most of the passersby were in ordinary clothes—tan shirts, brown pants—brushing past others in brighter traditional robes—usually women.

Pungent spice smells floated by, the scent of summer warmth, of secrets, of things long lost.

Up ahead, Simon was surprised to see what looked like a modern shopping mall blazing with festive colors and lights. Not far away, merchants waited wearily in marketplace stalls that looked like the forts Simon made as a kid, built of posts hung with colored sheets. Wealth and poverty mingled easily here.

An occasional Rolls-Royce or Mercedes trumpeted in the nervous traffic of yellow-topped black taxis, and gold-painted mansions lorded over the slums. Everything about Bombay offered perfect refuge to a Serpent.

The St. Georges had lost the scent of the Japanese Dragon, but its target was the same as theirs. If they could locate the Tiger Serpent, everything might come together perfectly—if you could consider facing two Dragons at once a perfect situation.

It sounded like a joke to Simon. What's worse than the two worst Dragons on earth? The two worst Dragons on earth *mating*.

The Ice Dragon was also out there somewhere. Simon and Key had been discussing how he played into these events, but neither could come up with an answer.

"Too many people," observed Taro. "Do they never consider how crowded this makes things?"

"This from a guy who lives in Japan?" muttered Simon. Aldric hushed him with a look.

"There are better ways to use our resources," Sachiko said to Taro. "I think we should split up and search for Dragonsigns."

"If we split up," said Taro, "we are less effective."

"We can always call for help," she answered.

Aldric looked at them. "Is this going to be another day-long debate session?"

Taro glared.

As the adults began to argue, Simon and Key stood together with their exotic pets in tow, looking at the crowd.

"A lot of sadness here," said Key.

Simon nodded. "It's going to be hard to see where it begins."

"Tourists?" said a voice. A very old Indian man astride a bicycle cab was staring at them, grinning a toothless smile.

"I guess you could say that," Simon answered.

"I take you anywhere," said the pleasant old man in English, but his knobby knees did not look capable of pulling them very far.

Key stared back doubtfully, but Simon asked him, "Where is the saddest place in the city? The worst of the worst."

The old man scowled at him, questioningly.

"We have our reasons," said Simon. "It's like a geography lesson. Are there any really rundown hospitals or orphanages we could take a look at?"

The old fellow regarded him. "You are not the average tourist."

"We want to see the places no one goes to—the real India," Simon explained. "We want to see the dark side of the city."

"This is a city with many dark sides," said the old Indian. "But I think I can find the darkest point. I can get you to the midnight place, if that's what you wish for."

"Yes," said Key, seeing what Simon was up to.

"We want the midnight place."

The old Indian nodded. He introduced himself as Rajiv, and Simon and Key climbed into the cart attached to his bike. Fenwick and Katana jumped in at their feet.

"We're not going to be too heavy, are we?" asked Key.

"Not at all," Rajiv said cheerfully, but Simon could see his skinny legs were straining hard, and the bicycle was going nowhere whatsoever. Simon actually breathed in, hoping to make himself somehow lighter. He worried his backpack alone could crush the wheels.

The bicycle remained firmly in place. The old driver was turning red from exertion. Auto rickshaws—motorcycles with canopies over them—zoomed past. Finally, Rajiv's cycle *inched* forward, and thankfully started to roll slowly down the street.

Sachiko had been watching the boys, her arms crossed in displeasure, as Aldric and Taro finally noticed them.

"*Where* are you going?" asked Taro, harshly.

"He says he can take us to the darkest of the dark places," explained Key, pointing to the driver. "Isn't that where we should start looking?"

Mamoru raised an eyebrow. No one admitted the boy was right, but Taro caught up to the bicycle cab.

"Move over," he said, climbing in beside the boys.

"Wait a minute. There's not enough room for us," said Aldric, irritated.

"No problem," Rajiv answered in his accented voice. "My brothers can accommodate anything, even large American rear ends."

"I'm an *Englishman*," muttered Aldric.

"So much the easier," Rajiv replied happily, and behind him, another bicycle cab rolled up, this one driven by an even older and even skinnier man. And behind him, more were coming, each driver older and less substantial than the last.

Mamoru found a seat in the last cart, which sagged so much it caused sparks as it rolled down the street.

The pace was slow, very slow, but it gave the Dragonhunters a chance to study the crowded streets for signs of a Serpentine presence, and Simon was pleased with Rajiv's knowledge of their surroundings and his amazing happiness in the face of all the city's troubles.

At last the bicycle cabs rolled into an area that did indeed seem darker than the rest of the city. Pitch-black smoke unfurled from many factories, coating the streets with an ugly mist. Several ancient palaces flanked the district, but they were so rundown Simon barely noticed their faded grandeur until he looked closely. One was adorned with simple columns; another with sculpted tigers; a third with curved swords holding up its terraces; and the last palace was a dull yellow with huge minarets.

Any of them might serve a Dragon well.

Chapter 27

A TIGER'S EYES

BOMBAY BELONGED TO THE Tiger Dragon. She knew about everything that happened here. She knew the Ice Dragon had crossed into her territory by airplane, for harmless snooping, scribbling in his book, no doubt—though he'd better keep out of her way until this was all over. She'd find some use for him in the new empire, or else find time to kill him, one or the other.

He was far down the list of challenges. She had learned about the arrival of the St. Georges and their new Asian partners within minutes of their entering the harbor. The news traveled along a line of beggars, thieves, and informants, paid to watch for odd happenings and foreign arrivals at all times. They'd seen the Dragonhunters arrive by boat, a strange assortment of tourists to say the least. Some of them were wearing armor under their coats, and the addition of a bobcat and a fox was hardly the way to blend in.

Issindra the Tiger Dragon was not amused.

From her magnificent Bombay palace, raised high on a hill by giant statues of roaring tigers, well above her complex of factories, Issindra heard the news from an old one-legged beggar. Looking out over the city, she considered how this would change her plans.

It was a bad day. Things were happening too quickly. She had been jolted to hear of a strange fiery phenomenon that had occurred in Tokyo, eating everything in its path, cutting a hole through the city. Odd conditions in the atmosphere, the news reports said.

The Dragon of Japan was on the run, headed for Bombay. They were supposed to begin talks on uniting their ventures, but they would take place sooner than expected. He'd sent her a message, a word written in blood that had formed on her mirror earlier in the day. *Rendezvous.* Imagine the audacity. It obstructed her view. Clearly, he wanted to show he knew how to get under her skin.

If he was so tremendously powerful, why didn't he just gut the Dragonhunters who were making his life so difficult? But she knew the answer. *You could try, but you could never quite snuff them out. You could crush them, and they'd spill out of your fingers somehow; you could burn them, but they'd rise from the ashes. Good fortune followed them. It was a puzzle, and a waste of thought. No sense in chasing them. Let the Hunters come into her trap of their own free will. Their time would come. They were no match for the speed and cunning of the Serpent mind. Sooner or later they'd burn.*

Her appointment with the Japanese Serpent would have to be kept, of course. She was planning to mate with him and kill him, and there would be no point in making the whole thing more difficult by putting it off.

One part of the plan she was certain of: Once the Japanese Creature saw her, he would surely find her suitable. On the wall, draped in jungle ivy, were huge oil paintings of her human self, and coiled in vines were sculptures of her elegant form. She was even more beautiful as a Dragon, she knew, even with the fire scars she'd received over the years on her tigerlike skin.

She noticed in a mirror the beggar was still awaiting his pay. Issindra looked him over, sneering. "What awful things you find to wear out there in the streets," she said. "Have you no sense of how you look?"

Playfully, she let fire roll down her throat, down the veins in her arm, and out her fingertip. Thin flames glided toward the beggar, wrapping around him, growing, until he was covered neck to foot in a flickering costume made of fire. Colors rippled in the flames as the beggar stood, terrified.

"Fear not." The Tiger Dragon smiled. "The flames are kept three millimeters from your skin. Do you not look stylish?" She laughed. "There's only so much I can do. Oh, stop shivering. I said I wouldn't burn you."

Without even looking at him, Issindra pulled the fire back into her finger. She dispensed with him by hitting a button on the floor, unleashing her tigers from the cage under her bed. Out they came, making a terrific racket as they took his one remaining leg. And then they toyed with him, throwing him back and forth, rolling him around. She could see them from the corner of her eye as she looked out at the city.

His misery pleased her and brought clarity to her thoughts. *The hours ahead will take some careful consideration. There is the Japanese Dragon on his way. The Dragonkillers will be on his trail, and mine. Any meeting I have with him endangers my own life all the more . . . unless I can make it all work to my advantage.*

Oh, why not, she thought arrogantly. *Let's finish them all in one delicious meal.*

She wanted to rest, prepare, and lay out a plan, but there was an awful noise from the tiger feeding. She turned to see the cats having trouble killing the beggar, trying to pull him apart but hardly doing a good job of it. She strode between the tigers, roaring to force them back, and quickly snapped the neck of the whimpering beggar. Sometimes you had to do things yourself.

The tigers moved in around her warily.

She watched them feed and considered the future.

Chapter 28

CITY OF A BILLION WONDERS

"WE'LL SPLIT UP," SAID Sachiko, stepping out of her cab.

"I don't remember agreeing to that," Taro said, getting out beside her.

"Neither do I," said Aldric.

She pushed past both of them. "We'll stay within a four-block radius, close enough to get help if we need it," she said, holding up her cell phone as she motioned Key to join her.

Taro and Aldric looked at each other.

"Seems reasonable," they said at the same time, begrudgingly.

Simon glanced at Sachiko's unusual phone, and whispered to Key, "That's a weird-looking one. Where'd she get that?"

"She made it," he answered. "The signal can penetrate anywhere, and it never stops working."

"Well, what if it *does* stop working?"

"Then we handle things ourselves," Sachiko answered.

The boys went with Sachiko, who refused any help from the quarreling warriors. As a result, Aldric and Taro were forced to join together as the other Samurai separated into pairs to see the other palaces.

The boys would investigate the area around the Tiger Palace. Simon wanted to lead, but Sachiko smiled and pushed him back rather roughly. He massaged his shoulder, surprised by her strength.

They ended up in an alley filled with well-tailored businessmen, all waiting to enter a tiny teahouse, which was hidden here with no entrance on the main street. One of the men looked at Simon with sunken, yellowed eyes. "The tea is miserable," he muttered, as if asking the boy for some kind of mercy. "But I cannot get enough of it. Five times a day I come here."

The scents of bonfires and cinnamon, chimney dust and burned sugar hung in the air. Simon had never known tea to smell so strongly. He and Key looked at each other. Dragonmagic, surely.

Sachiko had the boys sit at a table in the alley with their pets, under an awning made from a tattered blanket. "Do *not* move from here," Sachiko told them, "unless you absolutely have to, and even then, think twice. I'm going in."

She pushed herself through the mass of men, and disappeared into the teahouse. Simon felt nervous being Key's only protector, but Sachiko would only be away for a moment—if they were lucky.

"I feel like *we're* the killers. There's nothing we can do to stop what's going on," Simon said. He looked morosely at the crowd. "There's just too many of them . . ."

"We do what we can."

Simon looked at Key, thinking at that moment he looked like Taro. "He doesn't make it easy though, does he? Your dad, I mean," Simon said. "When we left him, he didn't say anything. And he didn't say anything after the fires in Tokyo. He never says anything to you. He's, like, pretty tough on you, isn't he?"

"No. He should be harder on me."

Simon rolled his eyes. *A glutton for punishment, this guy.*

"Is your father any different?" Key asked him.

"A little. I have to look for what he means, not what he says." *I wouldn't want to trade, that's for sure.* "Sometimes, though . . . when he says something cold, it's worse than when anybody else does, you know?"

Key nodded. Simon looked at him, waiting for him to say something.

"Taro worries about me badly," Key said. "He didn't say anything because he didn't need to, he has . . . confidence that I will do the right thing. He just never *gives* me anything to do."

"You must hate that."

"I think in America you might use words like 'hate' very easy. My father tries to keep me safe, that's all. He doesn't want any mistakes. See, look at me. . . . Here is my situation. I'm Caucasian, and I'm Asian . . ."

"A little something for everybody." Simon smiled.

"Well, you may see it that way, but in Japan, not everyone does. My father thinks I'm . . . there is a word for it. Damaged goods. But at the same time, he thinks I am some kind of great treasure that has to be protected. He's almost as bad as my mother. He is always with me. If I were to fall from this chair right now, one of them would be here to catch me."

"That's a good thing. I never had that."

"Hmm. Does that make you . . . enjoy being alone?"

"It makes you stronger." Simon tried to look into the busy teahouse. "I can't see your mom in there. She should've let us help her. She's brave, you know. Or else . . . crazy."

Key frowned.

"Even Akira stays with a partner," Simon observed. "And he's always the first one in, right?"

"Akira first, the front edge of the sword. He guards my father, because my father is the best at strategy. Mamoru is last, the hilt, the tireless one. Last one out, as well."

"But your mother fights alone if she needs to. We would never do it that way. Magicians are too valuable."

"And your father has gotten used to fighting alone."

"He lost everyone else. Anyway, you're wrong. *I'm* with him. I fight beside him."

"It is amazing that works for you. He does not seem able to work with people."

Simon wanted to change the subject. "We should go in after her," he said.

"She has not been gone very long."

"How long does it take for a Dragon to strike?"

"She said not to move," said Key.

"Then we should get help," said Simon.

"She did *not* tell us to get help," said Key.

"So what? She could need us. She's your mother."

"Which is why I am doing what she told me to do," Key answered, and he leaned back in his chair, eyeing Simon calmly. *I am not getting in trouble.*

"You know what happens to rule-followers?"

asked Simon. Key made no move to answer. "They die really old, and they never realize that they never really *lived*."

"If they never realize it," said Key, "then they die happy."

Simon blew out his cheeks. "She's in there right now. Probably getting eaten alive by some creation of the Dragon."

Key said nothing.

"Some kind of giant reptile," mused Simon. "Or a spider. She's probably being swallowed by a massive spider with acid dripping from its jaws."

Key's face held no expression.

" . . . and pieces of her," said Simon, "are now disappearing into the spider's stomach."

Key did not move. He had been given his orders. The orders had not changed.

"What kind of stomach does a spider have?" he asked Simon.

Simon was irritated. "I don't know. All gross with parasites and—"

"Tourists?" said a voice, but this time it was a young, quite beautiful Indian girl, maybe fifteen years old, with striking green eyes. She stood over their tiny table in the alley with an expression that was half excited, half superior.

"We are tourists," said Key, "who are sitting at this

table and not leaving it."

Simon frowned at him.

"That's too bad," said the girl. She had Englishman's English, proper and polished. "Not much to do here in this alley, unless you're waiting for a look at sweatshops. That's all there is here."

"Well, there is *you*," said Key.

Simon could see the girl enjoyed the remark.

She smiled at them. "I can show you something quite amazing, if you have the money," she said.

"How *much* money?" asked Simon.

"You should be asking, 'how amazing?'"

"All right, then. How amazing?"

"You have never seen anything like it," she promised. "If you are here in this part of the city, you must enjoy seeing the unusual, the exotic. The nasty." She snarled playfully on the word, and suddenly the sari she was wearing began to *move*, her blouse shivering, shimmering, and Simon nearly gasped as a large red snake emerged near her neck.

Tsssssss.

The snake was still half hidden in her clothes, its head craning out to stare at Simon. Fenwick leapt to attention, and Key's bobcat tensed.

Interesting. Did this girl have something to do with the Dragon?

"Not afraid of snakes, are you?" asked the girl.

"Oh, no," Simon answered coolly. "In fact, we're in the snake business." She looked at him oddly. "Pets," he followed up.

"If you like unusual animals, you're going to love what I have to show you," she said. "I know where you can see the most dangerous animal in the world.

"Come with me," she added enticingly, and wandered off down the alley.

She was so incredibly pretty. Simon looked at his cousin.

"I am not going," said Key.

"I am," said Simon. And he started after the girl. "And if I die somewhere out there by myself, your mother won't be happy that you let me go off alone." Key looked angry, but he rose from the table to follow him.

They headed down the alley. If Key decided to pass the blame later, so be it. Either way, Simon wasn't going to miss out.

He was going to follow that girl.

Chapter 29

SECRETS OF BOMBAY

FOLLOW HER HE DID.

Key came after him, reluctantly going after his bobcat, Katana, who was sniffing curiously at the feet of the Indian girl, as Fenwick trotted alongside.

"Your pets," said the girl, "will not be welcome here."

Simon stopped. "Why is that?"

"They might quarrel with the animal I have to show you."

Simon was becoming more suspicious, but he looked at Key. "Order him back to the ship. Fenwick will lead him."

Key did not want to leave the bobcat behind.

"Don't be such a baby," said Simon. "Let him go.

That little cat can't protect you anyway, right?"

"I don't want him to get eaten," said Key.

Simon frowned. "No one's going to eat your cat."

"In India, they eat cats."

"No, they don't. People say that about Japan, too—but you wouldn't eat a cat, would you?"

"I would if I was hungry enough," said Key.

"Come on," Simon groaned. With a hand signal, he sent Fenwick running down the street, and, to his satisfaction, the bobcat chased after the fox.

"They're going to make someone a fine meal," said Key sadly. "They'll bring back our parents, you know," Key added.

"If they don't get distracted somewhere. You don't know Fenwick," Simon answered.

The Indian girl, who said her name was Panna, kept going and led Simon and Key through a series of crowded alleys until they arrived at a doorway.

"This is where the party is," she said. "The most unusual creature in India. But it costs to get in, as I said."

She named a price that seemed beyond belief to Simon. "And you're not going to tell us what we see?" he said.

"The price is guaranteed."

"If we aren't happy, where are we going to find you?" asked Simon. "You'll be long gone."

Panna looked at Key, and winked at him. "This one could find a pretty girl in any city in the world."

Simon looked in amazement at his quiet companion.

"For you," she said to Key, "I'll drop the price a little."

"Oh, for him, you'll drop the price?" Simon was jealous, but curiosity was getting the best of him, and he went for his money. "I'll take your offer. I'm not stingy." Cost was really not an issue. He had plenty of rupees from his father stuffed into his backpack, and if this led to the Bombay Dragon somehow, it would be worth it.

Taking his money, the girl smiled at them both, and unlocked the door.

She led Simon and Key into a dark room where many other people were gathered together tightly. There was nothing else in the room but a closed theater curtain along one wall. Wealthy-looking Indian men stood waiting, alongside confused tourists from all over the world.

"Do you know what's going on?" Simon asked the man next to him.

"Not really."

"How did you get here?"

The man looked at him. "They promised me it would be amazing. Something I could only see in

Bombay. They said if I wanted to see a human being eaten by a strange and unusual animal, I could come here and watch it happen, for a price. I paid almost as much as my Mercedes-Benz, I think."

Simon could not help but look at him, revolted. He'd paid a fortune to see someone die.

The man did not seem a bit ashamed, just nervous with excitement.

"They're going to kill someone," whispered Key, fear in his voice now.

"It's a Dragon operation," said Simon quietly. "A little money on the side. The girl must be working with the beast."

But there was no sign of Panna, just a clicking at the door. Simon and Key were locked in the room with the crowd.

"If I know our enemy," said Simon, looking around carefully, "after the show, we're all going to die . . ."

Aldric and Taro were snooping around the outside of the decrepit palace with the giant minarets.

"This way," Aldric ordered, pointing to an alley.

Taro scowled. "I am not your Tonto."

He insisted on going the other way toward a busier road. Aldric went along; he had no better idea where to begin. There were people everywhere on the streets with terrible deformities, some shuffling along with their arms shrunken to nothing, others with missing eyes, and still others with no legs at all.

Taro watched them, a hand on his hidden pistol.

"I thought," observed Aldric, "the sword was the soul of the Samurai."

"It is. You may notice we carry two of them, long and short, honed to perfection. But the bullets contain Dragonfire, and that kills Dragons."

"Hard to control, though."

"Yes, but we manage it. We have all kinds of tricks, if you'd open your mind to them."

"What about tradition?"

"Tradition is good. Living is better. We follow *bushido*, the Samurai code, but we are not stupid. Now let me work."

Taro's eyes were focused on a young Indian couple.

"What is it?"

"You can find it anywhere," Taro said.

It was clear what Taro meant, watching the couple. Love, affection, human emotion.

"Even in the shadow of the Dragon," he muttered. "This woman in danger. Alaythia? I envy you."

Aldric looked at him. "Why should you?"

"She is in danger because of her feelings for you. You know it as a fact. She cannot hide it. Not so for me. Sachiko has developed the power to hide emotion from the Serpents. She has become a master of hiding these things, and who can ever tell what's in her mind now? Think of it. You don't even remember knowing her before."

He seemed to want an answer, but Aldric's memory of that earlier time was lost—gone except for a few murky images. Sachiko *was* powerful.

Taro cleared his throat. "I don't know whether Sachiko still has feelings for your brother, or not."

He moved on. Aldric had no way of knowing how to reply.

Sachiko had been delayed by a large group of bleary-eyed customers at the teahouse who had swarmed around her when their tea had run out. The staff at the teahouse had escaped her questions by ducking out the back way, but the dazed, tea-addicted men had seen Sachiko pass behind the counter to check out the back rooms, and some had mistaken her for the owner of the establishment. And they wanted more tea.

She tried politeness, but was forced to shove her way past the group, knocking some of the customers to the ground. She came out of the teahouse frustrated, having searched it thoroughly, seeing all manner of Dragonsigns—flies, wasps, and centipedes crawling from teacups—but no Dragon anywhere. It had departed, but only recently.

Now Kyoshi was gone. Sachiko was furious. *Simon St. George is a horrible influence*, she thought, pushing through the crowd, searching for the boys.

Nervously, she searched her heart. *If the Dragon had him, she would sense it, wouldn't she?*

She nudged past a heavyset businessman and slammed directly into Taro, headed the other way. He looked at her in surprise.

"I can't find them," she panted. "They were right here; I told them to stay put—"

"You lost the boy?"

"No. He lost himself!" She found herself fuming at Taro; it wasn't like him to blame her.

"Just calm down," he said. "We need to get everyone in one place, and we'll find the boy together. No more separations. Where are the others?"

"I thought Aldric was with you."

Taro shook his head. "He wouldn't stay with me. He came back to find you and the boys. Call the others to the corner, there, and we'll regroup."

But another voice called behind her. She turned to see Taro coming for her again, running through the crowd at a distance. How did he get *there*? And Aldric was with him, shouting, the sound absorbed in the rustle of voices. She looked back, and the *first* Taro had a sinister look on his face.

It wasn't Taro.

It just looked like him.

Sachiko went for her sword as the first Taro's form rippled away in a familiar mirage wave, transforming into the gold-silver Dragon of Japan. "Careless woman," hissed Najikko, and he calmly batted Sachiko's sword away.

Sachiko pulled back fast, narrowly missing a slashing claw.

With a swipe of her arm, she pulled one of the pins from her hair and stabbed the Serpentine forearm, buying herself the time to step back.

"Sachiko!" The real Taro was now standing with her, sword ready, as Aldric rushed out in front.

The people around them screeched in a fearful chorus.

The Japanese Dragon sneered at the crowd. *How sad for you all, losing your composure this way. There's no reason to be disturbed. Just a few human beings about to be mercilessly killed, filthy trash to be burned away. Go about your business. This is nothing more than a long-overdue roasting of flesh.*

Inside the building, the locked door could not be budged. Simon and Key shuffled through the collection of excited, tittering tourists, as they tried to find a hidden doorway. There had to be a different way out.

Behind them, the crowd gasped as the curtains opened to reveal a long window made of thick glass. From where he stood, Simon could just glimpse a tiger prowling beyond the window in a wooden cell. Then another tiger entered the arena. And another.

"It's about to happen," he told Key.

"I don't want to see it," Key replied, keeping his eyes on the wooden walls around him, searching for a latch or hinge or any telltale sign of a doorway.

But Simon could not look away. A trapdoor opened beyond the window, and a man fell into the tiger pit.

"I can't find anything," Key was muttering.

Simon stood on tiptoes, peering past the huddled onlookers.

"Wait a second," Key was saying, "There may be something here . . ."

But Simon was distracted, moving up, pulling himself a little higher by grabbing on two men's shoulders so he could see better.

The man in the pit rose from the ground, and Simon could see him clearly.

Oh, no.

It was Mamoru.

In a narrow alley not far away, Aldric and Taro rushed forward with their swords, seconds after

Sachiko emptied a small pistol of silver bullets. But the Japanese Dragon took the attacks unruffled and unperturbed.

He had recovered from their last battle. Now he hissed in pain, but held his ground easily. As fast as a switchblade, he kicked Aldric to the ground with his metallic leg, as Taro swung his *katana* sword, landing a blow on the Creature's artificial limb.

Quickly, two tongs clicked out of the Dragon's leg and grabbed the sword. The Dragon pulled back, the sword now latched to his leg and swiveled into position as if it were the Serpent's own *katana*. He lifted the sword by the handle, wielding it.

Taro was shocked. The Serpent grinned, trying not to be pleased.

You took my leg, the Dragon thought, *I'll take your life—with your own dirty sword*.

Sachiko saw her husband was left open. Hands shaking, she hurried to reload her pistol.

Aldric threw himself forward, his dagger splintering the Japanese Dragon's chestplate.

The Dragon spun, his wingblades whishing for Aldric's head. He missed.

In the steely Serpent's mind, the words of the fire-spell kept flashing. The power he held within wanted escape. *Burn it, burn it all*, the fire in him was saying. *You can cleanse this entire place of its sickening, diseased vermin.*

Calm, the Dragon thought, *perhaps just a touch, then, just a little fire to let out—*

Sachiko felt a sharp pain in her head as the fire-spell begged the Dragon to kill.

The Japanese Serpent opened its jaws to throw flames—but Aldric slammed his other hand into the Dragon's throat. The glove vanished deep into the creature's gullet, as it gurgled in shock. With his other hand, Aldric pressed the Dragon's chest, trying to begin a deathspell.

The Serpent spit fire—but Aldric had found its torching organ at the middle of its throat, so when the flames blasted out, they came in an uncontrolled, twisted torrent upward, blowing the Japanese Dragon's own head off in a silver-gold explosion, and sending Aldric flying backward in the alley.

Aldric's gloved hand smoldered as he rolled, fighting the fire on his armor.

A small blast of metallic-tinted flames burst open in the alley.

Simon shoved his way forward through the crowd to the window where he could see Mamoru struggling with the tigers. The oversized Samurai still had his body armor, but the felines were huge and muscular, throwing him about, slamming his unprotected head against the walls.

Simon banged on the glass. It was too thick to break easily. The patrons shouted at him and tried to pull him out of the way. They wanted to see this.

"Simon!" Key called. "I've found a way!"

He was staring through the slender slats of wood that made up the walls, at a series of butterflies slipping in, apparently out of nowhere. "There's something in here," Key was yelling. "Just beyond this room."

Simon barely heard him. He was calling to Mamoru, who threw back one of the tigers, which stunned the others for a moment, as he looked at the glass, frantic for help. The bulky Mamoru had an instant of recognition. "Simon!" Then he looked horribly confused. *What was Simon doing in there?*

But one of the tigers rammed into him, clamping his arm in its jaws.

"Mamoru!" Simon called.

Key looked away from the passageway he was trying to pry open. "Mamoru?"

Just outside in the alley, the Japanese Dragon had erupted in fire.

Aldric fell back and watched as the Japanese Serpent's body reacted. Headless, it remained standing as fire flooded from its neck in a blinding glow, flames of gold and silver leaping high in the narrow alley.

As Taro and Sachiko stared in shock, the beast

stooped, its seven-foot frame only half-visible amid the blindingly bright fire. Tendrils of silver and gold shot out of its neck, and quickly wormed through the fire beside it, snatching up the Dragon's roaring head. In one swift action, the wiry limbs pulled the Serpent's head through the flames and quickly restored it atop the towering creature's body.

And now, despite its Buddhist philosophy, it was angry.

The Dragon of Japan was very, very angry.

Simon finally remembered he had his sword, but, crowded by onlookers, he could not get any space to swing it against the glass. Mamoru was still struggling with the tigers valiantly, but the huge man was no match for them.

People were pulling at Simon, not sure *what* he was doing with the blade, and he fought against them viciously, furious at himself for not being stronger. He toppled one man, who fell against the crowd, shoving them back. Simon could hear Key yelp in response, somewhere behind him, pushed back against the wall.

But Simon's sword struck the glass. Once. Twice. The strong steel nearly shattered the window.

"Are you out of your mind?" screamed a fat American man, grabbing Simon's arm. "There are tigers in there!"

"That's why I have to get in!" yelled Simon, and he punched the man in the gut.

Mamoru was being pounced on, the tiger's fangs scraping uselessly on his chestplate, but the weight of the beast was crushing the hapless Samurai.

Simon swung for the glass again.

Crack! Crack! Crash! The window shattered, surprising the tigers.

They looked over at Simon, rattled and ready to strike, mostly out of sheer surprise.

Panicked and screaming, the crowd surged backward, and the pressure of their bodies on the rear doorway forced the passageway open, and an escape route presented itself.

"Simon!" Key shouted, fighting the crush of people. "There's a way out!"

Too late. One of the tigers leapt for Simon through the broken window.

The crowd screamed louder.

Chapter 30

CORNERED BEAST

OUTSIDE THE BUILDING, ALDRIC faced a challenge of his own.

The crowd was in a panic now, in a mad rush away from the Japanese Dragon and its unnatural fire. But there were too many people at the mouth of the alley, and they clumped together, crushing each other, as Taro, Sachiko, and Aldric together met the Dragon's fury.

Use the firespell. Cleanse this place, screamed the power in Najikko's heart. *You can destroy everything right now.*

Control, control, his mind cried. *Power spent is power lost.*

Somehow, he held his true power in check, heeding his own voice.

Still the creature's eyes burned with rage. It reached back into the bright glowing tower of fire and brought out a silver ball of flame.

The beast grinned. The fireball flew fast out of its claw—a blur of silver—and hit just below Aldric's head, scorching his armor at the neck, his tunic torched partly away as the fire again grew over his damaged clothes. He rolled quickly, tamping it out, and righted himself painfully, sword ready.

The Dragon let loose a second fireball, its golden light smashing apart as Aldric cut it with his sword. Tatters of flame spattered the alleyway.

Silver fireballs cracked at Taro's armor. Orbs of gold fire knocked Sachiko to her knees. They broke harmlessly over her armor, but the force battered her to the ground.

The Japanese Dragon was playing.

For all his apparent strength and control, however, he was weakening from this battle, and at least one observer had noticed. High above the fight, in the nearby palace, Issindra was watching. "Don't show yourself to be so foolish," she said to the Japanese beast, though he couldn't possibly hear. "We all know you brought them here to kill me. And now what? They hurt you more than you expected, poor darling?" *You'll need to heal,* she thought coldly. *You'll run. You'll hide in the slums, or in the sewers, or the rivers or the lakes, but I'll find you. Oh, but don't leave like this. Kill some of them, dearest, I know you can do it.*

Quakes rumbled the palace, the earth pained by the presence of Dragons.

Meanwhile, near the raging battle inside the building, Simon had just created a minor catastrophe by unleashing the tiger.

The big cat leapt at him, but he had room to fall back, now that the crowd was streaming out of the observation room. The tiger's body lodged in the window, struggling to get at him, clawing, brushing against the glass shards in the frame, as Simon ran for the back door.

Key stood there, awed by the massive animal.

Simon had to drag him out.

"What about Mamoru?" cried Key.

But the tiger was on their trail now, rushing into the room, chasing Key and Simon down a narrow wooden hallway, where the dozens of onlookers had fled, screaming in the darkness, clambering for escape.

Simon and Key ran right into the thick of them, but were pushed back, to the rear of the throng. Jammed in, unable to escape, everyone turned to see the tiger creeping forward, with too many choices to feed on, too much prey.

It was joined by a second tiger.

"You wanted him out," said an angry American to Simon, "you got him."

And he shoved Simon toward the tiger.

Out on the street, the Japanese Dragon, grinning with imminent victory, lifted his flaming claws to his spiked and armored head, setting it alight. The creature rushed at Aldric, its head lowered. He slammed into a wall as Aldric leapt out of the way.

"I feel no anger," the Dragon hissed aloud. *Like surgery,* he thought, *no anger, just clean, simple cuts, slash slash slash—*

The Dragon swung its head again, its flaming crown of jags connecting with Aldric, jabbing him in his side and burning his armor.

"I feel no anger," the creature repeated.

Taro howled, rushing in with a war cry, landing several blows with his sword on the Serpent's back. In the same moment, Sachiko struck at the creature with her sword, flashing in terrible efficiency.

But the Tokyo Serpent would not be held back. It angled its fiery, spiky head once more for a deadly blow to Aldric.

"I FEEL NO ANGER!" he raged.

Suddenly, there came a rain of silver arrows out of the sky, thudding into the beast with an angry patter. Confused, the Dragon halted, looking skyward.

Akira fell out of the sky first, then Kisho and Toyo, the Samurai dangling from cables hooked to a high building above the alley, firing crossbows down upon the Japanese Dragon, the whisk and clatter of their shots joining with the sounds of the whipping fire. Aldric looked up and smiled, blood dripping from his lip.

Partly veiled in the drifting smoke, the Samurai continued their onslaught. The Dragon was badly injured and wailed. His sense of control was lost. Inside him, the firespell begged for use, his new blaze urging release.

In a show of defiance, the Creature leapt up high into the air, and grabbed hold of Akira's line just above him.

Now the Dragon began to swing the cable back and forth as he viciously cursed the warrior, hating himself for taking time to play with his prey. *Never feel delight in the kill,* he told himself. *Nature punishes joy. Just kill them, kill them.* He swung the cable into the fire further down the alley, tossing Akira into the blaze.

The Dragon then crawled up the cable and jumped away, scampering over the rooftops.

Kisho got off one parting shot, but missed.

Far below him, Aldric rose with Sachiko's help.

Suddenly, Akira emerged out of the blaze on the ground, armored head ducked down, his body tightened up, hands around his knees. He stood up with a raised fist, crazed, screaming with rage and pain.

Taro pulled him away from the burning alley.

Aldric turned. The silver-gold fire had left only one escape route, and that was clogged with fleeing people. With no other choice, Aldric and the Samurai joined the pushing crowd, and eventually broke free into the city.

The rush from the alley became a riot of movement on the avenue, as a much larger crowd grew terrified of the smoke and fire.

The Samurai stood and watched in shock as the entire boulevard became a giant, raging ocean of people, running and screaming, throwing themselves against each other, thundering over cars and bicycles. Rats scurried in the street below them, driven out by Dragonmagic, while the ground rumbled dangerously.

Aldric's first thought was of Simon—fear that he was in that mess, carried away or crushed in the stampede of humanity unrolling before him. But a strange feeling made him look upward, and he saw the Japanese Serpent high above on a rooftop, its silver-gold chest heaving with breath. The beast would need somewhere to hide and recover. But for now the Dragon stood examining—enjoying—his handiwork.

The Thing was too weak to spin out his true fire, his full strength, but there were other pleasures in life. Almost as enjoyable as a fire . . . was a good riot.

Down below, Aldric tapped Sachiko, and began moving away from the rushing crowd, trying to track the Dragon. Sachiko, Taro, and the other Samurai, now on the ground, hurried to follow him.

There was still time to kill this monster.

Outside, part of the building was burning, but inside, Simon and Key hadn't even smelled the smoke. They had other distractions.

Simon fell back, as the other tigers tracked into the hall, with gleaming eyes and low growls. Feeding time had come.

The horrified people trapped in the hallway pressed back, quieting their shouting, awed by the creeping tigers.

Key yelled and started to come forward, as Simon motioned him to stay back.

Suddenly, Mamoru burst into the hall. He kicked at the rear tiger, and it spun around, roaring, while the others were jostled and turned in a snarling commotion to stare down the Samurai.

Key started yelling at the animals, trying to distract them. Simon watched him, amazed, not sure if he should respect him or call him the stupidest person on earth.

The tigers turned at the noise, seeming confused.

The shocked and confused crowd hung back,

whispering in terror, trying not to provoke the tigers. Simon and Mamoru were the ones closest to the angry creatures, and they could see the whispers were only agitating the beasts.

Desperate, Key climbed up to the low ceiling and began monkeying his way across the wooden slats, trying to get above the tigers. But his hand accidentally struck some sort of a trapdoor in the ceiling and a dark passageway opened above his head!

Everyone looked up.

Butterflies fluttered out of the dark opening.

It seemed to be a channel used for releasing prisoners to the tigers.

"Up here," said Key, and he put out his hand, helping Simon up. Wooden slats along the wall gave Simon a foothold, but he was hampered by his backpack. He looked back to see one of the tigers leaping at Mamoru, pinning him against the wall.

Simon looked at Key, desperate for ideas, but the Japanese boy had slipped into the opening in the ceiling, and was up there muttering something about levers.

"We need some way to bait them," yelled Simon, crawling up behind him. "What are you wasting time with?"

But Key stared back at him, looking over from a series of wooden levers. Calmly, the boy hit one and

Simon heard a clicking below. Looking down through the trapdoor, he saw a wooden gate lowering in the middle of the hall.

Mamoru saw it, too, and twisted free of the tiger, slipping to safety just as the big gate slammed down, trapping the tigers in the hallway.

"I thought that was the right lever," Key said simply.

All right, thought Simon. *From now on you handle the technical stuff.*

The crowd below broke into cheers for Mamoru. He smiled at them in tired triumph.

"COME ON!" yelled Simon.

Key found another lever, opening a gateway for the crowd to get out into the street. No sooner did the crowd shuffle onward than the wooden gate was rattled by the tigers, eager to get free from their traps.

Mamoru leapt upward to the trapdoor. Simon helped pull him up.

"You need to think about a diet," Simon groaned.

"You need to think about bigger muscles," the Samurai retorted.

He pushed away Simon's hand. "The Tiger Dragon's men, they overtook me on the street and threw me in there. I got lost from Taro and the others."

"Look," whispered Key. Simon and Mamoru

moved up to join him. He was pointing at a doorway up a ramp, where dozens of butterflies were clinging. The insects were bright blue and unnaturally beautiful.

"The Serpent is there," whispered Mamoru. "With luck, we can surprise it."

He took Simon's sword from him and moved up the ramp toward the door.

Mamoru forced it open.

A Dragon stared back at them from the dark little bedroom.

It was the Black Dragon of Peking.

Amid the chaos of the Bombay streets in the hot afternoon sun, Aldric ran, leading the Samurai toward the building where the Dragon of Japan had crouched. Sachiko barrelled inside just behind them. It was an office building, with rows of desks and telephones, but no one was inside—the occupants were now rushing away madly in fear of fire.

Aldric rushed up a stairway cluttered with papers and debris, and the others followed close behind him. The second floor brought the stink of something rotten and an infestation of flies. The insects swirled around in great swarms, the glass-paneled offices absolutely filled with the pests.

Aldric batted them away, bowing his head to

avoid the buzzing insects, and made his way down a corridor to a giant balcony, where a terrible stench mingled with the scent of fire and ash.

Looking out across the city, he could find no sign of the Dragon on the nearby rooftops. But on his right, nearly abutting the office building, was the palace with the carved tigers. He could see that on its side, the second floor was covered with many boarded-up windows painted with Indian scenes. And perched at the ledge there, several pigeons wriggled in unison, their wings opening and closing nervously in *exactly* the same way. All of the birds were black.

"Serpent," said Taro.

But Aldric was already sidling along the office ledge. He leapt across the narrow space to the Tiger Palace, and his momentum brought his body through the boarded-up window, which cracked apart easily, the pigeons scattering, as he landed in a dark bedroom.

His eyes adjusted quickly, and suddenly he was staring at the Black Dragon of Peking.

"Knight," said the old Chinese Dragon. A canary chirped at his shoulder.

"Dad," said a voice, and Aldric looked past the beast to see Simon standing at an open door with Key and Mamoru.

There was only a split second for them to react to

the shock of seeing each other before the other Dragonhunters burst through the window behind Aldric.

"Kyoshi!" yelled Sachiko, but the boy froze, afraid to step toward her with the Black Dragon in his path.

Taro raised his crossbow, but a hand materialized out of the darkness and pushed it down. Surprised, he didn't resist. It was a female hand, and Simon watched in awe as a ripple of light swept up the woman's arm, until it revealed her completely, lifting away the invisibility magic that had fooled even his St. George eyes.

"Nobody fire a shot," said the woman.

It was Alaythia.

Chapter 31

⚜

ENEMIES AND ALLIES

OUTSIDE THE PALACE, THE fire began to die out, its gold and silver mysteries instantly becoming nothing more than rumor and legend.

There had been some damage, but the real problem was the rampant fear that followed. Authorities arriving on the scene couldn't understand how flames could take on the colors of a metal junkyard; they couldn't see how the blaze had started nor how it had gone out. In truth, the Japanese Serpent had brought an end to his own fire—no doubt because of the Tiger Dragon.

Simon thought he had it figured out: the two were meeting in a cease-fire. If the Japanese Dragon burned down Issindra's den, it would certainly enrage her. It was risky enough for the Japanese Creature to be prowling and spying around the Indian palace. You couldn't know what she would do in response . . .

With just about everybody chattering at once, Alaythia kept the Samurai at bay as they stared in anger and amazement at the Chinese Black Dragon. Aldric took Alaythia's hands, pulling her away from the Dragon, not saying a word. As Simon watched them, he felt a surge of joy that she was all right, but he was soon distracted by the Samurai, who were clamoring to know what was happening. Alaythia soon quieted them, but it took some time for events and histories to be sorted out.

A few black buzzards drawn to the Black Dragon skittered and flapped about the storage room as Alaythia began to speak. It was much as Simon had thought. Back in New England, she had indeed gotten a powerful idea from her encounter with that Dragon skull: it was possible to contact a Dragon's spirit.

While Aldric and Simon slept, she dug up an obscure Celtic passage in the Book of Saint George that she'd never understood before, a spell for speaking to a Dragon. Using it, she began calling to the Black Dragon in her mind, on a plane of communication not understood by ordinary men. And the Black Dragon had answered.

"How did you know you could trust him?" Simon asked her.

"I didn't," she admitted. "But in that moment, we had the same mind—thoughts and feelings passed between us, and that made me feel somehow . . . safer. I was desperate. I knew the Serpents could sense my emotions and track me. I had to trust someone."

She had agreed to meet him in the Atlantic Ocean, a neutral place away from the territories of other Serpents. But the Ice Serpent *had* tracked him, and attacked them at sea. They escaped on her rented boat after the Black Dragon's vessel was destroyed in the fight, leaving Simon and Aldric to pick up the trail.

Alaythia and the Black Dragon had found refuge on an island near India. The Dragon told her he had been following the growing tension between the Tiger Dragon and the Japanese Dragon, and he knew a major confrontation was looming.

Simon felt himself grow cold at the prospect of telling Alaythia the Japanese Dragon had tremendous new power, that he probably planned to unfurl his fire all over Asia, and perhaps create offspring with the same capability. Luckily, Simon was saved from this anxiety; Aldric told her instead, and as she stood there, shaken, he related their encounter with the Ice Dragon.

She already knew the Ice Serpent was involved from their encounter in the Atlantic Ocean. She was not sure of his plan, only that he and the Black

Dragon had grown to despise each other.

Simon began to feel they were all being manipulated by the icy Creature, one way or another. But the Hunters had to admit, they didn't know how the Ice Dragon fell into the mix with the other two Serpents. Unfortunately, Alaythia knew little more than they did. Oddly, as Alaythia recounted her story there in the palace, no one—not a Serpent nor one of its guardians—attacked the Dragonhunters.

"They do not know we are here," said the Black Dragon. "This is the lair of the Tiger Dragon, Issindra. She believes all that happens here is the result of her own magic. She does not suspect I am living within her very palace walls."

They were directly above a palace death chamber, one of the feeding rooms for the Tiger Dragon. Simon could see through knots in the wood below him, a bare floor covered in human bones, and coils of snakeskin. He suppressed a shiver.

"She isn't here," Simon observed.

"She is searching for the Japanese Serpent in the streets now," said the Black Dragon. "We're safe. She'll not find me when she returns."

Taro eyed the Black Dragon suspiciously. "Maybe she doesn't find you because she doesn't want to. Maybe you and she have made a bargain."

"For what?" Alaythia asked. "If he meant to kill

us, it'd be easy enough with one blast of fire right now."

"I want no more of warfare," said the Black Dragon wearily. "There shall be no more battles for me. I am old, I have no children, and the only legacy I leave behind will be this help I bring to you. I have thought long and hard on this. There will be a place in the history books for me, perhaps, in *your* stories. Otherwise, as you say, I am ashes and dust."

Akira would have none of it. "You turn your back on your own kind?"

"That is the way of my kind. Always in struggle and hatred. But, it seems, even a Dragon can get old enough to desire peace and quiet."

"Peace and quiet is not what awaits us," Akira snarled.

"No. The Japanese Dragon's newfound power will plague us all. He stole that secret from my very own den. I am too weak to use the scroll's firespell, but I consider it my fault that it still exists. I should have destroyed it. I will do what I can for you now. That is all I can do."

Taro tapped nervously at his scabbard. "The Tiger Dragon cannot sense you? Cannot find you here in her own domain?" he asked the Black Dragon.

"Not even at this moment," said Alaythia. "It's this magic that I'm seeking from him. The ability to cloak a presence. I've been learning it slowly."

Alaythia told them the Black Dragon had allowed the tiger feeding to go on because he knew Simon and the others could fend for themselves and would be drawn to him. The servants of the Tiger Dragon put on this kind of spectacle regularly, and the Black Dragon had always saved the victims by putting the tigers to sleep. Simon could tell the Samurai did not seem willing to believe any of this yet.

"You trust this Thing?" said Taro sharply.

"I trust *her*," said Aldric, nodding at Alaythia.

Simon looked at the Dragon. "He helped us before. He's not like the others."

"How good is this hiding-magic? *We* seemed to find him without trouble," said Akira unhappily, staring at the Chinese Creature.

"I had hopes you would." The Black Dragon returned their gazes meekly, his tiny canary wriggling at his shoulder. "If I tried anything else to draw your attentions, that might have been overheard, detected. It was the best I could do."

"I didn't want you to come," Alaythia admitted to Aldric. "Dragons in a turf war is too dangerous for anyone. I wanted to handle this myself. But you kept poking your nose around."

"Your fear for me is what's dangerous," Aldric said, "to yourself and to all of us."

Alaythia frowned at him. "Guess what. I get to decide what's dangerous for me. I even get to decide if I want to put *you* in danger or not."

"Can you tell if she's trustworthy?" Taro asked Sachiko. She looked Alaythia in the eye, measuring her truthfulness, and Simon sensed the raw power in the air, two Magicians together for the first time in decades. The hair on his arms tingled.

"I can't be sure," Sachiko said. "She's powerful. If she wanted to, she could've struck us hard the moment we entered."

The Samurai were on edge, but for the moment they were appeased. They kept their weapons at the ready, watchful of the Black Dragon. But in the end, Simon felt they realized everyone had the same goal: to eliminate these two powerful Serpents before they joined together and created an army from their off-spring.

"The riddle and the problem," said the Black Dragon, "is how to strike at the Serpents now."

"What do we know?" asked Aldric.

He and the others huddled around the small Black Dragon in the dark room. The Japanese hunters never took their eyes off him. Sidelined, the boys hung back together and listened without drawing attention to themselves. According to Alaythia and the Black Dragon, who had eavesdropped on the palace for some time, the Tiger Dragon was now planning to meet with the Japanese Serpent to discuss how territories all over the world might be carved up. But Serpents never trust each other, and the situation could easily erupt into conflict.

"The Tiger Dragon may have the upper hand," Alaythia pointed out. "Now is the time for her to produce offspring; she's been ready for this her whole life."

"Her advantage is the sleep chamber," the Black Dragon explained. "At the top of this palace. It is as old as India itself. The jungle still lives within its walls, growing unnaturally. The room is covered in vines and overgrown trees, alive since the time when Issindra's grandmothers ruled the continent. The chamber was built to kill rivals. Exactly how it works is her great secret. I have read in rare journals of the Old Age that the room was built of pillars of carved-stone snakes, and that any outside Dragon who enters becomes hypnotized by the sounds the stone Serpents make, and can never leave again."

"There are stories of this chamber in our writings," said Taro.

Aldric raised an eyebrow. Simon knew there was no such information in the Books of Saint George. "How is it," Taro went on, "the Japanese Serpent doesn't know of this?"

"He is arrogant," Sachiko conjectured. "He believes he can overcome her power."

The Black Dragon nodded at her. "Your attack seems to have delayed their meeting," he said, "which is all to the good. We were not prepared to take them on alone."

"We've got a lot more to tell you. We've been gathering what information we could about her," Alaythia said. She pulled from a mess of boxes a map of Bombay. Parts of it were circled. "Her businesses, her system of operations, her haunts."

Simon wanted to see, but the Hunters crowded the boys out.

Aldric looked at Alaythia. "Would she go to one of these places?"

"Possibly. She might be monitoring them, making sure they were untouched by the Japanese Dragon, that he wasn't trying something behind her back."

"We should try to find a television, get some news reports," offered Sachiko. "It'd be the fastest way to find her trail in the city. We can't let them reach each other. Their children would be more than we could ever handle."

"Too many Dragons in one place," the Black Dragon murmured, "will send nature into a rotten fine chaos. We will find the two of them soon."

• • •

Did they think I was stupid? thought Issindra, the Tiger Dragon. *Did the Serpentslayers really believe they could take me on inside my own territory, right in Bombay? Did the Japanese Dragon really think he could lead them to me, and allow the humans to do his dirty work?*

She knew they'd entered her city, but she was not aware the Dragonhunters remained in her home at that very instant, in a forgotten part of her Tiger Palace, hidden by the Black Dragon's magic so that she could not even sense them.

Issindra, appearing as a flawlessly beautiful woman, was working her way through the dreary crowd, hoping to catch the scent of the Japanese Dragon and follow his movements.

That crippled, germ-obsessed Japanese Serpent had sent the Dragonhunters right to my lair. She was no one's fool. *You don't get on the cover of* Vogue *by being nice to people. There is calculation involved. Strategy.*

Her anger called to her; she wanted to blast a throatful of fire across the street in rage, but she could do nothing. With several Dragons in the city, one could never be sure how the flames might behave, what disaster they might bring. The living fire was a constant burden.

As it was, Bombay was being rocked by earthquakes.

Storm clouds were gathering fast, a strange heat

engulfed the city, and fat white worms had emerged from cracks in the pavement, carpeting the streets.

A summit between Dragons was not going to be a tidy affair.

She cursed the fact that somewhere in Bombay the Ice Dragon was adding to all this, as he jotted in his book, observing, pointlessly.

But there were stranger undercurrents than she had ever before known. The nails of her claws had begun growing at a shocking rate, lengthening, twisting together, warping her beauty. She gnawed at them to try to control the growth. Meanwhile, her skin was shedding right off her, leaving ugly raw patches. Her lungs needed more air. It was as if there was some unusually powerful force involved in bringing the Japanese Creature closer to her. What would this mean, if she were to have children with him? She refused to think about it.

This changes nothing, she thought. *The Japanese Serpent and I are going to face each other in my own palace, and I am going to win him over to my way of thinking. His life will be forfeited. The Dragonslayers will take time to find us, and by then, they will be ensnared in my trap. I will burn them, one and all. And I will get what I want, down to the last detail.*

I am not going to spend the rest of my life alone and childless.

While the Tiger Dragon hunted the streets for her Japanese counterpart, and the Dragonhunters considered their options, the Ice Dragon stroked his goatee and surveyed the city from the wide window of a grand old Indian hotel.

He licked at his little friends in his mouth, toying with the beetles in a quiet tussle at the edge of his jaw. He needed that extra bit of comfort. The decadent warmth of Bombay was doing him no good.

The pillar, and the hotel room around him, slowly dripped with white and black ice, fingers of crystal filled with grime and insects.

The heat in his veins was no match for that eternal frost upon him. Particles of ice crackled under his feet. His teeth ached from the cold. His age had brought a sickness he was finding it harder to fight, a winter that came inside his bones, and iced his very blood.

If only he could warm himself, if only his fire were stronger.

He had expected the final battle to take place at Issindra's palace, but the Hunters had changed matters, unfortunately.

Using rats for spies, he had seen the street battle from a safe distance. And he had not been pleased. The confrontation had come too soon.

Still, it's all gone well enough. This is the perfect city for such a masterpiece of death to begin, he was thinking. *Death is everywhere here. Today a crowd panicked over the smallest of fires. Imagine the chaos that will be created with a massive firestorm, blazes stretching to all the overpopulated cities of the earth. The Tiger Dragon will soon learn this power from the Japanese, and her children shall know it as well. It is going to be historic.*

The plan had not been easy to pull together, he admitted to himself. *But it was all working: The two most powerful Serpents on earth would join forces today and begin a new tribe of Dragons, renewing the entire species. The Dragonhunters had only to follow the trail and they would be swept up in flames, perishing along with that lying Black Dragon.* And the Ice Serpent would be there to see it all, to put it into his book, and be remembered forever as a hero to his kind.

His book would be found. The first man to find it would fall under an unbreakable spell and, possessed by magic, immediately copy it as quickly as he could, in every possible language. His book would go out into the world, where it would kill billions.

Now that, ladies and gentlemen, is a way to die.

Simon had held his tongue long enough.

He and Key had been patient for over an hour in the dim storage room of the Tiger Dragon's Palace. The scent of death leaking from the tigers' feeding chamber was getting to him almost as much as the fact that everyone was ignoring him. Sitting on a crate amid the cedar-and-rot smells of the attic-like space, he glowered at the others.

They were still chattering about the location of the Dragons, staring at the little television set Alaythia had managed to steal from an empty office up above. The news showed two growing areas of paranormal activity. On the northern edge of Bombay, flocks of birds were dying, dropping out of the sky, and people were wracked by painful convulsions, choking for air, suffocating amid buildings whose glass windows rippled and warped unnaturally. Meanwhile, the southern edge of the city reported an intensely hot rainfall, and people falling ill with a disease that rapidly blackened their teeth and fingernails, and left them unable to walk. Disturbingly, the news showed oceans of people crawling on the ground, as if held down by unseen hands. Insects and worms swarmed everywhere, locusts darkening the stormy city in deafening black tornadoes.

"It's the harbor," said Aldric. "The Japanese Serpent is going to meet the Tiger Dragon there, one coming from the north, one from the south."

"It looks that way," Alaythia nodded. "The Japanese Serpent could be headed to the harbor to get out.

It wouldn't surprise me if he tried to leave on one of his own medical syndicate ships to ensure it gets away. From what we hear, there's always a lot of money tied up on those boats—they carry everything from expensive medicines to a cargo of dead bodies for medical experiments—and Issindra has been targeting them."

"Care to guess what *she* is thinking?" Aldric prompted her.

Sachiko interrupted, looking out the stormy window at the distant harbor. "She would want to continue the rendezvous. A union with the Tokyo Serpent has been her aim all along, hasn't it? Why would she give up now?"

Alaythia looked at her, considering the idea. "I think you're right. And the harbor might be a perfect place to join forces, symbolically. It's where the Japanese Serpent has been invading her territory. Why not begin their truce in a place of strife?"

Taro seemed to affirm this in Japanese, and Simon saw many of the others nodding. Simon couldn't believe it, shaking his head, wanting to disagree.

Alaythia stepped beside Aldric, pointing to a spot in the harbor on the giant city map. "It's obvious they'll end up somewhere along here in the harbor. We have to cut them down right there, fast, eliminate them. Crush them before they proliferate. One assault, one result."

Taro raised an eyebrow to Aldric. "You were afraid for *her* safety?"

Akira pushed Aldric aside to get a look at the map. "What's the best way to get there?"

Simon had had enough.

"This is a *trap*," he said loudly. "This entire palace is a trap for anyone who comes inside it. The Tiger Dragon will *not* want to go into a difficult battle out there when she can bring her enemy *here* and get rid of him on her own turf, in her sleep chamber. She'll find a way to bring him to the palace."

Key looked like he wanted to hide.

"So what would you have us do?" Taro asked, point-blank. Simon hid his surprise that the Samurai was even interested.

"We can't *all* go out there," said Simon, pointing to the map, the harbor. "There's two of them, and they'd have us all at once, out in the open."

"Simon, if we gamble on them coming here, and they don't, we've lost our chance," said Aldric, "and it'll be very hard to bring down two Dragons in that sleep chamber of hers. It's a closed space, full of traps. We'd get sacked."

"Not if we let her take down the Japanese Dragon," Simon protested. "Then we face only one Dragon, and we can bait her into leaving the chamber. Then we get her."

Alaythia looked at Simon. "If we spend all of our energy preparing for them here, we could miss an opportunity to get them while they're distracted fighting each other. Having all of us out there now gives us better odds of surviving. You get what we're saying, don't you?"

"It's crazy to go where *they* would want us," Simon responded. "Right in the middle of a gathering of two Dragons— or worse: a crossfire. We'd be trying to work with two battle groups against two Dragons. At least we have a confined space here, Dad."

"Simon, in Tokyo, you thought we didn't know where to look for the beast, but we did. Things are not always as they seem. All the training in the world is nothing next to experience."

"You're wrong. The way to do this, is to put them where *we* want *them*. The Tiger Dragon will take care of the Japanese Serpent, and then we take on the Tiger Dragon, right here, where the Dragon would never suspect an attack. We'd start a fire, in her own palace, just before sundown. She'd leave her chamber, and we'd take her. She'd be cornered."

The Chinese Black Dragon looked at Aldric, his old eyes communicating agreement.

"You would leave the Japanese vermin to her, instead of us?" said Taro. "I can't say that I like this."

Alaythia shook her head. "Simon, you're counting

on a lot of things going right . . . but if we miss our chance at the harbor, the death they'd cause together could be devastating . . . What other choice do we have here?"

"Simon's choice. It's a good one," Key interjected. Simon looked at him, grateful, knowing how hard it was for him to speak up. No one seemed to know how to take this sudden alliance.

"Enough talk from children," rumbled Akira, in a voice that ended the matter. "We need to move on the harbor. We finalize our attack plan now."

In agreement, the Hunters drew closer, studying the map of Bombay as Key looked at Simon, frustrated. But Simon was looking at the Black Dragon, and all three of them realized there was another way of tackling the problem.

Chapter 32

꛰

WHERE THERE'S SMOKE

THESE ARE THE PIECES, thought the Ice Dragon, picking gnats from his frosty goatee and watching India quiver far below his hotel window. *And they are all in place now.* He had seen the two centers of destruction outside slowly moving toward each other at the harbor. *The Japanese Serpent is headed to the rendezvous. So is the Tiger Dragon. Look at the madness they create in their wake. And soon the Dragonhunters will be on their way as well.*

I need only to watch the fireworks, he thought. He laughed and snorted, and wanted to cry at the beauty of it.

This is the beginning of the end.

● ● ●

But another brilliant mind was at work in Bombay this evening.

Simon St. George had a plan of his own. His father had given him a mission, along with Key, and it was one of extraordinary importance. The mission was: *Stay out of the way.* He and Key were to stand watch with Mamoru and the Black Dragon, who insisted he could protect the boys in the event of an emergency. If they sighted anything unexpected, they were to report it, calling the others on their cell phones.

Now, that's excitement, thought Simon in frustration.

They were in some kind of factory, closed for the night or perhaps recently shut down, in a room filled with heavy machinery parts. Mamoru had found it, safely out of the way should the Tiger Dragon return home, but with a clear view of the entrance to her palace.

Simon watched from a window. The sun was abandoning India, and the bustling city was cast in gray from the storm clouds.

Aldric had taken Alaythia—he refused to fight without her—and Mamoru resentfully landed the job of watching the boys and the old Dragon. The big Samurai pinched the flab under his own chin thoughtfully, and eyed the Black Dragon with distrust.

"Mamoru, don't you think it'd be smarter if you were with them?" asked Key, staring out the open window. "They only left you here 'cause they still don't trust Ming Song." He looked over at the Black Dragon.

Simon listened, pleased, but he didn't take his eyes off the window.

"You're starting trouble again," Mamoru rumbled. "You listen too much to Simon. Simon is very bad. You know this. Why do you want to be trouble?"

This cowed Key a bit, but he didn't give up. "It's just a fact," he said simply. "Your skills are needed out there, aren't they? *Do* you trust him?"

"I don't know," said Mamoru, after a second's thought. "To me, he just looks like a little man . . ."

"He doesn't look much different as a Dragon."

"Really?"

"Yes."

The Black Dragon moved slowly to the window. He nudged Simon to take note of several guards at the Tiger Palace who were staring curiously up at them. The Black Dragon tapped his smallish claws together, *click, click, click*, and as they sparked, the guards were zapped by jolts of electricity from the lamppost they leaned against.

Mamoru watched carefully. To him, the Black Dragon looked more harmless than ever, an old Chinese man, chortling, amused. But there was something in his laugh that remained Dragonlike, and Mamoru couldn't see past it.

"There is still the matter of the Ice Serpent." Mamoru thought out loud. "We have not accounted for him, and what he might do."

Key looked disappointed, thinking. He brought out a netsuke, the ivory carving of the good Dragon, for emphasis, and Mamoru seemed moved by it, but only for an instant.

"Come on, let's not be totally stupid," Simon added. "We're safe. Hidden. We aren't going anywhere. Meanwhile, my dad could be killed out there. You could make the difference."

Mamoru glared at Simon. "What's the English word for 'talks too much'?"

"What's the Japanese word for 'pig-headed'?"

Mamoru would not continue the debate, settling into a rusty chair, resting his head on one hand, and ignoring the boys' arguments completely. Key continued talking, always respectful, and his heart was in the right place, but Simon could see this tactic was going nowhere. He quietly crossed to the back of the room, picked up a large piece of some unknown machine, and conked Mamoru over the head with it.

His eyes on the Black Dragon at the window, Mamoru never saw what hit him. He fell forward from his chair with a grim drumroll.

"Sorry, Key," Simon said. "Sometimes talking goes nowhere."

"I knew what you'd do. I was keeping him distracted," Key answered, but his eyes were filled with shock now that he'd actually seen it happen. He looked down guiltily at Mamoru, the babyfaced Samurai unconscious on the floor.

Simon made sure he was out cold, and then he turned to the Black Dragon. "Well. You're the new babysitter."

Elsewhere in the city, the other Hunters were rushing to the harbor, to try to stop a deadly rendezvous.

They had rented a weathered but sturdy off-road vehicle, and were doing their best to get to the harbor through the growing storm. Flooded streets were only one concern. Parts of the road cracked and lifted as Taro sped around the earthquake damage. They were at least half a city away from the harbor, but the supernatural tremors from the Serpents were reaching out, rippling through Bombay and even beyond.

In the backseat of the vehicle, Aldric and Alaythia kept their eyes on each other but neither said a word. It was the eyes of the other woman behind him that bothered Aldric. He knew what was on her mind. With the others preparing their weapons all around him, he looked back to Sachiko with what he hoped was a confident gaze.

"You can trust the old Dragon with your son," he

told her. "If Alaythia says he's honorable, then he is. And Mamoru will protect him as his own, I'm sure. He won't be alone."

"I left him," said Sachiko, "with a Dragon." She smiled, and the daggers shooting from her eyes were as sharp as anything carried by the Samurai. *You had better be sure of yourself.*

Issindra, the Tiger Dragon, let her tiger-striped tail swish back and forth. She was watching the Japanese cargo ship prepare to survive the storm. Facing a hard rain, crews worked desperately to load the last few crates from the dock, even as many of the men collapsed from a strange sickness. The approaching grayish clouds were turning black, like ink poured into milk. The Tiger Dragon licked her skin with feline arrogance. Her eyes tore into the darkness, waiting for the Dragon of Japan to move into her sights . . .

Come get your ship, she thought. *Come see who's waiting, dearest.*

The Japanese Dragon, appearing in his veiled form as a human doctor, was settled wearily into the back of a yellow-topped black taxi, but the driver had just stepped into the rainy street to push crawling beggars out of the way.

The Japanese Serpent watched as the cabdriver

fell to the watery road, succumbing to the terrible disease that had brought down everyone else on the road in front of him.

Nuisance, a sorry flaw in our design, thought the Dragon. *I've no control over this magic; it just pours out of me like a leaking faucet. . . .*

The Serpent had spent the past hours limping through the city's vast slums and neighborhoods, waiting for his wounds to heal. He had hoped for an easy, undisturbed passage to the cargo ship, where he could regain his strength quietly, but there was no escaping the supernatural madness gripping Bombay. He curled his mouth in disgust at the torrent of locusts swooping from above, the bugs pockmarking the windshield, and tried to restore himself to a calm, stoic resolve. *India is vile as death itself*, he thought, for he could see the tiny insects, bacteria, and viruses floating in the air, squirming over the buildings, living on human skin.

The world was a filthy toilet, and people lived in it without knowing.

He got out and left the car, ignoring the pathetic people crying for help and the cold dirty water rising around him. He realized his own body was being affected by his proximity to the Tiger Dragon. The bacteria on his own skin had grown, the tiny creatures now visible. Stunned, he watched the swarm of liquid blobs drip onto his metal leg. Shaking them off, he became aware that his vision was blurring. For several revolting moments, he could only see himself as a human. And the heat in his body was rising and falling erratically. He was used to supernatural ripples—but not ones that affected him.

He looked up beyond the human refuse ahead, and wondered what the buildings would look like wrapped in the coils of his beautiful silver-and-gold fires, with the embers of a dead Indian Tiger Dragon drifting across the sky. . . .

A bloated city burned clean and made sterile by the perfect efficiency of the flame.

Use me, his power beckoned. *You do have the strength. See what your fire can truly do.*

Chapter 33

⚜

NO SUICIDE MISSIONS

" E'RE GOING INTO THE palace. But we're not going in there to die," Simon told Key, his voice echoing in the machine shop. "You're going to need this."

He opened his backpack, revealing the black armor pieces he'd found in Key's room, along with a long silver dagger from the ship. The Black Dragon seemed to recoil ever so slightly from the sight of the weapons, tucking his fur-lined tail behind his back.

Key stared at the forbidden armor, looking both pleased and worried. "You carried that for me, all this time?"

"Didn't have room for the helmet," said Simon. "I wanted to give it to you before, with the tigers, but I didn't have time."

Armored under their coats, the three left Mamoru still restfully unconscious and headed for Issindra's domain. There they planned to bait her and catch her with her own trap . . . if they could figure out what that was. Simon tried to turn the worry in his stomach into excitement.

Once inside the Tiger Palace, Simon and Key were led by the Black Dragon past the floors of miserable workers, rows of them at sewing machines, who looked up at them with dull, spellbound eyes. Huge tiger's-eye sculptures clicked and rumbled above them. The boys kept moving, their St. George blood immune to the palace's power, but their fear was growing the deeper they went into the Serpent's domain.

And for good reason. Roaming guards approached, alert and suspicious, threatening to stop them. The Dragon, however, was a powerful ally, bewitching the guards to let them pass unhindered. Key let out a worried breath as they moved onward without a word.

It was at the sixth floor, after passing so many of the laborers, that Simon decided he couldn't stand to see any more suffering.

"We have to free these people," he said, his attention caught on a skinny young girl who was pulling a cart loaded with heavy rolls of fabric.

"How?" said Key.

"It will delay us," the Black Dragon cautioned.

"Are you drawing strength from this, too?" Simon accused him. "We have to take away the Dragon's strength. It's good to get her off-guard, but we need to throw her off-balance. We have to rob her of the thing that makes this place home to her."

"Can you break her magic?" Key asked the Dragon.

The Black Dragon moved into the workroom. He eyed the supervisor, a fat, slow-witted woman who approached with a pompous air. The Dragon raised his finger, and pointed at the door, and to Simon's surprise, the woman strode directly past them and out, her expression glazed by his sorcery.

Then the Dragon hobbled down past the rows of textile machines and workers, to the great tiger's-eye sculpture clicking at the back of the room. The eye burned down on all the workers, made them accept any pay, any job, any humiliation.

With a shaking hand, the Dragon swung his cane at the sculpture, but his strength alone was not enough. Seeing this, the boys ran up, hammering at the eye with their weapons, their blows ringing, clanging, until the cracks grew. The sculpture fell from the wall, rolling off to shatter into pieces; the sound a sweet symphony of destruction. In breaking the sculpture, they'd broken the spell.

The factory ground to a halt.

"Tell them the work ends early today," the Black Dragon told a foreman. In a daze, the foreman followed the Black Dragon's instructions. "Tell them to come back to the palace tomorrow," he said. "There will be gold for them to take. And silver. Overdue payments."

"Just what's going on here?" said a rumbling voice, and in came the security chief, a burly, blue-turbaned man with a killer's stare. His hate was no work of Dragon magic. He'd taken the job because he liked to hurt people, pure and simple. He moved to block the exit.

The Black Dragon raised his finger.

"Don't point at me, you old Chinese imbecile," the man barked. "I asked you a question. Do you speak English? What are you doing here?"

Key whispered to Simon, "He's too big. Make him fall, use his own weight to pull him down." Taking the cue, Simon strode up to the security chief and kicked him in the leg, snarling, "Why don't you just shut up and get out of our way!"

When the chief lunged at him, Simon tripped him, and the man tumbled past him into the wall and banged his head, knocking himself unconscious. Key nodded with satisfaction, as if finished with an algebra problem.

The Black Dragon lifted the security chief's walkie-talkie, and, mimicking his voice, he told the remaining guards to flee the building, go home, evacuate the workers, there was a toxic gas leak, nothing could contain it. The workers in the room stared in confusion at the old Chinese man.

He bowed and motioned to the door.

The palace was liberated. Workers flooded out of the building, like zombies restored to life but not yet believing it. They trailed out in the strengthening storm, the sky seemingly ready to collapse on them, the earth bucking as if to free itself from bonds of its own.

Inside, the sight of the chains in the factory made Simon sick.

He lifted the binds, small enough for children to wear. "Why do you do this? Why is your kind like this?" he said to the Black Dragon.

"That . . . is a simple question," said the old Serpent. "We feed on the pain. The riddle of it is why we are here at all. Why should nature seek to bring something like me . . . to life? But, then, is there not a reason for all things?"

"Do you have an answer?" pressed Simon. "'Cause I don't."

"No one will ever solve it," the Black Dragon said, holding his gaze. "But if there were no evil in humankind for the Dragon to feed upon, the Dragon would die out. Why is *your* kind like this?"

"People are evil. I told you, I don't like thinking about it." Simon sighed, and moved to the door.

"Ah," said the Black Dragon. "To think of such things makes us old. But wiser. To question makes you stronger."

"Then *you* think about it," said Simon, heading out. "It makes me feel weaker. I don't want to think about how sick the world is."

"Then truly evil has no purpose."

Mamoru had awoken in the parts factory with an almost instantaneous understanding of what had happened. He had been awake enough to have heard the voices of the boys and understand they were plotting something.

In disbelief that Key could do this to him, and cursing Simon St. George, Mamoru knew the Black Dragon could not possibly have dealt him the knockout blow. He'd watched its every move.

Simon had done it, he was certain.

Not sure where he'd find the boys, Mamoru immediately began walking to the harbor, where he suspected they were trying to get into the battle. He reached in his pocket for cab fare and found another object, the netsuke of the good Dragon, the ivory meant to reassure him, but it only made him angrier.

Mamoru alone had been left to protect the children. It was his only task. He knew Sachiko would be furious.

Facing the worsening storm, and cursing himself for being stupid, he hurried through the throngs of people toward a taxicab.

Simon, Key, and the Black Dragon had reached the top floor of the palace.

Before them were the giant wooden doors of the Tiger Dragon's bedchamber.

Simon hesitated. "You aren't afraid of what's in here, are you?"

The Black Dragon stared up at the towering doors. "I would be of little help if I stayed out here beyond the fray. I will trust that the legends exaggerated her powers and her trickeries."

Simon flung open the doors, and a huge open room with enormous windows, a pavilion atop the palace, greeted them. Jungle trees were rooted beneath the stone floor, and vines wrapped around snake-figure columns, while torches made for dim light. Exotic birds called from somewhere in the sinister greenery. The Black Dragon's canary hid itself in its master's fur. Simon could understand its fear. The entire room seemed to shiver and shudder as the dark leaves swayed in the hot storm winds, hiding untold threats.

Simon moved into the room.

Chanting, the Black Dragon forced the torchlight to grow stronger, and the boys found a panel in the floor, through which they could stare down at Issindra's prized animals.

The cages were very narrow. Tigers circled the tight quarters, restless, unaware of Simon and Key above. A thick glass shield engraved with Dragon-runes topped the cages. The runes slid around, words gliding over words, enchanted.

"Rune-writing," said Key, pointing to the glass top on the first cage. "It's meant to keep fires contained. This trap wasn't made for tigers—it was made for a Dragon."

"So this is how the Tiger Dragon will trap the Japanese Dragon," said Simon, taking it in.

"This is what I'm thinking."

"This is how she will *hold* him," said the Black Dragon. "But to *trap* him there must be something else . . . a spellchant, hypnosis. The room itself may be rife with ancient power. Perhaps she activates the sculpted snakes there along the walls, as the legends say."

The old creature looked down on the feline zoo. "The tiger is a solitary animal, it meets with others only to mate," said the Black Dragon slowly. "She has followed her enemy so long she loves him. Not unheard of, in Serpents or in humans. That's what the writing here really is. It is a sleepspell for a Dragon, to bring him here and keep him."

Not just the floor below them, but the bedchamber as well, was riddled with trapdoors and cages. The entire palace was filled with snares.

"*We* can use these traps, too," said Key. "One at a time. This is what I was hoping for. We let the Tiger Dragon trap the Japanese, and then we lock her in as well. They'll both try to burn their way out, and when they're out of energy—you send down your blackfire and finish them. Your fire *will* kill them, right?"

The Black Dragon thought for a minute, his dark fur rippling from the night winds, and then he nodded, grim. "There's good chances the Tiger Dragon never anticipated these traps would be used against her very own magic. It could work. It will be safer than any of you trying to use a deathspell."

"But we know the spell if we need it," said Key, "we studied all the Indian deathspells before we arrived here." The Black Dragon's eyes wrinkled in worry that it should come to hand-to-hand combat. "We memorized the Ice Serpent's as well, just in case, and the Dragon of Japan we've been ready to fight for a long time," Key added.

"We still need to get the Tiger Serpent *in* the

cage," noted the Dragon.

"You say she loves him?" scoffed Simon, looking at the traps. "You are very strange animals."

"As are you," said the Black Dragon. "Indeed, the Dragonkind loves human strangeness."

"Well, I try not to think about human strangeness very much."

The Black Dragon looked at him quizzically. "What has happened to you, Simon? You were always the questioner. Now you do not question things?"

Simon studied the traps. "I just want to know where to go and what the mission is. Let's get going. What do we need to do?"

"But do you ever wonder what the mission is for?"

"It just tires you out, questioning everything all the time. Takes too much."

The old Dragon looked disturbed. "The good soldier."

"That's right. What's wrong with that?"

"A soldier sees only targets. You are becoming like your father."

Simon shrugged him off, as he and Key looked down on the caged tigers anxiously. Where to begin. . . .

"Well, staring at it all night is not going to get the job done and finished," said the Black Dragon, leaning against the wall, smoking his long pipe. "We need all the trappings we can get. The tigers must come out, so the Dragons can come in."

"Do we *know* this will hold her?" wondered Simon aloud, and he peered closer at the glass. The tiger below sensed him, and looked up, leaping to scratch the glass. Key yelped and fell back.

"No guarantees," said the Black Dragon.

"I'll settle for some good odds," said Simon.

"Good odds, I think not," mused the Black Dragon, circling his pipe in the air. "But decent odds."

"What did I just say? I don't like 'decent,'" said Simon. "I want good. I want great."

"You want lies," smiled the Dragon.

"If that's the best you can do."

The Dragon blew away smoke and looked directly at him. "It's perfect."

The Dragonhunters had gotten as close as they could to the harbor, but rising tides had swamped the street. They leapt one by one from their car to a high, narrow wall beside a building. From here, Sachiko got a sobering look at the size of the growing storm, and the lightning menacing the Tiger Dragon's palace.

"They're out of there now. The boys are safe," Aldric said, worried himself.

"I know," she replied with a concerned smile, and,

in a consoling gesture that surprised Aldric, she reached out and gripped his arm. "They're all right."

Behind them, getting to the narrow wall last in line, Taro watched her. "She gives *him* comfort," his low voice rumbled, "very kind of her."

Sachiko was visibly unsettled. Alaythia seemed to want to say something in her defense, but at a loss, she began moving along the pathway.

Akira looked back at Taro. "You see torment in the smallest of things," he said. "Your house is strong . . . and what all of us envy."

Taro looked stunned.

"You should have stayed with the boy," Akira warned. "None of us have as much to lose."

Chapter 34

DRAGONTRAPPING

IN THE TIGER DRAGON'S PALACE chamber, a dangerous plan was being prepared.

"I'm trusting you that this will work," Simon was saying. "I never heard of it before. You can talk to each other in your heads—actually *in* your heads?"

"Not talk," said the Dragon. "Crysounds. Pleading noises. Like whalesong."

"They'll think you're held captive here. They'll know where it comes from?"

"Yes."

"They'll think the Hunters are harming you."

"They should. Yes. A thousand times, yes," the old Dragon said, irritably.

Key piped in. "Then we just stay calm. We bait

them to leave the harbor, and all we have to do is wait for them here."

"And then we have to *destroy* them," said Simon. For a moment, he was disturbed at the enormity of the task, but he thought of the fire roiling beneath Japan, of the chaos here in Bombay, and he regained his resolve. "Let's hope the trap works. Let's hope the Tiger Dragon's already thought of everything *for* us."

Key looked at him, unsure.

At the same time, his black-and-white frame shivering, the Ice Serpent was finally getting comfortable in a luxurious Land Rover, a taxicab he had gotten tailormade to his needs while in Bombay, the entire rear section darkened by Indian curtains and padded absurdly with high cushions for his old bones.

And then the noises started inside his brain.

The Ice Serpent heard the distress call of the Chinese Black Dragon deep in his wintery brain, a moaning in the oldest of Dragontongues. This was most unusual. In fact, to his knowledge, it had never happened before. Not in hundreds of years. Dragons hate each other. Even under the threat of death, they do not ask each other for help, not like this, not out of weakness.

This was a whole new chapter for him, an extraordinary development.

The low, echoing cry was unmistakable to Serpentine ears; he knew the Japanese Dragon would hear it, and the Tiger Serpent as well.

Indeed, Issindra had heard the call, as she waited in the harbor. *The Hunters have found the Chinese Black Dragon in the Palace. Hiding in my shadow, seeking protection without my even knowing. What cleverness. So the Hunters have found him there, instead of me. They have invaded. They must be holding him in the palace at this precise moment.*

Could she return there? Right into the hands of the Hunters? Her mind spun with possibilities. Leaning against the columns of an old temple, watching the harbor shudder from turmoil, she let the steaming rain run down her Serpentine skin.

Let them all die there, she thought. This was the opportunity she'd sought. A perfect bait.

Striding a narrow alley, knee-deep in filthy brown water, the Serpent of Japan heard the pleading, moaning song of the Black Dragon and did not know what to make of it. In the palace. In her palace?

What could it mean?

Simon and Key opened the doors on all the tiger traps. The levers were swung. The doors rolled open. And the tigers broke free, collected into a single large area used, no doubt, for the Tiger Dragon to watch her servants being eaten alive.

The tigers snarled and scratched at each other, none too pleased at having to share their space with others.

"This is why she keeps them separate," said Simon.

"Let's hope they stay put," said Key.

They moved to the window, where the Black Dragon stood watching the storm, waiting for the Tiger Serpent's return.

"Let's hope she gets here first," said Simon. "We have to let her take down the Japanese one herself, then we attack and throw her into one of these traps. She won't suspect us till it's too late."

"There is still the Ice Serpent, somewhere," said the Black Dragon. "Old crooked thing, in love with death, looking for his place in history. He will be mine to deal with. I owe him." He rubbed an old wound at his shoulder, growling deeply, and Simon remembered that, despite everything, the creature came from a dark, vengeful species.

"Everything will tumble into place."

"Oh, it won't happen like that," said the Black Dragon.

Simon frowned. "Suddenly you can see the future?"

"The part of it I can see does not go like your plan," said the Black Dragon.

"Lie to me."

"It's going to go perfect."

In a hammering downpour, the Japanese Serpent faced the Tiger Dragon, each of them sliding their tails back and forth across the watery harbor street. He had at last arrived at his ship, and there she was, waiting. The Serpentine female stood a full two feet taller, but she crouched respectfully, twisting her neck to peer up at him.

He listened to her low, scintillating voice, filled with promise and not a whiff of betrayal. "Set your fear of treachery aside and listen," she told him. "Listen to the promise of real power without either of us having to die. Listen to the truce I offer, and we shall make it reality. The Hunters have changed nothing. We can still form an alliance and pull from the wreckage a shining prize. How would you like to join me in being the only two Serpents on earth who could deliver the great traitor himself, the Black Dragon of Peking, dead in ashes to the rest of our race?"

And listen the Japanese Dragon did.

"He is mine," she lied. "Captive. Imprisoned."

Her adversary sized her up. "What is my part in this?"

"Your ship will leave port untouched," she promised. "The first of hundreds that will represent our empire. It begins here. Come with me to the palace and join me in killing the Black Dragon. You can see my sincerity; you can read it in my eyes. I have a vision for us—a future that will enrich us both. This unity, it doesn't have to be a dream."

The Japanese Dragon ground his teeth, regarding the Tiger Serpent with distaste, deeply suspicious of her docile behavior. Her snakeskin was topped with fur, and that, he knew, hides a whole slew of parasites. The street quivered under them as people in the distance screamed; the Hunters would soon be on the way. A decision needed to be made—join with her, attack, or retreat.

He felt hot, nauseous, as if a volcanic ocean was going to tear out of him, like nothing ever before. She was agitating the power he held within.

Nearby, his cargo ship was preparing to leave the dock. "Don't leave with it. Don't let the Hunters force you away," said the Tiger Dragon. The Japanese Serpent felt something new in the air, saw an unfamiliar element in her eyes. Was it desire? Was that possible?

"We can begin our partnership properly at the palace," she purred.

Equilibrium, he thought, as strange feelings surged

inside him, disgust and attraction in equal parts. He wanted to burn the Tiger Creature, knowing it would bring him the greatest joy. But at the same time, he wanted to keep her, to preserve her, perhaps in formaldehyde. In his head he calculated the difficulty of fixing the fire scars on her skin, wondering, *could plastic surgery work well on Dragonflesh? Fascinating challenge.*

He scarcely noticed the arrival of the Hunters.

The Tiger Dragon saw them first, as they scattered to take up firing positions at some buildings several yards away. They would have difficulty aiming in the storm, but she was taking no chances.

"The end, or the beginning—your choice," she hissed, and darted away across the water-glinting street into the flooded boulevard beyond. *He will follow,* she thought. *I have him.*

The Japanese Serpent looked back hatefully at the Hunters as their arrows split the rain water. "Now is not the time," he spat, and turned to follow the Tiger Serpent. *Such muck as this city has,* he thought, *cannot be worth enduring for her.* But he continued his pursuit, spellcasting in the direction of the Hunters to delay them. He'd leave them a nasty surprise.

Further ahead, the Tiger Dragon could feel his approach behind her. *Dragons and Dragonhunters. Too hard to deal with all at once,* she thought. *But there would be time enough to deal with each, one at a time. Could the*

Black Dragon already be dead? Did the Hunters leave him to rot in my own palace?

In the lead, ahead of the other Hunters, Aldric was watching the Japanese Serpent sprint away as the huge cargo ship rolled up on the rising tide, pushed forward by Dragonmagic. The ship now blocked Aldric, cutting off his view of the Creatures.

"Watch out!" cried Taro. The massive ship lodged against a building with a metallic groan and a tumbling and splashing of fallen bricks. Crates fell from the side of its deck, cracking open, tumbling dead bodies out everywhere.

Aldric waded away, trying to reach another alley and a way to pursue the Serpents. But the water rose up in the street before him, walling it off in a giant liquid sheet, impassable.

He started to move forward, to press himself through the liquid wall, but the water on the street began whipping around his legs with a whirlpool motion, as if there were hands gripping him, pulling him down by Dragonmagic.

He struggled, falling, trying to keep his head out of water, as Alaythia helped him up. Behind her, in the flashes of lightning, Aldric could see the wading Samurai also fending off the aquatic power of the Dragon, slashing at the water uselessly as it tried to pull them under.

"This magic can't last—the Thing is gone from here!" Aldric shouted over the rain.

But Alaythia had her eyes closed. So did Sachiko, and as they began spellchanting, the flood waters around the Dragonhunters began to recede.

Success. The two women opened their eyes.

"The storm's moving!" Toyo shouted, pointing.

Aldric turned. The monsoon was racing over the city, clouds split down the middle, yellow and black on one side, orange and black on the other, all flowing toward . . .

"The palace," Aldric said. "They're going to the palace."

Then he spied the arrival of a sputtering, waterlogged taxi from a side street, and Mamoru emerged from the back in confusion.

"Where are the boys?" cried Sachiko.

But Aldric knew. His boy was following his *own* plan.

The Tiger Palace was empty.

Issindra emerged into her bedchamber, and knew instantly something was wrong. There were no guards waiting for her. No servants lying dead under a tiger's claws. And no Black Dragon, captive or dead.

The Tiger Dragon closed her eyes, using her sorcery to search from room to room. Something trembled in the air, a veiled force that now weakened under her new intensity.

She turned as the Japanese Serpent stepped into the room behind her. Was *that* what she had felt?

"A jungle," he observed, "within your very walls. How . . . unique." His gold-silver head recoiled, as he tried to disguise his repulsion.

The beetles and insects inhabiting the plants and vines began to ooze out of the floor, trickling over Simon's hand as he hid in the darkness at the back of the chamber. Key winced as a fat roach dropped onto his head.

The Tiger Dragon gave a long-fanged grin. "This needn't be your home," she told her rival. "I know of your distaste for organisms. You may remain in Japan." Her wispy wings rattled in the wind, and she again bowed her head in respect. "With the wealth we create together, you may have as many homes as you like, wherever you wish."

"And the other Serpents will simply allow us to take their territories?"

The Tiger Dragon purred. "They will have no choice but obedience—or death. You know our bloodlines. They will fear us above all. They will *want* to serve us."

The Japanese Serpent stared back at her with suspicion and doubt. "Yes, we will deliver them their hated enemy—and where *is* the Black Dragon of

Peking, my sweet?" The word was a taunt, and made his mouth feel unclean.

"All in good time," she answered, sending her tigerlike tail sliding toward him. *First things first*, she thought. *One threat at a time.* "I must have confidence we are in this together."

He moved his own snakelike tail away from her instinctively. *Germs*, he thought. *Vileness.* "And just how will this union hold, when so many other Serpent alliances have failed?"

"It will hold," she answered, "because we will cement our agreement . . ." Her tail forcefully encoiled around his. ". . . As no one has before."

Equilibrium. He could feel heat rising in him.

Her eyes held his gaze. "Our children will keep us together, a Serpentine army of our own."

The thought disgusted him. Infant Serpents and the slime they created held little appeal. But imagine an *army*. If he could make them obey him . . . unlimited riches and power would follow. This female tiger-skin, she made him feel something new, an emotion he'd never known. *What was it?* He wanted to destroy her, but he wanted somehow to do it over and over, forever. Could he even dream of a partnership? *Ah, but she would make a lovely flame, wouldn't she?* Such strength, such impertinence. *Torch her*, his whole body was thinking. *You can't keep her as a slave.*

• • •

Across from the palace at that very moment, in the steaming rainfall, the Ice Serpent had crawled onto a rooftop to watch what was happening. *Unity?* He wondered. *Is it possible? Can there be such beauty, creating life to create death?*

Meanwhile, the Tiger Dragon sensed the doubt in her companion.

"It may be, Najikko," she said playfully, "that we shall try to kill each other a thousand times in this alliance. Who knows? All that lively fun can wait. But how will we ever know what we're capable of achieving, if we don't even try?"

She whipped her tail across the floor and away from him. Best not to pressure him too much. She needed him to stay put a few moments longer. He'd scarcely heard the hissing of her snake sculptures, but they were doing their hypnotic work. He was tiring.

Momentarily calm, Najikko wondered, *Was she disgusted by my artificial leg?* But his eye followed the path of her tail, and he saw the trap in the floor. His head shot forward, snapping at her face. "You wretch." He hissed.

She pulled back, yanking out a silver fang that had lodged in her snout, and with a sweep of her arm, knocked the Japanese Serpent to the ground. But the distraction caused her trance-spell to fail; her hissing snakes quieted.

For an instant, Simon could see the Japanese Creature squirming, winded, trying to get up, but the Tiger Dragon struck once more, driving his head down and pulling out one of his horns. She had broken his crown. Howling, the Japanese Serpent unfurled its steel wings, slicing her as they emerged from his back.

With a flash of desperate strength, the Dragon of Japan launched into the air and flew out the great open windows, disappearing into the storm.

The Tiger Dragon roared, lifting the crescent-shaped horn she had taken from him.

Simon took a breath. *New plan. Time for action.*

The Tiger Dragon waited for the other Serpent's return, but it did not come.

There was only a blast of arrows from two young boys, huddled in the rafters of her immense room.

Simon's first arrow slammed into her arm, his second into her side, and his third, into her great clawed foot. The bolts fired by Key missed their mark, and studded the wall behind her.

The Tiger Dragon roared. She moved deeper into the room, angrily trying to get a look at them, her mind going wild. *Boys? They sent boys against me?* She crouched and prepared to attack.

Suddenly, black fire rolled out of a dark corner, and the river of flame carried her out of the room, sending her out of the window toward the courtyard.

Instantly, she recovered and clawed around the building, entering through another panoramic window.

Simon cursed. By using fire, the Black Dragon had revealed himself to her. He'd be vulnerable to her trance-spell now, if she could attempt it. Instead, she shot forth her fire, catching the Black Dragon by surprise. Her tigerlike flames, ribboned with orange and black, forced the Black Dragon to dive behind one of her statues of herself. His little canary flew for cover, terrified.

"Traitor . . ." hissed the Tiger Serpent. "You will die for your betrayal."

"Their world is worth living in," said the Black Dragon, crouching tighter behind the statue. "Yours is not."

The words stunned Issindra. She had not realized he had entered the human world, been welcomed into it. She did not know it was possible.

Suddenly, Key threw one of the ceremonial lances from the wall, and because he was close, he hit the target. The Tiger Dragon howled as the shaft stabbed into her chest. She stumbled back in shock, pulling at the long handle.

The Black Dragon tried to throw fire again—but his energy was gone. Simon jumped down from the rafters to the marble floor, where puddles of flames were flickering, circling, and devouring furniture in long, curling wiry strands. Fire climbed the jungle vines, the trees began to burn. With smoke for cover, Simon rushed at the Tiger Serpent, but she kicked him back. He went sliding across the floor, directly into the pouncing form of—*the Japanese Serpent!*

Chapter 35

❦

CHAMBER OF HORRORS

THE JAPANESE DRAGON SLAMMED its claws into Simon's arms, pinning him down. "I will not unsettle my mind with you," the Creature hissed. "I will gently cut you open, quick and quiet."

"Kill him, my sweet," said the Tiger Serpent, sneering. "My gift to you before you die."

Eyeing her cautiously, the Japanese Creature lifted a sharp claw, but Key began firing his crossbow, and an arrow hit the Dragon's arm, yanking it back.

Najikko screeched, and then very calmly pulled out the silver arrow so it was pointed at Simon, ready to stab him, and down came the blow—

But suddenly he screeched again.

A sword slashed into his armored back, releasing a spray of sparks. Aldric burst into the chamber! He slashed the arrow out of the Japanese Serpent's claw, and it skidded across the room. Furious, the Dragon of Japan blew fire at Aldric, but the Knight lifted his shield, and the flames were sucked *into* the shield and vanished.

The Japanese Dragon leapt at Aldric, knocking the shield loose, and rolled with him onto the floor. Simon snatched up his sword, but the Tiger Dragon had her sights on him. She lunged at Simon and carried him into the wall, banging his head roughly.

Dizzy, Simon fell.

Above, Key fired another shot. The arrow went right into her shoulder.

He shouted with joy.

The Tiger Dragon leapt high, snatching the boy from his spot in the rafters. Key landed hard on the floor. Simon heard him yell in pain. The Tiger Dragon grabbed hold of Simon, throwing him beside Key, and then she paused, preparing to burn them both in one terrible jet of fire.

Instead, she felt a new spray of arrows thud into her hide.

A war cry filled the chamber.

Crawling in from the night were the other Samurai.

In from the giant open windows they came, in full battle gear, a surprise assault from behind.

Taro and Sachiko led the charge, calling orders to

the other Samurai, who leveled their crossbows at the Tiger Dragon.

But it was the Japanese Serpent who threw his fire, breathing it out in a great silver-gold flood. The Samurai lifted their shields, but the Warriors were tossed back as if from a firehose blast.

The silvery, gold-lashed flames slapped them backward. The fire tumbled through the palace, and outside, growing in the night, swirling and rising as it flew outward, away, through the square of palaces. The Japanese Serpent began chanting.

Yes, called the burning in his core, *Now is the time, now is my moment. Now. Now.*

The spinning plume of fire, like smoke from a factory, began to rise quickly in the night, until it stood the height of skyscrapers, a huge funnel cloud made of silver-and-gold fire. Terrific winds whipped around it.

This was fire like nothing on earth; a grand, twisting, sinuous lifeform; a single, thinking, eating, hating destroyer. A colossal tornado made of fire.

The Japanese Serpent calmly smiled. "There is no escaping this," he said calmly. "You witness the power of the ancients. The firespinner will devour all things in its path. I alone shall live through it."

Issindra glared at him, hissing vengefully in the Dragontongue, and blasted him with her black-orange flames.

Her tigerfire was met on the floor by a tide of nearly formless men made of metallic flame. Najikko's fire was coming to life, combatting Issindra's blaze! Serpentfire hates Serpentfire, and Simon feared their contact.

But the two fires actually *merged*, melding into one, the flames married together. Then the burning figures seemed to drift, carrying all the flames outside through the open windows, into the path of the returning cyclone of fire.

Simon watched in wonder as the huge twister, now burning its way back toward the palace, sucked up the flames, joining with them, as oxygen was pulled away from the chamber and into the burning whirlpool.

The sound the cyclone gave off was of millions of roaring tigers.

Everyone fell to the ground. Simon could see in dreamlike splendor the silver-gold light flashing on the awed face of his father.

But he could also see the most astonishing thing of all: Key had run toward the levers rising from the floor, and, seizing his chance, shoved them back.

The Tiger Dragon screamed as she was sucked down by a trapdoor and fell into her own trap. The glass shield slammed shut, and, although she blew fire at it, the flames helplessly burned away, starved of oxygen. She was caught.

Her own trap held her now.

But the Dragon of Japan was in his glory. Leaning back, his sterling tail flashing in the light of the cyclone of fire, he closed his eyes and fell into a meditative state. *The beauty of it all,* he was thinking. *The cyclone shall burn away all but my own life. . . .*

The beauty of it all, thought the Ice Dragon. *The Japanese Dragon must be teaching her the ancients' secret power. Their unity is sealed. And once the offspring are created and hatched, the Tiger Dragon shall surely destroy her Japanese mate, and I shall be here, ready to raise the children, advise them, make them do as I wish. As I die, they will carry my history books out into the world. I will never be forgotten.*

He sat perched on a ledge outside the palace, watching the cyclone of fire grow and gyrate, whipping up new cyclones in its wake. Perhaps he should be leaving now; perhaps the Tiger Dragon should stop this fire from going too far. The people down below were getting sucked into the flames. They were so small, so very small. He was staring, eyes wide, his freezing hands scribbling down everything he could think of . . .

Meanwhile, the Chinese Dragon fired a slender, careful beam of blackfire at the Serpent of Japan, but the fire simply twisted away, shooting off toward the cyclone, which was now traveling backward, almost playfully, taking in the ebony burn with a scream of joy.

Simon took hold of Key and pressed him against the wall, grabbing onto the curving iron base of a light fixture, desperately resisting the howling tornado.

Amid the whipping winds, Taro charged.

The Japanese Serpent saw the motion and, with a wave of his hand, simply cast Taro down.

Seeing her husband had fallen, Sachiko closed her eyes. Using a mindspell, she drew the shattered glass from all the surrounding buildings—thousands of glass shards swirling around outside—all together. To Simon's wonder, the shards formed into dozens of animal-like beasts, vague wolflike creatures all loosely held together, which flew toward the palace with a vengeance.

Alaythia saw what Sachiko was up to, and closed her eyes. Working in unison, she and Sachiko pulled the glass predators into the palace to slam furiously into the Japanese Serpent. The jagged glass creatures began snarling and biting at Najikko.

There were so many.

Simon watched in awe as the glass predators rushed at the Serpent in waves, throwing themselves against him, tugging at his metal leg with teeth made of shards.

The Dragon began tossing the glass creatures

away, spinning with his blade-wings, cracking their clear flesh apart.

Seeing an opportunity, Aldric threw his sword, which spun around and around before the Dragon's unconcerned eyes, before being pulled into the firestorm and melting in the air.

Simon's father was disarmed.

Without thinking, Simon yelled, catching the Japanese Serpent's eye, and it moved for him, reaching out past the glassy creatures around him.

Shocked, Simon's hold weakened, and he nearly slipped away—but he was shoved back into place by Akira.

The fiercest Samurai fighter had managed to fight the winds and step in, raising his sword to protect Simon. He rushed forward, straight for the Dragon and the orbit of glittering glass around the Creature. The glass-shard animals, now completely out of control, were ripping into everything in their path. And they found Akira.

Sachiko screamed.

Fighting the crackling shards, a savaged Akira managed to block the Dragon from reaching Simon and Key, striking it twice. But now caught in the swarm of flying glass, Akira fell to the ground, his armor pierced by the glass splinters, his body unmoving and lifeless. He lay in a heap, rattled by the wind.

Key and Simon clung to the wall, watching in horror.

The other Samurai called out in shock, but amid the spinning glass shards, the Dragon's glare turned to Key.

"They have to hit the Dragon's heart, weaken him—we can still get him into one of the traps," Key said, his voice drowned in wind and chaos. Simon was already yelling to the other fighters. "Fire at the Serpent's heart!" he shouted. "Everyone fire! Aim for the heart!"

But Taro was getting back on his feet and shouting over him, "Don't fire—it's a waste, move in, move in!"

Aldric was hollering at the same time, "Fall back! The fire's too strong! Fall back and regroup!"

"Fall back! Get out while we can!" Alaythia echoed him. "We'll get another chance!" The air was getting thinner as it was pulled into the fiery cyclone, all sound dimming and becoming absorbed.

If either side had trusted the other, either plan might have worked.

Instead, the Dragon of Japan calmly stalked through the wind-blown hail of glass toward Akira.

His gold-clawed foot kicked the Samurai's body out of the way, heading relentlessly for Taro. The beast threw out its hands with renewed energy, and under its spell, the shards of glass separated like chaff and blew away into the cyclone. Taro braced for a one-on-one attack.

"They're not listening," cried Simon, and he exchanged looks with Key, the two realizing what needed to be done. Key let go of the wall, and was dragged upward, clinging to a chandelier of molded brass—a tiger's claw.

The Dragon of Japan immediately moved toward him, his eyes excited by the easy kill. The Samurai instantly rushed forward in defense, but their bodies were pulled and scraped across the floor in the wild winds. They grasped for anchors, or stabbed at wood with their blades to avoid being sucked out of the building by the growing twister.

Key dangled above them, as Aldric reached out to help him.

All attention was riveted on Key, up high.

Simon saw his chance, kicking free of the wall, and sending himself rushing into the Japanese Dragon from behind. He landed at the Creature's back, and the Serpent tripped, his wounded leg giving in. Simon took advantage. He reached around the shocked Serpent and locked his hand directly on its heart.

If he had forgotten the words, the split second would've cost millions of lives.

But he did not.

Simon called out the deathspell, and the Japanese

Dragon's heart seized up.

The Serpent's body went limp and flew backward, its shocked eyes collapsing into resignation as it was pulled toward the cyclone of fire. Simon screamed in exaltation. Suddenly afraid he'd be sucked out of the palace, he tumbled end over end, and found a hold at the top of a pillar. He watched as the Serpent clawed desperately, on all fours, fighting the vacuum, snarling, roaring, jaws gleaming, teeth gnashing. With no energy left, it spat—and a silver-black residue splatted onto Simon's face, burning him. Simon cried out, but he had won. The Japanese Dragon's claws scraped across the floor as it was suctioned away, exploding in silver-gold energy, pieces of its body spinning, burning, in the twister of flame.

Meanwhile, the glass-shard animals turned into a glassy liquid, their bodies fusing together and then dripping apart in the dizzying fire.

The Ice Dragon saw it all happen. He realized his masterpiece of horror had turned into a complete failure. He watched his books, laid beside him on the ledge, sixteen magnificent volumes, get pulled into the cyclone and burn. He could not believe it. He had enchanted those pages *never* to burn. He could not be this weak.

He could see the Black Dragon staring at him from

the Tiger Palace, an angry smile on his face.

The Ice Dragon did not react. He had only one power left in the world. To choose his moment.

He stepped forward off the ledge, and let the cyclone pull him into oblivion.

Fire, loss, death and flame, burn the bones, end of game. . . .

He died instantly, though the hellish whirling pillar of fire was losing strength. Its master had died, and so the cyclone began to fall apart, becoming mere flashes in the night, horrible flames turning into tiny wisps of fairylight in a cascading, spinning fall to earth.

Air rushed back into the palace.

At the top of the pillar, Simon breathed. His arms were wrapped around the coils of a Serpent statue. Small areas on his cheek and neck had been burned, but he could hardly feel it under the shock of victory.

Aldric stared at his son.

Simon stared at Key. The boy still clung to the vine-wrapped chandelier, his knuckles white. Beneath him, Issindra remained locked in a very small cell, staring up out of the glass. Trapped.

The Dragon was in terror.

Chapter 36

The Way a Fire Dies

OKYO'S SUBTERRANEAN FIRES FIZZLED out at exactly the moment of the Japanese Dragon's death in Bombay. The nightmare was over.

For days afterward, the sound of the screaming flames stayed in people's heads, lingering even in their dreams, until at last subsiding.

In Bombay, recovery was already underway the morning after the cyclones struck.

When Simon and Key went back through the streets to get to their ship, they saw rubble being cleared. It was apparent, as Sachiko and Taro trailed a distance behind, they were giving their son more space than he'd ever been given before. He'd earned it.

But everyone's mood was dark; the Samurai had been deprived of giving Akira a proper funeral. His body had been thrown to the fire by the Japanese Serpent, and nothing remained of him but a memory. No one spoke of it. The pain was too fresh. They were simply relieved to be going home.

As the boys weaved through the crowds, they were startled as Fenwick and Katana leapt from the Ship with No Name and darted *past* them. The creatures had seen the Indian girl who had led them to the tiger trap, and who was now shadowing them as a pickpocket.

"Let me go," she moaned, kicking at the snarling bobcat. Indignantly, Aldric took his wallet back from her. She explained that she and her father worked in the Tiger Palace caring for the big cats. They had begun doing the tiger feedings on the side because they were in terrible need of money.

Evil has so many colors, thought Simon. *So many layers.*

They left her behind in the street without a word, hoping she would find a better way of making a living than robbing or killing people for profit.

Simon and Key traveled the street in quiet back to the docks.

Trying to catch up, Fenwick climbed a crate and shot Simon a glance, a burning link to his mind, allowing him the fox's version of all that had happened: the animal's travels through Bombay, trying to find help for the boys, his own view of the terrible storm, and how he ended up returning to the ship for shelter.

Fenwick leaned forward to lick at Simon's burned cheek, which hadn't yet healed completely under Alaythia's power.

With a sigh, Simon lifted the fox, and in this way they forgave each other for the mutual abandonment. Key's bobcat nuzzled his legs. Neither boy wanted to admit their closeness to the animals. They'd headed over to the Ship with No Name, which was battered from the storm but seaworthy. As he made his way impatiently, Simon heard a street vendor's radio.

BBC News was reporting on the atmospheric disturbance that had hit Bombay and Tokyo, "a mystery scientists will puzzle over desperately for many, many years."

The Black Dragon had been given the task of disposing of the Tiger Serpent of Bombay. He asked for it, as a sign of trust, and the Warriors had agreed; it was the ultimate show of confidence in him that they would let him do it alone, keeping themselves free of danger as he requested.

However, while she remained trapped in her own palace, Issindra was still useful. She possessed information about all manner of illegal and wrongful operations around the world.

But it was no simple matter, stealing information from a Tiger Dragon.

It was a high-risk business.

It required touch.

The Dragonhunters had been sent away, to protect them from a dangerous—and, in fact, secretive—endeavor. Dragons did not like to give away the secret to thought-theft, a most shameful practice in their culture. The Black Dragon would meet the Hunters in three days' time to share information.

So Ming Song, the Black Dragon, now stood alone before Issindra, the Tiger Dragon of Bombay, watching her from above the glass-roofed cell.

"You know what I'm here to do," he said.

"You have to touch me," she purred. "And to do that, you must open my cage."

"You have, by now, exhausted yourself of fire. My own flames can destroy you if you try to escape."

"So you say."

The Black Dragon pondered the predicament.

"You have left me no choice, Issindra," he said in sorrow. "If you will not speak, I must break your mind."

He opened the cell, and clambered down, blocking out the light, filling the cage with darkness. She was weak, and he moved fast. His claws struck at her head, and tore at her thoughts. What he saw surprised him, for there was a loneliness and sorrow that filled her, and—if it were possible for a Dragon—he saw gentleness, even playfulness. She was not a kind soul, but over the centuries, she had killed relatively few, and that mattered to the Black Dragon. He knew the taste a Serpent had for pain and misery—they fed on it to survive—he knew how difficult it was to resist these hungers, because he had them himself. She could have done far worse to the world.

And then he saw in her mind's eye that over the years, she had captured several Indian police investigators and left them imprisoned somewhere in the jungle. They had to be freed. The problem now, of course, was how to locate them? Where were they? He could not find it in her head.

In the end, she agreed to show him, if he spared her life. "Even if it means living in a prison forever," she pleaded.

He gave in to her demands. But as she gave up the location of the imprisoned men, he climbed away, and with the cage open for a mere instant, she called a spell to her ancient palace.

The Black Dragon found himself hypnotized and convulsed, as the enchanted hissing of a thousand snakes echoed in the vine-wrapped chamber. Cinders blew from the mouths of the carved snakes.

As his canary twittered helplessly, the old Dragon rolled in the ashes of the burnt jungle plants, folding his arms and legs up into his chest, unable to move.

"How they despise you out there," Issindra said, rising, coming close to his face, "but I have come to respect someone of such cunning. You have bested the greatest of the Dragons, and you have won over the hearts of human beings—no one else has achieved such greatness. I think . . . perhaps . . . there is more to you than treachery."

Bestilled by magic, he looked into her eyes, and only the fire within him moved.

"Such genius should not be lost," she said, "but passed on."

She purred, a rasping sizzle in the throat, like a cat and a snake together. "Don't trouble your mind. I don't plan to kill you, old one. But I do have need of you. The goodness in you can be a blessing . . ."

The Black Dragon's skin wanted to shudder, but he could not even blink.

"You still have a use to the Dragon world," she said, and her tail looped around his, coiling . . .

Simon and Aldric, along with Alaythia, escorted Key and his family and protectors to Kyoto on the Ship with No Name. The way back was heavy with grief. Simon and Key promised to keep in close contact;

having gone through battle together, they had new common ground. Key couldn't wait to get back to his Windmill School. He began writing in a journal. The Ice Dragon had given him the idea.

Alaythia was protected now from her emotions by the power of the Black Dragon's spellcasting. The Serpents would no longer find it easy to locate her. She told Simon she had learned the Dragontongue words, and the secret of the "turning," as she called it. She said it was something you did in your head, like trying to imagine what your heart looked like as it was functioning. Simon didn't really know what she meant, but he understood what she'd done was difficult.

In his hand, Simon had a letter from the Black Dragon, left behind to be read later. "The cost of fighting evil can be great, it can be small; it can take something from you in a quick, iron grip or in a slow, greedy pulling out, as from a needle taking blood; but there is always a cost. To fight the darkness, you must enter the darkness. What you lose first is the foolishness that says evil is far away, that evil will always be vanquished and destroyed. You rid yourself of that. And then you become a man."

Simon looked up, not sure what he was getting at, and read on: "The purpose of all you are doing is not to make you more closed-off, closed-in, and selfish, but to get you to serve others . . . without losing yourself. You need not become your father."

Become his father?

What had he done to deserve all this? He didn't think of himself as a cold person. He tossed the parchment into his pack.

To pass the time, Simon sat in a hammock on deck, quietly pondering Akira's sacrifice. Simon, and all of them, would be dead if it hadn't been for this one Samurai, who bought Simon the few extra minutes he needed. Before now, Simon hadn't thought much about Akira at all. He gave him no more thought than a toy soldier; he was almost an adversary. The Warrior had never even liked Simon, never said so much as a kind word. And yet he had died protecting him, protecting them all.

Simon looked at the other faces.

Would they have done the same thing? Give their life for a stranger? Attack when it meant suicide? Could I have done it?

Simon was not sure he could answer even for himself. In his moment of terror in the cyclone's path, he could hardly think, but his mind was clear in one purpose: survival. How had he set that aside to attack the Dragon? He knew he would not have had the courage if it hadn't been for Akira showing him the path . . . *using* his anger to a purpose.

"What are you thinking about?" Key asked from across the deck.

Simon tried to smile. "Girls."

Hours later, they said good-bye at Sachiko's mansion, and while Taro tried to stop Fenwick from tearing up a garden trellis, Aldric glanced over at Sachiko. "It's strange, isn't it? You knew the spell that hides emotion. You knew it from the start. I keep wondering if there's a word for 'irony' in Japanese. I mean, you would've helped Alaythia if she'd known to come here in the first place, wouldn't you?"

"This group doesn't welcome people easily," she answered. "In the end, we may have *needed* to battle a Dragon just to know she was trustworthy. Taro would have needed a long time to make that decision."

"He's that selfish?"

Sachiko's face hardened. "'Samurai' means to serve others. It means sacrifice. He is not afraid of that. He has a responsibility to Japan above all else; it is written in the code we follow. Loyalty number one is to the island. I do not know what he would say, but he is learning to trust more as time goes on."

"I can tell you one thing," said Aldric, and he looked over at Alaythia across the Japanese garden. "This Warrior code has not been served well by keeping secrets."

Sachiko smiled. On this they agreed.

Mamoru gave Simon the Dragon netsuke, to show he forgave him for conking him on the head, and Kisho wandered over, crushing flowers onto Simon's shirt, for reasons no one understood. He told Simon, "Always set your clock by nature's hand." Whatever that meant.

Simon just nodded. "Thank you, Kisho. Thank you." Key seemed relieved Simon withheld his laughter, and treated the man with respect.

Later on, Simon watched Alaythia and Aldric find each other in the garden, and they seemed right together, as maybe they always had.

The evil wrought by the world's Dragons would be divided now, Simon knew, by two sets of Warriors on either side of the globe, though it was likely their paths would cross many times over. In this conflict alone, two entire cities had nearly been burned away. Unity was needed.

The war seemed limitless. On the journey back to Japan, Simon had remarked that there seemed no end in sight to their battle, with scores of Dragons in the White Book of Saint George still remaining. And Taro had replied, "Why should we want it to end? We would have no purpose."

It seemed they saw the world as fighting to achieve balance, not as a war in which one side would dominate. It was the fight itself that mattered. It was supposed to go on and on.

It was Simon's honor, before he left, to see Key given his proper swords of battle, long and short, the *daito* and the *shoto*. Taro placed them in his son's hands, and Sachiko laid before him two beautiful fabric containments for the swords, and atop them, *fusahimo*, ornate gold cords used to tie the bags closed.

It was the beginning of something, and the end.

At last, when the Ship with No Name was finally ready to leave the island, Sachiko gave Simon a gift, too. It was a package of ordinary pills for his stomach, marked in Japanese, though he hadn't ever told her about the anxious, burning pains he suffered. She said to him, "The trick is to bear the weight of the world, and still smile *despite* the burden." At the time, it seemed like she was joking, but Simon would think about it for a long time afterward.

Chapter 37

SMALL SACRIFICES

SIMON RETURNED TO NEW ENGLAND, and to Emily, the girl from the novelty shop.

He rode his horse beside her on the way to school. But it was as if, in the months that had passed, she had forgotten him. She behaved as if he were a passing acquaintance, as if they had never spoken to each other. Life in this little town had gone on without Simon, and there was no way he could fit himself back into it.

"I thought," he said, "you might want a ride."

"A ride?" She gave half a laugh. "I don't think so. It's a long way to fall."

He would rather she had been disappointed in him, or angry. Instead, she was polite, and sort of looked at him sidelong with half a smile, as if he were an odd quirk of Ebony Hollow to be enjoyed, but at a distance.

"I was afraid, all this time, people were, like, going around thinking I was a pyro or something," Simon said, letting the horse set its own pace. "I didn't start that fire at your shop."

"No one really thought that," she said. "The fire-fighters said it was a freak accident."

And so the conversation went. He wanted to explain everything to her. Every last detail. But she was keeping him so far away.

She had been flirting with him, that's all. She was a nice person. She wasn't going to be rude, but it was all the same to her, whether he was there waiting on the morning walk to school, or not.

When he returned home, Simon tried to tell Alaythia what happened with Emily, but the words couldn't find a way out.

On the television, there were images of war in Africa, and coal miners lying sick in Virginia who were kept away from doctors by the company they worked for, and there were reports of children in a North Korean orphanage who were starving because their headmaster had taken the food and resold it.

And it seemed incredible to Simon how many Serpents there must be to have caused all of this rottenness in the world. How the Dragons must love this planet, what pleasure they must have felt in finding so many people who, instead of adding candles to the darkness, were blowing out the light.

Epilogue

THE DYING EMBERS OF THE DAY

HE RODE HIS HORSE out beyond the Ebony Hollow forest to the seashore.

And he thought about evil.

eXTRAs

Samurai

A Note from Jason Hightman

A Q&A with the Author

A Sneak Peek at Goodraven

A Note from Jason Hightman

This book exists to get boys to read.

In an age when male readership seems to be getting smaller, and the reading choices for that audience seem to be dwindling, I set out to try to capture a part of that group with the most intense kind of storytelling I could manage. This book was intended to be LOUD. It was made for speed, gleaming with sharp, twisting angles, and roaring with energy. Maybe it was crazy to try, but the reasons for this approach are obvious.

Grabbing attention is not easy these days; books have to compete with an astonishing array of entertainment— interactive games, comics, music, blockbuster movies and television shows, even website creation and custom video-editing projects.

A book, any book, has an incredible uphill climb.

It's enough to make a writer commit *seppuku*.

When faced with such a challenge, any author might resort to the use of an arresting image like . . . a samurai.

It all started with the simple question, what if the St. Georges were *not* the last Dragon hunters? I wasn't interested in repeating the same events as in *The Saint of Dragons*. I wanted to strike out for new territory, for this adventure to stand on its own. This is how *Samurai* was born.

Medieval history has always intrigued me. The Asian soldier of the period has all the trappings to fascinate

3

young people, especially boys—the strange and magnificent armor, the meticulously crafted weapons, the complex modes of conduct, the unique, imposing castles, and the mystical temples wreathed in fog.

I decided for the sequel to *The Saint of Dragons*, I would do something that would work in Japanese history. The location gave me a chance to explore new avenues of danger for the hunters—Tokyo! Bullet trains! India! Tigers!—as well as providing new emotional worries for Simon and offering a fuller picture of the history of Dragon slayers.

The image of a modern samurai instantly appealed to me. How would a samurai fight the ancient battles in cities of neon and concrete? How would he view the use of a gun when faced with such a terrible enemy? We know from history that the rise of the firearm spelled doom for their warrior way of life, but what if circumstances pushed the hunters to accept the new weapon, or face certain death? How would the warrior incorporate the gun, and with what reservations? How would people from this tradition deal with other technology, and the expanding role of women?

But the idea was to not only imagine how a samurai would meld his ways with changing times and the Japanese "group dynamic" of the present day, but also to smash together an American/European way of thinking with the Asian fighter's ethics and styles. Simon St. George represents just about all American- and Western-born kids, who so often consider themselves as individuals first, without thinking very much about service to others or the community around them. On the other hand, the Japanese character, Key, must discover the power of individuality and witness the glory of being the lone hero.

With *Samurai*, I also entered a new world of Serpent lore. It was interesting for me to consider how Dragons— who hate each other fiercely—would *have* to deal with each other sooner or later or face the extinction of their entire species. Questions of good and evil play a big part in this series. I've received mail from readers who loved the idea that the wickedness in the world could be chalked up to Serpent influence, while others complained it took human beings off the hook for their own immoral actions. For me, allowing Simon to wonder about the chicken-and-egg relationship of humans and Serpents was more important than drawing a final conclusion. In this way, of course, the issue is much the same as accepted Christian ideas about people and demons: can the devil *make* you do evil, or does he just offer you the opportunity?

At the end of the book, Simon is beginning to question why evil exists on Earth. While he may never quite figure it out—since no one really can—pondering the reason is going to make him a better, stronger, tougher, and smarter person.

Where the story goes from here is certainly left open.

But I feel there are enough hints and clues as to the way Dragon hunting will continue in the future to satisfy a reader. The kindhearted "Light Dragons" that the Chinese serpent once proposed may finally come into being. One can only guess how Aldric would deal with a castle full of Dragon children who are learning to combat their own kind in the interest of a common good. That story may never be written, but the raw materials are here to stoke anyone's imagination.

Jason Hightman

A Q&A with the Author

What initially attracted you to writing about Dragon fighting?

Dragons are an interesting and time-honored symbol of evil. I was drawn to the chance of enriching our understanding of how these evil creatures might interact in a modern setting. *The Saint of Dragons* was all about a group of Serpents trying to work together, but thwarted by their own instincts to lie and cheat each other. I was intrigued by the obvious issue that arose out of that: How does such a hateful species ever reproduce itself? How do the rival Dragons ever set aside their differences long enough to create new young?

Do you identify with Simon St. George? Is he based on anyone you know?

Simon is a pure creation of fiction, but every writer finds parts of himself in his characters. I can relate to his feelings of aloneness, his worrying about the world. But Simon is angrier, tougher, more rebellious, and quicker to action than I ever could be.

How did you happen to find inspiration in the Far East (or Japan) for Samurai?

With so much going on in Japan's manga and anime culture, it seems amazing more mainstream books don't merge the worlds of East and West, of knights and samurai. Once I started thinking about warrior culture all over

7

the world, I saw all-new possibilities in a focus on the Far East.

What do you like about writing for teens?
The audience is less jaded. Teens are more open to different ideas and reinvention. I've found adult readers sometimes object to the whole concept of Dragons and Serpents in contemporary culture. They are trained on traditional fantasies with more familiar-looking creatures, and don't want anyone messing with the usual elements of these stories. Young people are more willing to let you experiment.

How does your background as a screenwriter influence the way you write novels?
Action, action, action. Quick writing, painting a scene with few words—that's what movie writing is all about. I don't know if my background helped or hindered this particular novel. Sometimes the demands of a story ask for a different approach. This time I was trying to concoct a dose of literary adrenaline.

Your next novel, Goodraven, is quite a change from Dragon lore. What intrigues you about this new topic?
The Saint of Dragons and *Samurai* try for a reinvention of Dragons, and *Goodraven* aims for a reinvention of witches, but that's where the similarities end. With *Goodraven*, I wanted to create a monster that evokes the primal

response a reader gets from Dracula and Frankenstein, but in a fresh adventure, presented specifically for a younger crowd, with youthful heroes.

At its heart, *Goodraven* is a shivery ghost story about a teenaged Victorian couple who find themselves lost in a bitter snowstorm, with a legendary Salem villain stalking them. Just forget everything you know about witches. You've been told only lies.

A Sneak Peek at Jason Hightman's Latest Novel, Goodraven

Tobias and Tess stood apart from the flow of people through the station gates; as always, the two of them against the world, watching it pass by.

"Last chance to turn back," Tess murmured.

"Nonsense. We're about to find out if there really *are* witches up there."

A stooped old conductor ambled past them. "A lot of out-of-town folk here; train's crowded," he muttered. "You may need to sit apart."

Tobias looked down at the train worker. "Oh, we're never apart."

"What do you mean, never?" barked the old man. "She'll be sitting with other women . . . no scandal to it."

Tess felt her heart flutter, but Tobias calmed her panic with confidence. "She'll be sitting with me, sir. Thank you."

"Dangerous to need each other so much," the old man replied. "I'm a widower; I can tell you a thing or two about that—"

"And no new lady has snatched you up?" mumbled Tobias, under his breath. "You wonder how this could be possible."

"You'd better get in. They're boarding up," the old man said, not listening, heading into the gates.

Hiding a smile, Tobias imitated the man's fearsome voice, "They're boarding up . . ."

Tess considered him. "You don't have the right inflection. You have to sound more like you're hiding a human head in your coat."

Tobias tried again, darker, more convincing. "They're booooarding up . . ."

"Much better. The human-head element was right there. Palpable."

"Tobias! Tess!"

Celia Harnow, the innkeeper, shouted from behind them, her golden curls bouncing as she ran. She was a bubbly, boisterous woman whom Tess found somewhat likeable, for all her stumbling kindnesses, and whom Tobias found quite annoying, which he openly admitted.

"You forgot your train tickets!" she said, her baby face flushing red from running. "Here, now, they might've had to seat you apart—"

"Thank you, Miss Harnow," Tess said politely.

"I'm so jealous of you two, tighter than two doves. Me, I'm stuck with the old goat, he wants me to stay with the inn and feed him and his firemen friends. I can't even go to the Carnival." "The old goat" was her husband, the usual target of her complaints.

"Yes, thank you, ma'am, we've got to be going now," said Tobias, moving Tess along as he whispered, "The Dead hate to wait."

11

As they neared the line for the train, Tess saw four little girls near a scowling, thin woman arguing with a porter over some boxes. She was saying, "Be careful with those, they have my dolls in them. I'm going to display them for sale at the Festival." And Tess saw the woman rudely warn one of the girls, "Don't touch these, they're not for playing with."

Tobias watched one of the sweet, tiny girls turn sad. Out of spite, he reached over and swiped one of the thin woman's boxes. Tess hid her amusement. As the woman fussed over the loading, not even noticing him, Tobias broke open the box and pulled out a boy doll. He looked at the little girl. "What do you want for Christmas?" he asked.

Tess watched the little girl stammer. "Mmm, something . . ."

Tobias grinned, handing her the doll. "Like this?"

"Something scary," the tiny girl giggled. Tess laughed with her.

"You're a strange man," said the girl.

"Yes," said Tobias, good-naturedly. "Yes, I am."

Tess shook hands with the little girl. "Tess Goodraven," she introduced herself, and gestured to Tobias. "My husband, Tobias Goodraven."

"Husband?" the girl laughed. "You're too small to be married."

"Not at all." Tess smiled back.

Just then, the girl's father turned, calling the child angrily, and Tess could see Tobias tense up. "What I love about Christmas is it always brings out the best in people," she said, hoping to ease the situation.

Tobias took on a mock-scary voice. "And all the ghosts get homesick."

She kissed him. "I feel brave."

They moved toward the train. Its magnificent, huge black engine breathed steam over the beautiful station, itself a tiny jewel of architecture, covered in dazzling latticed iron and crowned with a small glass dome. Steam unfurled over the waiting crowd.

Several youngsters turned to her, shocking her with their gaze, for their eyes were pearly white and fixed upon nothing in particular. Others nearby stood with closed eyes, she noticed, and carried canes to help them along. They were blind children, from a school in Salem, she knew. They stood with their chaperones, and Tess felt a pang of sadness that they could not see the beauty that the train and the station created together.

Everyone was silent, in plain black and brown coats. Tobias and Tess stood out brilliantly, as always, he in gray, she in white. They looked around at the crowd, observing every detail, as the snow crept down around them all.

Tess realized sadly this was what normal people looked like to them.

Odd little curiosities.

The train would take them to the Winter Carnival in the old town, deep in the woods. Passengers were eager to be on their way, moving as one to come aboard. The train was a masterpiece. Tess and Tobias moved through several parlor cars, beautifully appointed, bordered in mahogany. The trip was a short one, but the Festival organizers had spared no expense in trying to attract visitors.

Car after car grew more opulent. Tess found herself wanting to sink into the chairs of each car, for they were truly rooms, unbelievably beautiful, dripping with Victorian grandeur, plush sofas, dazzling chandeliers, wide windows.

Then came the showpiece dining car, ornamented with cherry wood tables, brass fixtures, silver and linen and china the finest restaurant in New York would envy—a feasting place for kings. The second dining car was less expensive, but only slightly less extravagant.

There was a smoking car, complete with an upright piano, a harp, pre-Raphaelite paintings, and a high ceiling made of glass so that Tess could see the snowflakes drifting down upon them with fairy-tale delicateness.

Finally Tobias and Tess reached the elegant, day-trip passenger cars, and found their seats, together as always. Tess had traveled quite a bit in her few short years of life, and this train was as perfect a creation as she had ever seen in New York, London, or Paris.

It was a shame it would all be smashed to pieces.

DISCOVER THE TRUTH...
DRAGONS ARE REAL!

JASON HIGHTMAN

the SAINT of DRAGONS

EXTRAS INSIDE

DON'T MISS JASON HIGHTMAN'S
FIRST EPIC DRAGON TALE

An Imprint of HarperCollins Publishers

www.harperteen.com